FRIENDS OF THE
SACRAMENTO
PUBLIC LIBRARY

THIS BOOK WAS DONATED BY

**FRIENDS OF THE
GALT LIBRARY**

The Sacramento Public Library gratefully acknowledges this
contribution to support and improve Library services in the community.

SACRAMENTO PUBLIC LIBRARY

THE SPIRIT-EATERS

BRAVELANDS

BRAVELANDS

THE SPIRIT-EATERS

ERIN HUNTER

HARPER

An Imprint of HarperCollinsPublishers

Library of Congress Cataloging-in-Publication Data

Names: Hunter, Erin, author.
Title: The spirit-eaters / Erin Hunter.
Description: First edition. | New York, NY : Harper, an imprint of HarperCollinsPublishers,
  [2020] | Series: Bravelands ; 5 | Audience: Ages 8–12 | Audience: Grades 4–6 |
Summary: "The true Great Parent has finally risen and must unite all the animals of Bravelands
  to prevent an ancient evil from taking root"— Provided by publisher.
Identifiers: LCCN 2019027320 | ISBN 978-0-06-264218-9 (hardcover) | ISBN
  978-0-06-264219-6 (library binding)
Subjects: CYAC: Baboons—Fiction. | Lion--Fiction. | Elephants—Fiction. | Adventure and
  adventurers--Fiction. | Africa--Fiction.
Classification: LCC PZ7.H916625 Spe 2020 | DDC [Fic]—dc23 LC record available at
  https://lccn.loc.gov/2019027320

Typography by Ellice M. Lee
19 20 21 22 23   PC/LSCH   10 9 8 7 6 5 4 3 2 1
❖
First Edition

Special thanks to Gillian Philip

PROLOGUE

The water was still and green and placid, its surface dappled by the shifting shadows of the overhead branches. Gulper the white pelican paddled lazily through the shallows, watching for movement beneath him. Around him, his brothers and sisters fed busily, ducking below the surface to scoop up fish. Spotting the flash of a silver shoal in the murk, Gulper arched his wings and plunged his own head underwater.

The fish he caught was fat and sweet; Gulper threw back his head and swallowed it down, eyeing the bank for possible dangers. But all was peaceful. What a beautiful day it was at the watering hole: the sun beating down from an almost cloudless sky, a gentle breeze ruffling his feathers. Herds milled on the bank, churning up the mud as they stamped and flicked their tails and shook flies from their eyes. Two zebra mares groomed each other's backs, scratching with their teeth. Buffalo plodded lethargically into the water to stand thigh-deep, enjoying the blissful coolness. A little way off, a pod of hippos wallowed in the deeper water, yawning to show their teeth and occasionally diving down to find the sweet grass at the lake bed.

Gulper wasn't too afraid of any of the big animals, though he and his squadron would keep their distance from the hippos. It was the crocodiles he really had to watch out for. Some of the huge scaly predators basked on the shore not far away, their cold eyes scanning the lake for unwary prey. More than once Gulper had seen a croc drag a pelican under to drown and eat. He stretched his wings, plunged for another fish, then surfaced to eye the crocodiles once more.

A high-pitched three-note call distracted him suddenly, and he looked up, water streaming in rivulets from his feathers. A little whistling duck was flapping quickly overhead, wheeling away from its flock, its white face bright as it called down to the pelicans.

"Have you heard?" it piped. "There's a new Great Father!"

Gulper's heart surged with excitement as his squadron paddled around him, staring up at the duck. It had been so long since Bravelands had known a Great Parent. Since the death of Great Mother Elephant, the animals had known only False Parents—first the rhino Stronghide, and then the evil baboon Stinger, who had tricked and doomed Stronghide before taking the role for himself.

Did they at last have a true Great Father who carried the Great Spirit of Bravelands? Gulper hardly dared to believe such good news.

"Really? Are you sure?" he called up.

"It's true, true-true-true!" whistled the duck. "We heard it from a stork!"

"A stork?" Gulper's friend Scoop tilted his head skeptically. "I wouldn't take their word for anything."

"You'd be wrong!" trilled the duck. "The stork heard it from a kite, who heard it from a vulture. They don't lie!"

"No," agreed Gulper, giving Scoop a thrilled glance. "They never do!"

"So it's true!" exclaimed Scoop. "After all this time!"

"True-true-true," piped the duck, spinning away with her flock in search of other birds, their wings a blur of flapping. "Spread the word!"

"This is too good to be real," cried Scoop. "A new Great Father!"

"I trust the ducks," said Gulper happily. "If this news came from the vultures, it's time to celebrate."

"I hope so," said young Skimmer. "I don't even remember a time when we had a Great Parent's guidance. Does it make such a big difference?"

"It changes everything!" Gulper told him. "A Great Parent guides, advises, settles disputes. All Bravelands' troubles would be over!" He stirred the water's surface with his huge beak. "Everything has been in such uproar recently. You'll see, Skimmer, we'll—"

"Gulper! Look out!" Scoop reared back, flapping his wings.

Gasping, Gulper twisted his neck to glance back sharply, then paddled furiously away from the huge scaly back that drifted toward him. Beating his wings hard, he rose up out of the water, squawking an alarm.

But the crocodile did not submerge for a sneaky attack, and it didn't lunge from the water to strike. As the frightened pelicans milled above it in a flurry of white wings, it drifted on, oblivious.

"Its eyes . . ." Scoop grunted, shocked. "Look."

Gliding back onto the lake, Gulper paddled warily closer. Scoop was right. Now that it was floating into shallower water, Gulper could see that the croc's eyes were milky and lifeless. Its stubby legs hung in the murky water beneath it, not moving at all.

"It's dead." He clicked his beak in relief as the crocodile's body bumped into the bank.

The pelicans gathered around it, curious. No pelican would mourn a dead crocodile, but Gulper couldn't help wondering what could have killed it. The croc didn't look old, and it was a big one—in what should have been the prime of its life. He risked prodding its hard flank with his beak, but it did not stir.

"Biggest croc I've ever seen," remarked Scoop, his eyes wide.

"I'm not scared," crowed young Skimmer, lifting himself into flight. He flapped triumphantly onto the crocodile's ridged back, his webbed feet unsteady.

Under his slight weight, the dead croc tilted and rolled onto its back, exposing its pale creamy underbelly. With a squawk of alarm, Skimmer took off again, but Gulper didn't look at him. He could only stare at the croc's belly.

A great ragged gash had been torn in its tough hide. There were no traces of clotted blood—it had all washed away in the lake—and Gulper could clearly see the cavity within its rib cage.

Scoop beat his wings furiously, driving himself backward. Gulper clicked his beak frantically.

"I've never seen anything like that," he murmured.

Around him his flock bustled and flapped and grunted; he could sense their bewilderment and fear.

And no wonder. His own feathers rose at the roots, and his skin beneath them felt cold with dread.

Let the coming of the new Great Parent be true, he thought. *So many things are bad now, and wrong.*

It seemed Bravelands had entered a new and terrible era. And it would take a very special Great Parent to put it back on its true path.

CHAPTER ONE

Sky drew a breath, stunned. She took a moment to gather her confused and scattered thoughts. The air was thin up here, in this shallow cleft at the peak of the stony mountain; the sun was hard and bright and high, and it was all too easy to believe that her eyes were deceiving her.

But why would her mind invent such an odd and startling sight? A baboon, crouched in the sacred pool, his eyes closed and his expression blank. Vultures were hunched in a circle around the pool, their black eyes riveted on him. It was a baboon she recognized.

Sky blinked, slowly, and tensed. Hesitantly, she extended her trembling trunk.

"Thorn?"

His eyelids fluttered, then slowly opened. He gazed at her, a trace of confusion in his eyes. Yet as she stared at him,

6

wondering, her strongest impression of his mood was one of peaceful resolve.

"Sky Strider." His voice seemed to come from very far away, but there was nothing weak about it.

"Thorn . . . what's happening?" She flapped her ears, bewildered. "I've come to find the Great Parent. I have to speak to him."

His dark eyes looked straight into hers, seeming to pierce her to the center of her being. Deep inside her, Sky felt a tremor of powerful emotion she couldn't identify.

"Then," said Thorn calmly, "you've come to the right place. And the right creature."

Sky stared at him, unable to speak. Did Thorn truly mean what he was saying? Did he know what he was saying?

Yes, of course he did. Sky knew it with certainty, and a thrill of realization: this made sense.

I saved his life, she remembered. She had charged at Fearless the lion when he was on the verge of killing Thorn; the instinct had been sudden and irresistible, and Sky knew now the Great Spirit had been working through her all along. The Great Spirit had needed Thorn Highleaf, and it had trusted Sky—its bearer since Great Mother's death—to do its vital work.

Was it strange that the Great Parent was a baboon? *Especially*, Sky thought with an inward shiver, *after Stinger, the False Parent, had snatched the role for himself?* Yet Bravelands lived in troubled times. A clever, innovative baboon might be a far better guide through those times than a stoic elephant.

That thought brought back to Sky her whole reason for coming here. She took a deep breath, dipped her head, and closed her eyes.

"There is a terrible new menace in Bravelands," she told Thorn softly, "and you are the only one who can thwart it."

Sky's eyes flickered open once again, studying his. A strange feeling came over her. It was as if, in only a moment, the troubles of Bravelands did not seem so insurmountable anymore. There was a new calmness inside her that made up for all the confusion, all the torment, all the terrible anxiety of the months since Great Mother's murder. The world around her—the mountain, the stone, the sky—seemed to thrum with a bright hope, and Sky knew the Great Spirit was near her once again. It felt a little as if family had come back to her: family she had loved and feared lost.

Great Spirit, I've missed you.

"Please help us," she begged Thorn. She bowed her head, then raised it to gaze at him. "Great Father."

She saw him tense, his jaw clenching, and for the first time, he did not seem so serene. *And no wonder,* she thought. Thorn Highleaf had just taken on the greatest and most terrifying responsibility in Bravelands—and she had brought him instant proof of that burden.

Shaking himself, Thorn began to climb out of the pool. Sky hurried forward, extending her trunk to help him, and though the ring of vultures tensed, their feathers bristling with alarm, Thorn held on to her.

"I've carried the Great Spirit too," she told him, gently

withdrawing her trunk to let him stand alone. *It's no surprise he looks overwhelmed,* Sky thought: the Great Spirit was a burden for an elephant, let alone a small and nervous baboon. "I understand a little of what you're feeling, Thorn."

"I know you do." His voice was hoarse and quiet, but his eyes were filled with gratitude.

"You're not alone," she said. "I will help you. All your friends will."

Thorn let his head droop and took a few deep breaths. When he raised his gaze to hers again, he was smiling ruefully. The young baboon looked much more like his old self.

"Honestly, Sky?" he told her. "I know this was right. I resisted it for long enough—till I knew I had no choice." He gave her a wry grin. "But I haven't got a clue where to begin. Tell me, what news were you bringing me?"

Sky sighed. "The strangest things have happened these last few seasons in Bravelands. You know that as well as any creature, Thorn. But this . . . this might be odder than all of them, and even more horrible. There's . . . there's a pack of golden wolves. They came to Bravelands recently." She hesitated. How could she possibly explain?

"Go on," Thorn urged her gently.

"They're breaking the Code," she said.

"We've known many animals recently who have done that," Thorn pointed out.

"But this is different." Sky stirred the white dust with her trunk as the vultures looked on, impassive. "Thorn, they are killing animals for no reason but to take their spirits."

He frowned. "They're doing what?"

"They don't eat anything of their kills—nothing, except the heart. These wolves, they believe that when they eat a creature's heart, they take its spirit and its abilities."

"Storm and stream," murmured Thorn, shocked.

"And the worst of it is, they're right." Sky raised her troubled gaze to his. "I don't know if it's true that the wolves can take their victims' strength, but they certainly kill their spirits. And by taking an animal's spirit, they prevent it going to the stars. Those essences are lost . . . forever."

Thorn clenched his fangs. "This is true evil, Sky. It's clear these wolves don't follow the Code, so it's unlikely they'll listen to the Great Father, but that's not the point. I have to try to stop them. This can't go on."

"So many have been taken already." Sky's voice quavered as she remembered Rush, the brave cheetah who had joined them in the Great Battle against Stinger. After surviving all that, Rush too had been taken by the wolves, her heart ripped out and her two cubs left orphaned.

"Then we need to warn all the other animals," pointed out Thorn, smoothing down his damp fur. He picked in agitation at his lip. "But how? Bravelands is huge—it would take weeks to cover it—yet I hate to think of one more animal falling to these creatures."

"Then you must call a Great Gathering," said Sky firmly. It was how Great Mother had reached out to every inhabitant of Bravelands; even those who could not attend would have news and advice brought to them by those who could. "There should be a Great Gathering anyway, Thorn. All of Bravelands needs to know that you are our new Great Father."

Thorn rubbed his muzzle with his paws. "I don't—the trouble is, Sky, I don't know how to do that. I don't even know how to call a Great Gathering."

"The vultures know." She turned to Windrider, the austere old vulture who stood in front of the others, dignified and watchful. This was the bird who had carried messages and bones to Great Mother. Sky felt a little shy in the bird's presence, and she could not quite meet those brilliant black eyes. "They know what to do. The birds can spread the word to more than their own kind, I think, in spite of our different tongues."

Thorn took a step forward and rose onto his hind paws. He gazed solemnly at Windrider. "I believe Sky speaks the truth," he said, with a respectful inclination of his head. "Can you and your flock herald the Great Gathering, Windrider?"

The huge vulture spread her wings, extending her neck toward Thorn. Opening her savage beak, she gave a sharp, drawn-out cry. Sky had no idea what she was saying, but it was clear that Thorn, like all Great Parents, understood Sky-tongue. He waited for Windrider to fall silent, then nodded and murmured, "Thank you."

Thorn turned to Sky. "We should begin as soon as we can," he said. "We must leave the mountain now."

"Ride on my back," Sky offered at once. "It'll be faster."

Nodding with thanks, Thorn scrambled up her extended foreleg and onto her shoulders. *It did not feel too odd to have him there,* Sky thought as she set off up the short bank of the summit crater. After all, she had carried many animals on her back—most recently those poor orphaned cubs of Rush. Thorn settled easily between her shoulder blades, his fingers gripping her ears, and he seemed to adapt quickly to her swinging stride.

The way down the mountain was long, but Sky discovered she wasn't tired at all, not yet—the new Great Parent coming forward gave her a thrill of swelling hope. Of course she could never have anticipated that it would be her friend and ally Thorn Highleaf.

I fought beside him in the battle for Bravelands, even as I carried the Great Spirit inside me. Yet it gave me no hint. I never once suspected the Spirit would pick Thorn. . . .

And all her life, Sky had believed one thing above all: the Great Spirit always acted wisely.

Around and above them, the vultures flew, Windrider at their head. Sky was grateful: no danger or predator would escape those searching eyes, so she herself could concentrate on finding her footing down the gritty rock and through the dry scrub of the lower slopes. The sun beat down fiercely on the shadeless landscape, but she barely felt its glaring heat.

"What's next for you, Sky?" asked Thorn after they had walked and ridden for a while in silence. "Will you find your herd and go back to them?"

Sky sensed unease in his voice; Thorn must be worried she would leave him alone. *That,* she thought firmly, *would not happen—not until he no longer needs me.* She still owed her allegiance and faith to the Great Spirit, after all, and now it resided in Thorn.

"My herd can wait," she reassured him. "And besides, I'm not quite sure what my plans are. I've been sidetracked for such a long time—first in the aftermath of Stinger's tyranny, and then with my quest to find the Great Parent. Now I'm focused on keeping the Great Spirit safe. . . . I'm almost too used to being without my family."

Of course there were things she didn't want to tell Thorn, too: her disastrous love for Rock, the bull elephant who had murdered her herd-cousin River in a blind rage; her doomed mission to deliver Rush's cubs to safety with the cheetah's sisters, when one was dead and the other would have nothing to do with them. And after fleeing in grief and horror when the bull's herd had revealed Rock's crime, Sky had taken on another lost cub: Menace, the daughter of the lioness Artful and the mad lion Titan. Sky had barely had time to think, let alone find her family once again.

Yet Thorn was right—she should be with her herd. An elephant of her age should be with the other females, raising a calf, protecting the family, learning the migration routes till she could follow them on a starless, moonless night. . . .

Perhaps I will never live the life of a normal elephant, she thought sadly. It wasn't as if she could take a mate now—her impetuous betrothal to Rock meant that she was bound to him for life. Was there even a place for her with the herd anymore?

Realizing she had nearly reached the foot of the mountain, Sky blinked and took a breath. Waiting just below the final shallow slope was the bull herd, with her brother Boulder at its head. He turned to watch her approach, his ears flapping forward in welcome. Not far from the bulls were the cheetah cubs Nimble and Lively and, keeping herself a little apart, the bossy little lion called Menace.

Thorn's baboon friends were there too—at least, Sky assumed they were his friends. Two of them she didn't recognize, but she knew that shy little Mud was Thorn's best friend. The other pair must be trustworthy, then, although they looked very different. One was heavily built, strongly muscled, with a badly scarred face that told of a violent past. The other . . . Sky pinned her ears back, startled. He was a gangly baboon with an unfocused gaze, and he appeared to be babbling away in some form of Sandtongue to a bright red-and-blue lizard on his shoulder.

All the waiting animals, except for the one chatting to the lizard, stared skyward in awe as the vultures circled and swooped. None of them had time to ask questions, because Thorn was already scrambling down Sky's extended foreleg and bounding forward. He paused to call up to the vultures.

"Call everyone!" he cried. "Bring Bravelands to my Great Gathering."

For a fleeting moment, Windrider caught Sky's gaze; the

old bird's stare was intense. Then the vulture dipped her head toward Thorn, flicked her wings, and turned at a steep angle to rise into the sky. Her flock followed her, and in moments they were invisible against the glare of the sun.

What had that look from Windrider meant? Sky swallowed. She thought she knew, and guilt stung her. *Windrider knows I'm uncertain.*

But Windrider would never have doubts; the old vulture's trust in the Great Spirit put her own to shame. Sky straightened, lifting her head a little higher.

Windrider knows my faith has been shaken, yet she is passing on guardianship of the Great Father. She trusts me to protect Thorn with my life.

She would repay that trust. Renewed determination filled Sky as she watched Thorn embrace his three oddly matched baboon friends. *I will protect him*, she promised herself. *And it will be an honor to do it. I served and guarded the Great Spirit. Now I will do the same for the Great Parent.*

Sky felt a prickle in her hide that told her she, too, was being watched. Swinging her head around, she noticed her brother Boulder.

"Well done, sister." Ambling closer, he twined his trunk with hers.

"We have a new Great Parent," she whispered, pressing her head to his. "It's the beginning of a whole new season in Bravelands."

"It is." Thorn had padded close to them both, and he smiled up at her. "Now we will head for the watering hole.

The vultures are summoning the herds."

Leaving the other two baboons, Mud bounded over and clapped his paw on Thorn's shoulder. His eyes glowed.

"Yes. It's time," he said, his voice brimming with happiness. "The first Great Gathering of our new Great Father!"

CHAPTER TWO

Titan could not have survived. It wasn't possible.

So where was his broken corpse?

Fearless paced across the valley floor, still cast in deep morning shadow. In the cooler air beneath the steep walls of the ravine, the young lion felt a chill ripple through his muscles. That monstrous, black-maned lion had fallen from that high ridge above them, vanishing in the mist.

"He's nowhere," called Keen, lifting his head and flaring his nostrils to sniff the air once again. "We've lost him, Fearless. He must have escaped, unless a giant hawk took him."

Fearless shook his head. "There are no giant hawks," he growled. "He's got to be here somewhere."

"We've searched every scrap of ground." Keen hunched his slim shoulders. "There isn't so much as a scent. We've done all we can. I'm sorry, Fearless."

Frustration burned Fearless's throat. He stared up at the impossibly high ridge, snarling. "He has to be dead."

"Agreed." Keen licked Fearless's muzzle. "There's no way he could leap across the ravine; no lion could do such a thing. And no lion could survive such a fall! Not even Titan." He shot a guilty look at Ruthless, Titan's young estranged son, who was trotting dejectedly toward them. Lowering his voice, Keen muttered to Fearless, "Maybe he wasn't quite dead when he hit the ground? Titan must have dragged himself away, to die in a hole somewhere."

"No." It was galling for Fearless to admit it. "If Titan was here, dead or alive, we'd have found him." He had missed yet another chance to avenge Gallant, the lion who had raised him, and he'd failed to get justice for Loyal Prideless, too, his true father.

Fearless sucked in a bitter breath. "Titan survived, I can feel it. He'll probably try to get back to Titanpride now. We should go and see."

"Yes," said Ruthless in a small voice. "We really should."

Despite his own disappointment, Fearless's heart went out to the cub. Ruthless had loved his father, had spent his young cubhood confident that his father loved him too—but that was before Titan had gone mad with hunger for power, heedlessly breaking the Code of Bravelands and killing beyond any need for food. Even Ruthless had now come to terms with the fact that Titan had to be stopped.

"I think it's a mistake to challenge Titanpride," Keen growled. "We are not strong enough to take them on."

Speak for yourself, thought Fearless, though he didn't say it aloud.

"I don't want a direct confrontation," he replied. "We should be able to get close enough to see if Titan is there."

Keen licked his lips. Across his neck, the first fine hairs of his mane were coming through, Fearless noticed. For a moment, he felt inferior, though he knew that his own would appear soon enough.

"Very well," said Keen at last. "Let's just be careful, yes?"

Fearless led the climb back the way they had come, placing his paws cautiously on the loose scree and slippery rock, wary of the dampness that lingered from the morning dew. Ruthless trailed a little way behind them; when Fearless glanced back he noticed the cub looked sad but resolute. *Poor Ruthless,* he thought. *This must be tearing him apart.*

Higher up, the sun's rays found the cliff faces and turned them gold; the last of the mist that had hampered their search was burned away. Fearless was panting with heat and effort by the time he bounded over the lip of the ravine and onto flat grassland. He still sensed Keen's reluctance to continue on their course of action.

"I was supposed to kill him," Fearless muttered as they walked across the grassy plain. "That was my moment, there on that ledge. And I messed it up."

"He backed out of the fight, you mean," Keen reminded him gently. "Titan was clearly afraid of you, Fearless, and you're not even fully grown. Your time will come."

Fearless was not so sure. Titan had been within reach of his claws and teeth, and he knew he would have gotten the better of him eventually. "Let's not discuss it too much in front of Titan's son," he growled. Raising his voice, he called back to the cub, "Are you all right, Ruthless?"

"I'm fine," panted Ruthless, picking up his pace to walk beside the two older lions. "It's just, well—it will be strange seeing the pride again."

Fearless felt a pang of guilt. Of course Ruthless was troubled. His mother, Artful, had been the most powerful lioness in Titanpride, and he had only recently heard of her death at the feet of the elephants. *How could I have been so cruel? I was only thinking about myself.*

"Perhaps you should stay at a distance with Keen," Fearless said.

"What's that?" At his side, Keen came to an abrupt halt and growled.

Fearless stopped too and sniffed the air. As a thick, rank, and deathly scent reached his nostrils, he curled his muzzle in disgust.

"It's the wolves," he snarled. "Those brutes that have been feeding on spirits."

"It doesn't surprise me that they chose to come this way," said Keen, shaking his ears. "This is the Dead Forest."

The three lions stood unmoving, staring at the trees ahead of them. *The Dead Forest was well named,* thought Fearless. Its trees were skinny and broken and lifeless, their bark gray with an unhealthy mottling of pallid white fungus. Even the grass beneath the trunks was stunted and limp, and the whole place seemed infected with that fetid scent of wolf.

"Perhaps," said Keen, his voice hushed, "it was the wolves who took Titan's body."

"Why would they?" Fearless hunched his shoulders. "They don't eat whole corpses, only hearts."

Keen grunted in resignation. "True."

"We have to keep going and find Titanpride." Tensing his muscles, Fearless padded forward through the sickly trees. Even the ground beneath his paws felt sticky and soft, like rotting meat. He picked up speed.

They seemed to walk a terribly long way, as the sun rose higher in the sky beyond the skeletal branches, and the Dead Forest becoming no more welcoming. Its silence felt oppressive, growing heavier with every pawstep. When Keen spoke at last, his voice seemed to break a horrible, deadening trance.

"You're quiet, Ruthless," Keen told the cub lightly.

"Sorry." Ruthless twitched his whiskers ruefully. "I was thinking about my father."

Fearless shot a glance at Keen, who looked as uneasy as Fearless felt.

"He's a bad lion," Ruthless went on, his paws trembling with each pace on the yielding ground. "He's done terrible things. I know he deserves to die, and I know Bravelands would be a better place without him." His voice dropped to a whisper. "But he's my father . . . or, he was."

"We know, Ruthless," said Keen. "And we understand."

"Cub," said Fearless, pausing to turn to him, "you need to understand what must happen. What I plan to do. I know how you feel—I lost my own father—and I know this is difficult. But if Titan is still alive, I will kill him."

"Yes," said Ruthless softly. "I know."

"Titan took two fathers from me." Fearless walked on, letting the cub follow behind. "He murdered Gallant, stole his pride. He tormented my mother, Swift, and let Artful blind her. Then he killed my true father, Loyal. I made an oath of revenge, Ruthless, and I have to follow it through. No lion should ever break an oath." He hesitated, feeling a twinge of guilt. Loyal himself had been an oath-breaker. *My own true father.* He never meant to break that oath, and it was one of his greatest regrets, but he did.

Hurriedly, he went on: "But Ruthless, I do know this is hard for you. You don't have to stay with us. And you certainly don't have to help me."

The rapid padding of Ruthless's paws ceased, and Fearless turned in surprise. The cub was gazing at him levelly, his eyes dark but determined.

"Fearless, you and Keen have shown me more kindness than my father ever did," Ruthless told him. "It will be hard, you're right. But I'll stay with you. Whatever happens, I'm at your side."

Fearless found himself swallowing with emotion. He nodded, then turned swiftly away and strode on, his tail-tip flicking in consternation. Who would have predicted that one of his most loyal friends, the pride-mate who would follow him no matter what, would be the son of Titan?

* * *

Fearless was beginning to think the Dead Forest was endless, that they would never escape it, when at last an odor that wasn't rank wolf-scent drifted to his nostrils. Lions. Just as he recognized the scent, he saw the open plain beyond a last line of trees. Fearless shook himself, as if he could dislodge the clinging foulness of the forest.

"We're close to Titanpride territory," murmured Keen at his flank. "Let's take care."

Lowering their shoulders, slinking through the long grass beyond the Dead Forest, the three lions made their infinitely cautious way toward the familiar camp. There was no stir of movement in the grass, no tossing of golden manes, no flick of a tail swatting flies. No black-maned monstrous pride leader rose to his paws to roar a challenge, and Fearless was torn between relief and disappointment. But where were the others—Resolute, Glory, Artful, and the rest?

A breeze whispered across the plain, bringing a scent that stung Fearless's nostrils and caught in his throat. He stiffened, halted, and rose higher in the grass to stare.

"Look at the flies," whispered Ruthless.

The camp was abuzz with them, black masses of flies like shifting storm clouds. Fearless shuddered. Vultures circled overhead, landing one by one, and he saw a lone jackal glance at him, freeze, then scamper off into the far brush. It held a rib bone in its jaws, fringed with tatters of blackened flesh.

"What happened here?" breathed Keen. Seeming to throw

caution aside, he straightened up and strode forward.

Fearless trotted to overtake him, staring in disbelief at the carnage of Titanpride. The corpses of lions were strewn across the grassland. He jerked his head around and growled at Keen.

"Titan may be among the dead. Keep Ruthless back!"

Reluctantly, Keen halted and swung his forequarters to block the cub's path. Fearless paced on toward the ruined corpses of Titanpride.

The stench made his gut churn, and he wasn't even among them yet. His pawsteps slowed, his blood feeling heavy in his veins. As he crept closer, he recognized a muzzle here, a twisted tail there; a distinctive mane, an old scar. Not just the weak and old, but strong males too.

Fearless tried to close his twitching nostrils. But in this sluggish heat, there was no escaping the noxious odor of death and rot. Walking among the corpses, for a moment he paused, his head reeling. He recognized so many of these lions. He'd liked very few of them, but what kind of end was this for a feared and arrogant pride? There was Merciless, one of Titan's lieutenants: his fierce golden eyes staring lifelessly, set in rigid terror at some unseen enemy. He lay sprawled on a dry patch of red earth, a stain of much darker red clotted beneath him. Flies danced ecstatically around the dried blood, their buzzing almost deafening in Fearless's ears. Shuddering, he backed away and walked on.

He spotted a misshapen lump of unusually pale fur—Glory,

once a Gallantpride lioness. Fearless almost choked on the stench. She lay on her back, paws curled up as if she was basking in the sun. But her tail did not stir to flick at the crowd of flies, and her eyes, like Merciless's, stared at nothing.

Shaking his head violently, Fearless edged closer to Glory. Feeding vultures backed away, gulping down strips of furred meat as they watched him with wary eyes. One of them cawed in offense at the disturbance. In his peripheral vision, Fearless noticed the jackal creeping closer once more.

But his attention was focused on Glory and her ripped chest. The lioness's rib cage was exposed, fragments of bone gleaming white against her dead flesh. Her heart was gone, ripped out.

Fearless swallowed hard. Silently, Keen had crept to his side. Together they stood among the corpses. So many corpses. This was almost all of Titanpride.

But where were the rest?

"Was it sickness?" rasped Keen. "Or did they starve?"

"Neither." Fearless stood aside to let him see Glory's wound, and his friend gasped.

"The wolves?" breathed Keen.

"It must have been." Fearless stalked between the bodies, trying not to inhale too deeply. "These lions all have the same wound."

"But those golden wolves, they're so small." Keen shook his head in disbelief. "How could they have done this to Titanpride, of all lions?"

"I don't know. I don't know what's happening in Bravelands. I don't know what's happening to it."

From above them came an unearthly, piercing cry that sent ripples of dread along Fearless's spine. He jerked his head back and stared into the sky.

"More vultures," observed Keen. He shuddered as his paw brushed against a corpse, and he drew it quickly back.

Of course, thought Fearless; the stench of this carnage would draw rot-eaters from far away. He watched the new flock circle. The birds that had been feasting on lions shifted on their talons, then stretched their black wings and flapped into the air.

Without a word, Fearless turned and bounded back to Ruthless, Keen at his heels. The cub was shivering, staring up at a sky that was now dark with beating wings.

"What's that call? The vultures sound different."

"I don't know what it is," growled Keen, "but you're right, Ruthless. It's different. And I've never known a vulture abandon its meal like that."

"I think I know." Fearless felt a surge of excitement that drowned out even the horror of Titanpride's ruin. "That's the herald call to a gathering. A Great Gathering!"

The other two lions stared at him, confused. "A what?" asked Keen.

"A gathering of all the creatures of Bravelands," Fearless said. "Only one animal sends out such a summons."

Ruthless's eyes widened. He stared at Fearless, then up at the vultures once again. They were forming into an organized flock, aligning their broad wings to fly south. The cub blinked in wonder. "And that means . . . ?"

"A true Great Parent!" growled Fearless, slamming a paw onto the ground. "That means Bravelands has hope once again!"

CHAPTER THREE

Borne forward on Sky's shoulders toward the lake, Thorn watched as crowds of animals parted to let the two of them through. It wasn't for his benefit, of course—they simply wanted to avoid the stomping feet of an elephant. Above, the air was loud with birds. There were the vultures, of course, but so many more: a glittering flock of brilliant blue starlings, a dignified squadron of pelicans, bee-eaters that flashed and whirled. A single marabou stork flapped down close to Thorn and clattered its beak as it eyed him.

"Welcome!" the birds cried as one. "Welcome, Great Father Thorn of the Bright Forest! Welcome, new hope of Bravelands!"

As he listened to them, strength surged through Thorn's bones, even as a knot of fear tightened in his belly. To the animals on the ground, he knew, the birds' squawking and screeching would mean nothing. For every moment of his life until the day before, they had been nothing but squawks to him too. But now, invested with the power of the Great Spirit, the poetry of the sky was revealed to him, inspiring and chilling at the same time. The fact that he now understood Skytongue was all the proof he needed: however unlikely it seemed, he really was the Great Father of Bravelands.

But how can I do this?

So many hopes to be fulfilled, so many expectations to be met. Where did he even begin to understand how to lead Bravelands?

Already the herds were massing at the lake, their movement stirring up great clouds of dust that obscured both horizon and sky with a milky ocher haze. Scanning the horde desperately, Thorn at last made out Nut, Mud, and Spider. The three of them were making their way with difficulty toward him, negotiating bodies and hooves and swinging horns. The sight of his friends was reassuring. But Thorn's hide still tingled with nerves.

Zebras, gazelles, antelopes, and buffalo were crowded so thickly on the shore, the herds were intermingled, and bellows and brays echoed as they bumped into one another. Giraffes loitered on the edge of the crowd, gazing rather smugly from their high vantage point. A few gerenuk had propped their front hooves against trees to browse while they waited. A leopard sprawled on a branch, watching it all with detached curiosity. Even the earth was alive with scurrying rats and ground squirrels and guinea fowl; a fat little hyrax craned his head up to watch Thorn and Sky as they passed.

"The Great Father is with us!" chorused the birds above their heads. "All will be well now! All will be well!"

"They expect me to solve everything," Thorn muttered to Sky. "They're putting so much trust in me. I'm not sure I can ever live up to this."

Sky curled back her trunk to touch him, lightly but distractedly. "The Great Spirit knows what it's doing. Believe that."

It sounded a little like a command. It also sounded, just very slightly, as if she was talking to herself.

Thorn furrowed his brow, about to ask her if she was all right—but at that moment his eye was caught by a distinct movement beyond the tree line. He started and clutched Sky's ears tighter.

"Dawntrees Troop!" he gasped. "Over there."

The baboons that had once been Brightforest Troop, now led and renamed by their Crownleaf, Berry, were bounding down the shallow slope toward the gathering place. Thorn felt a lurch in his heart at the sight of them. They were his family, his friends, but he and Nut and Mud had been exiled with the stranger Spider. How would the troop react to their disgraced comrade being Great Father?

Berry—their Crownleaf and his mate—hadn't been happy about it. Their relationship had already been troubled, but when he'd at last confided his greatest secret, Berry had turned away from him in disbelief and shock.

"I need to go to Dawntrees Troop," he whispered to Sky. "Let me down, please?"

She nodded in understanding, and half knelt to let him scramble down her shoulder. Just at that moment, Nut, Mud, and Spider at last pushed through the crowd to his side. Their eyes shone with excitement.

"That's quite the entrance, Thorn." Nut grinned.

"Spider thinks this elephant is a very fine one," announced Spider, patting Sky's leg. She snorted at him, amused.

Mud embraced Thorn, then drew back, furrowing his brow. "You look worried, Thorn. Remember, you're in charge now."

"Maybe that's why his fur is going gray before our eyes," said Nut.

Thorn knew his friends were trying to make him feel better, and he appreciated their efforts. But it wasn't the burden of his future responsibilities that was making him anxious—it was the past. He swallowed hard.

"Don't let them intimidate you," boomed Nut, with a hearty slap of Thorn's shoulder. "You're Great Father now."

"We'll come with you," offered Mud.

"Thank you." Thorn nodded with gratitude and turned. With Nut, Mud, and Spider behind him, he bounded through the milling animals toward his former troop.

Thorn's heart clenched as he picked out Berry's golden fur among the crowd. She marched at the head of Dawntrees Troop, flanked by her loyal and fearsome Crown Guard. Thorn shuddered at the sight of them. He had never approved of the formation of a personal bodyguard for the Crownleaf, and the powerful baboons looked no less hostile than they had when some of them had driven him out—all because he and his friends had stopped them from murdering Tendril, the Crownleaf of their rival troop.

"Berry Crownleaf." There was a catch in Thorn's throat as he greeted his mate. Was she still his mate? He didn't know if she still loved him, or if resentment and bitterness had killed what they had had.

"Thorn." Berry halted and gazed at him. There was not a twitch on her face to betray what she was feeling. For a long moment they watched each other, and then simultaneously they both averted their eyes. Thorn felt his heart lurch with misery, and his throat went dry.

"Hey, you!" Viper shouldered in front of Berry and glared at Thorn. "What do you think you're doing? You don't belong with Dawntrees Troop."

Creeper, thuggish and one-eyed, pushed forward to stand beside Viper. "Get away from our Crownleaf, exile."

"That's not why I'm here," growled Thorn through clenched teeth. "I know I don't belong with Dawntrees anymore."

"We'll make sure the four of you understand that." Viper rose onto her hind paws, her fur bristling. Peeling back her muzzle, she snarled at Nut, who reared up to face her with a defiant growl. "A beating should remind you never to approach us."

"Viper, Creeper," snapped Berry. "Stand aside." She stalked between the two Crown Guards, giving each of them a reproving look. "Whatever else has happened, Thorn is my mate. Treat him with respect." Her eyes narrowed, and she gave Viper a particularly savage glare. "And no one attacks any baboon without my say-so. Understand?"

Viper looked away sullenly. Nut smirked at her.

Thorn gave Berry a nod of appreciation. He couldn't speak; his heart was too full at the sight of her.

"There's something I want to say to you, Thorn," said Berry. Her voice was still haughty, but there was a trace of the old warmth in her golden eyes. "You were right about Tendril. Her killing would have been an unforgivable breach of the Code, and you and your friends risked a great deal to stop us. You always were wise."

Viper shot her a look of rebellious outrage, but quickly blinked and suppressed it. Creeper simply glowered.

"Who cares about Thorn or Tendril anyway?" muttered Viper. "Both are irrelevant. We're here for the new Great Parent."

Berry's eyes widened a little, and she swallowed hard as she met Thorn's gaze. She knew already what her Crown Guard did not. Her expression was pained, and it cut him to the bone.

How can this possibly work? he wondered dismally. *We'll never get back to the way we were.* To be Berry's mate and Great Father to Bravelands: it seemed impossible now. *Oh, Great Spirit . . . What have you done to me?*

"You'd better go, Thorn Highleaf," Berry told him quietly.

"Yes . . ." He hesitated, then turned away and made his trembling way through the herds.

"Thorn?" Sounding anxious, Mud touched his flank.

Thorn didn't turn or respond. He couldn't meet his friend's eyes, and he had nothing to say.

The four baboons padded back to Sky, who was by now standing at the shoreline. For a fleeting instant, Thorn thought she looked worried. But as he drew closer, she blinked, and her expression became calm.

"Are you ready, Thorn?" asked the young elephant softly.

He nodded. Sky raised her trunk, stepped back, and let out a great trumpet of greeting.

One by one the animals hushed their chatter and yelling, and the low thunder of voices subsided. The rumble of shifting hooves and paws was stilled, and the dust began to settle as every creature turned their attention to Sky.

"Animals of Bravelands," she cried. "The Great Spirit has returned to us and has found its home once more. We have our new, true Great Parent!"

Thorn watched between her legs. Every creature seemed to hold its breath. Their excitement was like an energy Thorn could feel in the air; it thrummed like the beating of a thousand hearts, like the pulsing rhythm of Bravelands itself.

"I bring him to you today." Sky lifted her head, scanning the herds' suspenseful gazes. "He is the future of Bravelands, of us all." She paused, then took a few steps to one side to reveal him. He felt the fire of a thousand burning stares on his fur. "Salute your Great Father—Thorn of the Bright Forest!"

A gasp went up from the throng, turning swiftly into cries and hollers of excitement and surprise. The sound of voices rose in a rustling crescendo as the news spread through the herds, reaching the rearmost animals faster than Thorn had thought possible. The giraffes at the back began to bray, stretching their necks skyward. Rhinos pawed the ground and snorted; gazelles bounced; a zebra stallion whinnied shrilly; hippos opened their jaws and gave resonant bellows. Two cheetahs mewled harshly, and the leopard in the tree roared a reply. Thorn had to shut his eyes briefly, overcome with the din.

But he couldn't close his eyes forever. He had a job to do, the most important job of his life. He padded to Sky, turned to face the crowd, and rose onto his hind paws.

Once again, the noise faded, and an expectant hush fell over the herds. For a moment Thorn hesitated, and his gaze fell on Dawntrees Troop. Their faces almost made him bark a nervous laugh, but that would have been inappropriate: the moment was too solemn. They looked as if a chimpanzee had smacked them with a branch. Viper and Creeper wore matching expressions of horror, their jaws hanging open to exactly the same degree. Berry, though, scratched apprehensively at her muzzle, then stared at the ground.

It was more comforting to look at Mud, Nut, and Spider at the front of the crowd, their chests puffed out with pride. Thorn cleared his throat. It felt tight.

"I . . . thank you, animals of Bravelands. Thank you for your trust. This is a . . . a proud moment for m-me. . . ." *No, that's wrong—*

He swallowed. The silence was like a pressure on his ears.

"I didn't expect this. I don't think any creature in Bravelands would have."

Beside him, Sky shifted uneasily. There was a little ripple of laughter from the crowd, but it wasn't the unkind sort. Thorn let himself smile. He drew himself up straighter.

"Animals of Bravelands, the times are hard. Things have been wrong for a long time; we all know that." He felt his voice growing steadier, stronger. "I'll be honest: I don't know if I can fix it. On my own, I certainly couldn't. But I'm not alone. And it's not just that I have good friends to help me, friends who love Bravelands as much as I do." He turned and gave Sky a smile, then nodded fondly at Mud, Nut, and Spider. "I'm not alone, because the Great Spirit is with me. The Great Spirit is with all of us. It has come back at last. It is the Great Spirit that will rescue Bravelands, and I am honored to be its host."

The herds erupted. Stamping, neighing, tossing their heads, they bellowed and squealed. It was long moments before the hush settled once more. Thorn waited, feeling the warmth of their delight flowing into his blood and bones. Their excitement was for the Great Spirit, he knew, but it put strength in his spine all the same, made his head feel clear and purposeful.

"Our troubles are not nearly over, that's the truth of it. I wish I could tell you otherwise. There are still hard times ahead, friends. But I believe, I honestly do believe, that good times are just beyond the horizon—if we have faith in the Great Spirit. We've all worked together before to defend our home—remember the Great Herd that came together as one to defeat the False Parent?"

A buffalo bellowed, "Indeed. A good and honorable day."

"Even the smallest of us had a part to play, even the weakest." Thorn glanced down at a little ground squirrel and inclined his head. "If we remember who we are and what we fight for, we can bring peace back to Bravelands. If we follow the Code and uphold it in our lives, we honor the Great Spirit and follow its will. With all the strength that's in me, I swear to you I will fight for that."

Sky was watching him intently; her eyes seemed brighter and happier now. Thorn coughed again, pausing for a moment.

"But I have to tell you that a new threat has come to Bravelands—yes, friends, another. The golden wolves have come to dishonor our Code, to steal the spirits of the strong and the clever and the sprightly. In other words, they've come to steal everything we are. But we're not going to let them. Together, we will defend the Code, trust the Great Spirit, and defeat them."

A halfhearted cheer rose from the herds. *They don't quite believe in me yet. And why should they?*

Thorn lowered his head. "I know many of you will be wary of a baboon Great Father."

"No!" neighed a zebra.

"Never!" squeaked the little ground squirrel in agreement. "You're not Stinger!"

"Thank you," said Thorn humbly, "but it's true that many other animals will be nervous." He raised his head, trying to meet as many troubled gazes as he could. "I want to promise you all, in the sight of the Great Spirit, that I'll never betray you as he did. I'll never lie, nor will I turn the animals of Bravelands against one another. I will never, ever break the Code. I am not Stinger, and may the Great Spirit strike me down if I ever become like him."

Thorn hesitated. He couldn't help his eyes straying toward Berry, the daughter of Stinger. Her gaze remained fixed on him, but it was impossible to read her expression. *I had to mention the False Parent*, thought Thorn, *I had to repudiate him!* Thorn could only hope with all his heart that Berry understood.

He took a deep breath. "My friends. I serve the Great Spirit. I honor the Code. And I swear to protect Bravelands all the days of my life!"

He closed his eyes, suddenly more afraid than he'd ever been in his life. But he couldn't let it show.

"So. Who will follow me as Great Father?"

The silence seemed charged by the threat of lightning. No creature moved, none spoke. An impala exchanged glances with a wildebeest. A solitary cheetah stared past Thorn toward the lake.

Then Berry Crownleaf stepped forward. She padded through a herd of zebras and rose to her hind paws, staring at Thorn. His heart was in his throat.

"I accept Thorn Highleaf." Her voice rang through the air, clear enough for all to hear, yet her eyes never left Thorn's. "I accept him as Great Father, and I have faith in him. He is wise and compassionate; he is the furthest from my father Stinger it is possible for a baboon to be—and I speak as one who knew them both. I would trust him with my own life, and I trust him with the future of Bravelands."

Thorn gulped hard, feeling a turmoil of emotion in his chest. *Thank you, my love*, he wanted to say, but he found he couldn't speak.

"If our Crownleaf accepts our new Great Father, then so do we." Lily Middleleaf bounded forward to Berry's side.

"We do," chorused all of Dawntrees. Even Viper and Creeper joined the shouts, though their faces were surly.

"And I accept Great Father Thorn, on behalf of my herd," declared Sky, taking a determined step forward and raising her trunk. "My family is on migration now, but I have the right to speak for them, and I do."

"And I on behalf of my own bull-herd," bellowed her brother Boulder from the back of the crowd. "Great Father Thorn is our leader."

"We follow you, Thorn!" A zebra stallion sprang forward, tossing up his head.

"As do we!" brayed one of the gerenuk, rearing high on its hind hooves and flailing its forefeet.

"We too!" squeaked a pack of rats.

"And the hyenas."

"And the hippos." Wallow, whose pod had joined the Great Gathering, plunged through the shallows in a massive shower of spray.

"The rhinos agree!"

"The impalas agree!"

"The leopards follow you." A lazy growl from the branches.

"The serval cats follow."

"And the bushbuck!"

Thorn stood in awed wonder as one by one, the animal herds shouted their acceptance. He felt buffeted by their support, proud and humbled at the same time. But no declaration meant quite as much as Berry's pledge of loyalty; the memory of her words glowed warm in his breast.

There was a stirring in the herds, a startled shifting of bodies and clatter of hooves as animals dodged out of the way. Some even gave cries of fear. A golden-furred body hurtled forward through them, and for a moment Thorn froze in shock.

Then a lion sprang on him, bowling him over, licking and nuzzling him and panting hot breath happily in his face. Thorn grinned and giggled, play-punching Fearless's heavy body. He remembered the last time Fearless had knocked him over on this spot, when the young lion's intent had been far more deadly.

It was so different now. Thorn hugged his old friend. Suddenly Fearless bounced back, shaking himself, his face anxious and uncertain.

"Sorry. Sorry, Thorn. I shouldn't have done that. You're Great Father now."

"Oh, my friend. You can do it any time." Thorn laughed. "So long as you're not trying to kill me."

For a fleeting moment Fearless averted his eyes in embarrassment. Then his muzzle twitched with amusement, and he nodded at Thorn.

Sky's trunk nudged Thorn's shoulder, and he turned to her.

"You must make it official," she murmured.

He nodded. He'd seen Stinger do it, and it was time to cleanse the Great Parenthood from that evil baboon's noxious legacy.

Getting to his paws, he padded forward into the lake until the cool water lapped around his chest. He rose onto his hind legs and cupped his forepaws, scooping up the water. Tipping his head back, he drank.

Around him all the animals were moving forward now, stirring up the water and splashing happily as they plunged their muzzles in to drink. But Thorn was only vaguely aware of them. In the dazzling sunlight that dappled the surface, he saw shapes form: animals whose ghostly bodies did not disturb the water's surface—great spectral elephants, a bounding cheetah, a noble giraffe.

The others weren't seeing this, he knew. Only Thorn could see the spirits of the Great Parents of the past. Pacing across the water toward him came a dignified, elderly baboon, his shape shimmering against the lake's brightness. He gazed into Thorn's awed eyes, nodded, and smiled.

I am Bravelands now, Thorn realized. *I am all of its creatures. I am linked to all these ancient Parents, and through them to the land itself.*

He stood very still, letting the joyful herds plunge and drink around him, and allowed the Great Spirit to bind him to Bravelands forever.

CHAPTER FOUR

It felt strange but quite pleasant to stand up to his belly in the lake, feeling it tickle his fur, as herds of prey animals splashed and waded in the watering hole nearby. Fearless lapped at the water, then lifted his dripping jaws and tried to spot Thorn in the melee. At last he glimpsed him, talking earnestly to a couple of hippos as a bushbuck waited his turn patiently. Fearless felt a tingle of pride.

He's one of my best friends, and now he's Great Father of Bravelands!

A rhino gave Fearless a sidelong stare, and a young kudu looked particularly nervous. *That was natural,* he thought. It was most unusual for a lion to attend a Great Gathering; his kind followed neither the Great Spirit nor the Great Parent who embodied it. But he had been raised by baboons, and he felt at home here. After all, he had been to Great Gatherings before—though those had been Stinger's, and the thought of those scandalous charades in honor of a False Parent now made him cringe with shame.

Thorn's dry joke had bitten him sharply: a reminder of the day Fearless had tried, on Stinger's orders, to kill Thorn. Looking back, that moment seemed to Fearless so symbolic of Stinger's dreadful tyranny and deceit. Thorn might be able to make lighthearted jibes about it now, but Fearless knew he would carry the disgrace of it for the rest of his life.

How could he have fallen so hard for lies and pretenses and turned against his lifelong baboon friend? Looking back, it seemed so clear that the wily Stinger had been a charlatan and a murderer. Yet Fearless had believed in him utterly. He'd felt loyalty and love for the baboon who had adopted him as a cub, and he remembered those emotions every bit as well as he remembered his shame. It was confusing enough to make his head ache.

"Don't look so dejected, Fearless," growled Keen. He and Ruthless had refused to get into the water, but they stood close by on the bank. "You made a mistake, that's all. I think your baboon friend has forgiven you. And it's not surprising you believed that other one. Stinger was like your father, wasn't he?"

"My mentor, for sure." Fearless glanced back gratefully at Keen. How was it that his companion could so often read his mind? "Are you coming in, by the way?"

"I'll stay right here, thank you." Keen laughed.

Ruthless shuddered at the mere suggestion. "Me too. What are they all splashing around for anyway?"

"It's a tradition," Fearless explained. "They think it connects them to the Great Father, and through him to the Great Spirit. I don't know how it works, but it's been the custom forever." He slid his eyes mischievously back to Keen. "And it feels great. The water's so cool. Very refreshing. You two look as if your fur's smoldering."

Keen sagged dramatically. "It is hot," he said.

"You're missing out," taunted Fearless.

With a sudden spring, Keen plunged into the water beside Fearless, showering him with spray.

Spitting out lake water, Fearless shook himself. Wading closer, he licked Keen's face, then settled to grooming his slender back. He felt Keen reciprocate, and they basked for a moment in the cool water under the sun. It was so good to have a moment of peaceful respite amid all the troubles that had afflicted Bravelands and their own prides.

"Oh, fine!" yelped a voice from the bank. Ruthless flung himself into the lake, splashing them both. His shorter legs took his out of his depth quickly, but he adapted straightaway, paddling quite confidently around the two older cubs.

"What?" he said defiantly. "I was feeling left out."

Fearless gave a throaty growl. "Told you you'd like it."

Ruthless immediately looked distracted, though. He was staring back at the bank. "What's happening there? Is it another Great Gathering thing?"

Fearless and Keen stopped grooming each other and turned to look at the shoreline. Other animals were turning too, and there was a ripple of uneasy murmuring.

Two leopards were prowling down the shallow slope of bank, dragging something heavy and limp between them. The thing was shapeless, bumping along the gritty sand, but every animal in the lake grew silent as it became clear what it was. The leopards dropped it from their jaws and raised their heads to look at the new Great Father. Their faces were set hard with grief and anger.

Fearless stared at the limp corpse of a third leopard. Why would they bring that here, and on such a day?

Thorn was already wading back through the crowd, dropping to all fours as he reached the shore and bounded forward. He halted in front of the leopards, staring in horror at the body. Sky had followed him, and she gasped, flapping her ears in distress.

Fearless ran to join them, Keen and Ruthless at his heels, shaking water from their fur.

What did this? Fearless was about to ask, but he only had to look at the wound to know what had killed the leopard. Its rib cage had been torn raggedly open, and where its heart had been, there was a bloody cavity.

"The wolves," snarled one of the leopards hoarsely. "They took her heart. Now she will never hunt among the stars."

As the thick silence deepened, Fearless felt his own heart wrench. *I should have told Thorn at once about Titanpride.* But now wasn't the moment. The leopards' distress was painful.

Soft cries and squeals and a horrified muttering were rising once again from the herds that were now emerging from the water. Thorn crouched over the dead leopard, his fingers gently brushing the edges of its terrible wound.

Abruptly, he stiffened and rose to his paws. He turned to the other animals. Fearless almost didn't recognize the expression on his friend's face: it was full of such cold fury.

"These wolves," he declared in a ringing voice. "I will stop them, and I will put an end to the evil they have brought to Bravelands."

"How?" cried an impala, stepping forward and shaking his horns. "This same thing happened to one of ours, not three days ago. She too has lost her spirit, and she will never run along the silver way that lights the night sky."

"I heard," rumbled a hippo angrily, "that they have even done this to great and powerful animals. A crocodile. A rhino. More than one buffalo. How can a baboon stop them?"

"I'll start with the only thing I know," said Thorn. He gazed around the herds, and it struck Fearless how open and honest his face was compared to Stinger's; there would be no crazy boasts from Thorn. "I'll find the leader of these savages and tell him it must stop. They cannot stand against the united animals of Bravelands, and they know it. We defeated Stinger's army. Perhaps these creatures don't know how much they have to fear."

For a moment Fearless felt a nip of anxiety in his gut. How would the herds react to Thorn's first, peaceful proposal in the face of such brutal provocation?

But a rumble of approval went round the gathered crowd. "Well said, Great Father!" bellowed a buffalo.

Fearless took a pace toward Thorn. "I'll help," he said, "and so will Keen and Ruthless." The two lions nodded at him. "We can track down this golden wolf leader and bring him to you. You are a fine Great Parent, Thorn, but you need strength and muscle behind you."

"And that'll be us," added Keen.

Thorn exchanged a look with Sky and nodded. "That's a good plan. Thank you, Fearless."

"It's the least I can do," said Fearless, his head drooping slightly. "Perhaps it'll help make up for what I did the last time we all gathered here."

"Stop thinking about that," said Thorn kindly, rubbing his friend's head. "What matters now are the wolves."

"We know roughly where they are," Keen told him. "We scented them at the Dead Forest. We'll start our search there."

There was movement between the long legs of the zebras, and a small shadow sauntered out, her tail held arrogantly high. Fearless stifled a groan. It was the irritating daughter of Titan: Menace.

"I want to hunt wolves too," the little cub demanded haughtily. Her nose tilted high, she looked around. "I am the daughter of Titan, born to hunt and kill my enemies."

"You're too little for this mission, Menace," said Sky kindly.

"I didn't ask for your advice, elephant," snapped Menace. "I am going! I'm not staying at this stupid gathering a moment longer. My father says it's all a load of hyena dung anyway. I want to hunt."

"You can want all you like," said Fearless irritably, "but you're not coming."

"My father said I—"

"Your father isn't here!" roared Fearless. He lunged his face down to hers, peeling back his lips from his fangs and trying to look as furious as he could. "You—are—staying—put!"

Menace did not flinch much. She glared at him until he had no option but to draw back.

He turned away, flicking his tail at her. "Keen, Ruthless— let's go."

"Good luck," called Sky.

"You'll need it," muttered Nut.

Thorn, though, shook his head as he raised a paw in farewell.

"Luck does not matter so much, Fearless. Not when the Great Spirit goes with you."

"Can you hear that?" Keen halted, one paw raised, flaring his nostrils.

Fearless paused too and glanced around. "What?"

"That sound. There's something following us."

Fearless's muscles tensed, and his claws sprang from their sheaths. "Yes. I hear it. In the long grass behind us." He swung his head toward Ruthless. "Stay back, young one."

"Ha! I'm not much younger than you two." Ruthless

padded to his side and turned to face the danger, his gentle muzzle curled in threat.

Keen caught Fearless's eyes over the younger cub's back and wrinkled his muzzle. They'd been moving for half a day after the Great Gathering, over empty plains. With so many animals at the watering hole, the rest of the Bravelands belonged to them.

The breeze sighed across the grass, making the long blades sway and rustle gently, but it was coming from behind them. There was no way to catch the scent of whatever trailed downwind. But there was definitely another sound: a compact body, the pad of paws, the huffing of breath. Fearless coiled his shoulder muscles and lowered his haunches, his tail-tip twitching. No golden wolf would take them by surprise. . . .

The creature blundered out of the long grass, coming to an abrupt halt as she caught sight of them staring at her. A fleeting look of guilt crossed her face, replaced quickly by defiance.

"Menace!" Fearless's snarl was exasperated.

"You young fool," snapped Keen.

"Sister!" exclaimed Ruthless. "You were supposed to stay behind. This is dangerous!"

"No chance," said Menace smugly. "This is what Father would have wanted. And I know that much better than you, Ruthless. Besides," she added, unconsciously quoting his own words, "I'm not much younger than you."

"Yes, you are," Ruthless growled. "Fearless, she has to go back!"

"Indeed," said Fearless, swatting a paw at her. "Get back to the watering hole!"

"You're not my pride leader," she retorted, "and you're certainly not my father."

As Fearless glowered at her, wondering whether to grab her scruff in his jaws and drag her back, he felt Keen nudge his neck.

"Fearless," his friend murmured, "she can't go back on her own, and we've come too far already. Our mission is urgent. We can't spare the time." Keen looked at Menace. "We'll have to let her come. It's not safe, with the wolves around."

"I can hear you, you know?" snarled Menace. "I'm not scared of a puny wolf. If I see one, I'll tear its—"

Fearless growled. Keen was right, and he knew it.

"Fine," he snapped. "You can stay with us. Ruthless, don't argue, we don't have a choice—she's safer here. For now," he added, as Ruthless shut his jaws and glared at his sister. "But mark my words, Menace, you'd better do as I say. You may not consider me your pride leader, but for the purposes of this mission, I am."

"The only lion who can tell me what to do," Menace sneered, "is my father."

Keen took two paces forward and swatted her muzzle with the flat pad of his paw. Menace staggered sideways and laid back her ears at him, hissing, but he stood over her, four square and tall. The blow had been a warning—clawless but firm.

Fearless gave a growl of approval.

"Fine," said Menace after a moment. "I'll behave."

Keen nodded and stalked back to Fearless's side; Fearless gave him a grateful nuzzle as they turned and set off once again.

He hoped he wasn't going to regret this decision.

CHAPTER FIVE

The sun was beginning to drift down from its midday zenith, but Thorn was still surrounded by a great crowd of animals, stamping and snorting in impatience as they waited their turn to talk to him, to seek his help or ask his advice. The herds had moved up onto the shore, and the water of the lake lay still once more, gleaming rose and silver. But there was no quiet afternoon peace for the new Great Father.

As Sky watched, Thorn backed away from a couple of impalas, nodding and smiling and muttering some reassurance. As soon as he could detach himself from the throng, he turned and beckoned Sky closer, his eyes pleading.

How could Thorn be expected to focus on all these complaints, wondered Sky, on his very first day as Great Father? There had been no letup in the petitioners who surrounded him, not since Fearless, Keen, and Ruthless had left on their mission to find the wolf leader. It was true that giving advice was a vital part of being Great Father, but Thorn was so new to this, and he had so much on his mind. Sky's heart went out to him.

She trod carefully to his side, dodging guinea fowl and an indignant hyrax. "Excuse me, little cousin," she murmured to it as it glared at her. "Coming through. The Great Father needs me."

The hyrax harrumphed and backed off a little, and Sky dipped her head to Thorn.

"What do I do now?" he whispered to her. "What happens next, Sky?"

"Try not to worry, Thorn." She stroked his shoulder with her trunk.

"I can't help it," he muttered. "These animals don't have a great deal of patience when it comes to their problems. There's much more to this than I expected, and I expected a lot."

Then I'll try not to worry, too. Sky suppressed a sigh. Thorn seemed so unsure of himself. . . . But whatever happened, she had to support him. "I watched Great Mother for years," she told him. "She might have been confident when I knew her, but she told me often what a terrifying burden it was to begin with, when she was only a young elephant like me. I saw how she dealt with the practical matters, too, so I can help." Turning to face the waiting animals, she raised her trunk and smiled.

"Please, will you give the Great Father some space for a little while? He wants to address all your questions, help you with your problems, but he has only just begun."

The creatures exchanged glances. A hippo gave a grunt. "All right. That's fine with us."

"He will help us, though?" asked the hyrax. "Won't he?"

"Of course he will, little cousin. Give him time, that's all I ask." Sky raised her gaze to the others. "Even our beloved and wise Great Mother needed space to gather her thoughts."

With some reluctance, the waiting animals dispersed, flicking their tails and murmuring together. Only Mud, Nut, and Spider remained, hovering at the edge of the little clearing by the shore. Spider was chattering to his lizard, though it seemed to have fallen asleep on his shoulder.

"I'm going to have to make a more sensible arrangement." Thorn looked around at them all. "I need to be accessible. Every animal needs to know they can talk to me. Great Mother roamed the plains freely, Sky, but I'm not used to being away from the forests. I don't know if I can do it."

"You don't have to," she told him. "Don't live like an elephant. You're a baboon! Find a baboon way of being Great Father."

Thorn scratched his jaw thoughtfully. "Honestly, Sky, I have no idea why the Great Spirit didn't choose you. You're so wise."

"The Great Spirit always chooses the right host," she said firmly. "And it's so much wiser than I am. You simply need to find a place where all can reach you—the largest and the smallest. Somewhere they'll know where to find you, where you can be safe."

"What about Baboon Island?" suggested Nut, picking a tick from his elbow and squashing it. "I know bad things happened there, but it was a perfect setup."

Thorn shook his head. "No, I don't want anything that could link me in the herds' minds with Stinger. That would be a big mistake, I think."

"How do baboons usually find their camps?" asked Sky.

"Well." Thorn considered for a moment. "We'd find a quiet clearing, with shelter and access, but safe from unwanted intruders. . . . Somewhere that can be defended . . . We look for good strong trees to sleep in."

"And plenty of fruit," put in Spider, licking his lips.

"Yes." Thorn laughed. "Plenty of figs and marula nuts— and preferably mangoes."

"Then that is what we do next," Sky rumbled. "We look for somewhere just like that."

"And there we have it," declared Nut, dusting his paws together with satisfaction. "An excellent Great Father Clearing. That wasn't so hard to find!"

Sky raised her head and cocked her ears, gazing around at the dense green forest that ringed the clearing. The ground rose toward the east side of the glade, providing a prominent hillock where Thorn could wait to hear the petitions of the animals; that was perfect. Fruits gleamed between the thick green leaves: no mangoes, unfortunately, but they'd found figs, passion fruits, sour plums, and a big jackfruit tree. A little way away, Sky could hear the sound of Boulder and his herd-brothers as they began to smash and tear down saplings and scrub, creating a path that would allow even the bulkiest of animals to reach the clearing.

"I don't know what Dawntrees Troop will think," mused Thorn, looking around. "They're in the same forest. Viper and Creeper won't like it."

"But much farther to the west," argued Nut. "They should barely notice us here. They might try to drive us out, but they won't."

"Look what I found!" exclaimed Mud, bounding out of the brush. He held out his paws, filled with yellow fruits. One was crushed and leaking yellow pulp. "Mabungo."

Thorn licked his lips. "This is the perfect glade." His eyes gleamed. "And Nut, I don't think even Viper and Creeper would try to drive the Great Father away. Not if we don't encroach on their boundaries."

"Spider loves mabungo." The odd baboon loped forward and took one of the fruits from Mud, picking a little pulp out to offer it to his pet lizard. The lizard stared at it, perplexed.

Sky smiled to herself and turned her head to watch the bull elephants at work. With the scrubby bushes cleared, a big stinkwood had been exposed, right in the middle of the proposed path. Noticing that Sky was watching, a big young male called Forest bunched his muscles and slammed his head into the trunk, then drew back and tore at it with his creamy tusks. The other bulls paused to watch him, chewing and crunching on the branches they'd torn down. Forest butted the stinkwood again, and it creaked and swayed.

Sky caught his hopeful eye. *He's showing off for me*, she thought, with a slight sinking of her heart. Didn't all these young bulls know there was no way she could take a mate? Her relationship with Rock might have been doomed to failure from the start, but he was still her betrothed. She was not allowed to choose another partner.

Not wanting to encourage him, Sky turned away and ambled toward a thin old elephant who was curling his trunk and tusks around a huge uprooted mahogany stump. His feet slithered on leaves, and he dropped it, panting.

Sky walked to his side. "Can I help?"

He shook his deeply wrinkled head. "I'm fine. I've done this before."

He looks so very old, thought Sky, *and tired.* "We all need help sometimes," she said, and shoved at the stump with her curled trunk. At last it thudded over and rolled, and together they pushed it deeper into the undergrowth away from the new path.

"Thank you," the old elephant muttered. "There was a time I could have picked up that stump and tossed it clear of the trees. But years go by, I suppose, and there's nothing we can do to stop them."

"There's honor in age," Sky pointed out, "and wisdom."

"But not much extra muscle," he said wryly. "Tell me, Sky Strider, why do you stay away from your herd? It's an unusual path you've chosen, for a young elephant."

"You know my name?" She blinked in surprise.

"I do. And I suppose I have you at a disadvantage there. So: my name is Flint."

Sky frowned. That name seemed familiar. "Flint? But that means you—surely you aren't—"

"Yes." He nodded, blowing idly at the tree dust on his flank. He met Sky's gaze once again. "I was close to your grandmother, Sun. That was before she accepted her destiny as Great Mother, of course."

Sky stared at him, her heart lifting in happy surprise. "You are my grandfather," she whispered. "Flint was the sire of my mother, Mist. That's how I know your name. My grandmother told me about you . . ." She hesitated. "After my mother died."

He dipped his head in sad acknowledgment. "Yes. I had many offspring, Sky, but your mother was special. It broke my heart when I heard the lions had taken her." He looked up, studying Sky's face. "You're as special as she was. I can see it."

Sky's heart turned over at the memory of her mother. It had been so long since, weak and ill after Sky's birth, Mist had fallen victim to a lion pride; yet the grief still lived with Sky.

"I miss her too," she said softly.

"Sky! Sky!" Two energetic balls of spotted yellow fur came crashing through the undergrowth toward her. Sky turned, almost glad to have her memories interrupted.

"Nimble. Lively." She nuzzled the cheetah cubs with her trunk. "What is it?"

"We can't find Menace anywhere," Lively complained. "She's vanished!"

Sky's stomach lurched. *No.* What if the wolves who had taken Artful had taken her daughter too? No one knew where the golden wolves prowled. . . . Often it seemed they appeared and disappeared at will.

"Did I hear that right?" Thorn padded toward them and sat back on his haunches, dusting bark and dust from his fur. He peered at the little cheetahs. "That Menace is missing?"

The cubs nodded unhappily. "She's a nuisance," said Nimble in a small voice, "but we don't want anything to happen to her."

"Don't worry, cubs. And Sky, relax. I'll find Menace." Thorn closed his eyes, a frown creasing his brow.

The two cubs turned to each other, perplexed. Then they stared at Thorn again.

"Well, you'll have to get going," pointed out Lively.

He opened one eye and wrinkled his muzzle. "I don't have to," he told her. The cub's eyes opened wide with fascination.

Sky watched him, her anxious heartbeat calming. She did not know what Thorn was doing, but he was Great Father. She had trusted the Great Spirit while she herself carried it; now that it lived within Thorn, she must do the same.

Mud patted her foreleg to get her attention. "He's searching with his mind," he whispered as Sky lowered her head to him. "Thorn can do that now. The Great Spirit, you know?"

"Oh!" breathed Sky. She watched Thorn with renewed fascination.

Leaves dipped and rustled overhead, dappling Thorn's fur with sunspots. High in the canopy above the silent glade, birds whistled and called, a distinct note of annoyance in their voices. *Well*, thought Sky, *the elephants are destroying some of their trees.*

Thorn's eyes blinked open. He smiled at Sky. "You don't have to worry," he told her. "Menace is with Fearless."

"She is?" Sky flapped her ears. "Why?"

"I'm not certain. But she has the protection of him and Keen, and her brother, Ruthless, so no doubt she'll be safe."

"All the same." Sky blew nervously at the dusty ground. "I'm not sure Fearless and Menace make a good combination. Menace is devoted to Titan, and Fearless wants to kill him."

"True." Thorn laughed. "But Fearless will protect the cub; you know that. He has a good heart."

"It's a relief, but never mind Menace just now." Sky studied him. "Mud told me what you were doing. You can look across the savannah with your mind?"

He nodded, looking modest. "It's just something that came. When I was with the vultures."

"The Great Spirit's gift." She nodded. "I remember Great Mother telling me about a baboon Great Father who had a similar power."

"That's right. Great Father Creek of the Goldenforest," said Thorn proudly. "I was a bit shocked at first—it's frightening—but I've been practicing a lot, and it's getting easier. More natural."

Sky hesitated, her heart thumping. At this moment, she

wanted so much to ask Thorn to find Rock; to enter his mind and to confirm for her that somewhere out there, her former mate was alive and well. She had rejected him, but it had been the hardest thing she had ever done, and Sky still missed the dark-hided bull with the green eyes. Rock had done so much to help and guide her, and she had been so happy and content in his company. If she hadn't found out that he'd killed River, they would have been together still, striding side by side across the plains. He'd have been here now with the other bulls, helping prepare the Great Father Clearing, casting loving glances her way as he worked. . . .

But he had killed River, Sky told herself angrily, and he wasn't here, and she could not dwell on him. She had squandered her chances of a life-mate on a killer. That was all she needed to know of the elephant she had loved. She would not ask Thorn to find Rock, she thought, clenching her jaw. *I need to forget he ever existed.*

Boulder plodded toward her, looking tired but content. "Sky, there you are."

"Hello, brother," she greeted him brightly. "How's the work progressing?"

"It's going well," he told her, butting his trunk against hers. "In fact, it's nearly done. My herd is growing restless. We'll be leaving in a day or two."

"I understand," she said, pressing her face to his cheek. "You can't stay forever."

"You could come with us," he suggested. "We're traveling

to the mating grounds. You'd find your own herd again—the Striders are sure to be there."

Sky was aware of Flint watching her closely. She lowered her head.

"I don't think I'm ready to leave yet, Boulder. The Great Father still needs me."

"Sister, you're not responsible for the Great Spirit anymore," Boulder told her gently. "Thorn has been chosen. He needs to find his own path."

"I know, but—oh!" Sky swung around at the sound of rustling leaves and snapping twigs.

The baboons of Dawntrees Troop were approaching, some padding along the forest floor, others strutting along branches or springing from rock to rock. At their head strode Berry Crownleaf, the soft golden sunlight glowing on her fur. Her expression, Sky realized with relief, was not hostile.

Berry stopped in front of Thorn, and for an awkward moment there was silence between them. Then they exchanged a slow nod.

"We've come to see how you're getting along," Berry told Thorn. Her voice was calm and warm. "Is your new camp suitable? We can offer you any help you need."

"That's kind, Berry Crownleaf," said Thorn softly. There was yearning in his eyes, but he didn't reach out to touch her. "I think we're almost settled. The elephants have cleared a path for the other animals."

"That's exactly the problem," growled Viper, slinking forward. "They're knocking down good trees!"

"Viper," warned Berry, "we came here to welcome the Great Father."

"The Great Father's made a mess," complained Splinter. It took everything Sky had not to flick her trunk at him. Thankfully, Berry had something to say about it:

"Splinter!" she snapped. "Behave."

Splinter gave her a surly look, but he shut his jaws.

"The Great Father's got no right to be here, actually," snarled Creeper. "Thorn, you've picked a spot that's way too close to Tall Trees."

Berry glared at him, but Creeper took no notice.

"Creeper's right." Viper nodded. "Those elephants of yours are making such a racket, they're scaring the small prey. The mice and rats are fleeing—even the spiders and beetles are hiding themselves."

"They'll be gone soon," promised Thorn. "I know it's an upheaval, but it'll be worth it."

"Oh, will it, now?" Creeper rose onto his hind paws, glaring. "You don't care if you harm this troop, do you? Now that you're Great Father, you think you can do anything, you power-hungry—"

"That's enough!" Berry spun around, snarling at her lieutenants. "That—is—enough! Thorn is Great Father of Bravelands, and how long has it been since a baboon was chosen for that honor? You should be proud! Respect his decisions—and respect mine! I am your Crownleaf—and I say that we are privileged to have the Great Father make his home in our forest!"

Thorn looked taken aback by her vehemence, thought Sky, but not nearly as shocked as Viper and Creeper and the other complainers. Muttering and grumbling, the troop turned one by one and went back the way they had come, their fur bristling at Berry's scolding.

Berry herself, though, lingered behind. Sitting down on her haunches beside Thorn, she peeled the bark from a twig. She looked troubled.

As the last noises of the retreating baboons faded, Berry glanced up at Thorn. "I'll be honest. . . . I'm not happy with the destruction of trees either."

Thorn nodded, looking shame-faced. "I swear to you, Berry, we've removed only what was necessary. I had to find a place to give counsel."

"I know." She gave him a sidelong smile. "I know you have to please everyone, and I know you have responsibilities none of us can imagine. Just . . . please think of the troop sometimes."

"I will, Berry. I promise."

She lowered her eyes and murmured, "And think of me too. Sometimes."

Thorn stared at her, a little shocked, as she rose to her paws and bounded after her troop. Her tailless haunches vanished among the undergrowth, and for a long moment there was an awkward silence.

"Oh, Sky." Thorn gave a great sigh, and his shoulders slumped. "I know I have duties, and I have a huge responsibility to Bravelands. But I can't shake my loyalty to my old troop.

I owe them something too, don't I?"

"Of course." Sky paced closer, reaching out her trunk, but she was suddenly afraid to touch him. "Thorn, I know this is difficult. Believe me, I know. But you'll find a way. The Great—"

"Ah, yes," he interrupted, a hint of weary mockery in his voice. "The Great Spirit doesn't make mistakes. Does it?"

Sky went still, not knowing what to say. It was a relief when she heard the sound of clopping hooves, thudding feet, and a great rustle of branches.

She took a deep breath, cocked her ears brightly, and nodded at him. "I believe you have your first petitioners, Great Father!"

Thorn already looked worn-out, thought Sky with a twinge of pity. Since the first buffalo and impalas, the stream of animals had been constant throughout the afternoon. What could Thorn possibly do for the giraffe who complained his neck was too short to reach the most tender leaves? How could he explain to that rhino that the evil rhino who lurked in the pools was his own reflection?

And as Thorn complained to her when the warthog turned its stiff little tail and trotted off: How could he advise a warthog on its love life when his own was such a mess?

Yet Thorn had listened patiently, and Sky had watched in admiration as he gave gentle advice, stern instructions, and warm consolation for lost herd-mates. Even a Dawntrees baboon had come to complain of ill treatment from Creeper, and Thorn had resisted the urge to crow about his enemy's unpopularity; instead he had quietly advised the young male to speak to Berry, ask for her protection, and trust her sense of justice.

Thorn Highleaf had been born to help other creatures, Sky thought. He had a kindness that softened his cleverness and wisdom; not a single creature had left the clearing angry or dissatisfied or resentful. She had to crush that niggle of doubt that lived inside her.

"You're doing so much better than you think you are," she told Thorn, as a hyena trotted off, tail in the air, to make the suggested compromise with his leader.

"You think so?" Thorn glanced at her sidelong.

"I know so."

A queue of animals still waited to bring their troubles to him, and she saw Thorn suppress a sigh. He would get used to it, Sky thought. She vividly recalled the crowds who had waited on Great Mother, the inconsequential complaints that were always addressed patiently and fairly. At least in this one respect, Thorn was just like the wise old elephant matriarch.

And Thorn had his friends to help him, after all. Nut was in his element, bossing the waiting crowd into some sort of order, scolding queue-jumpers, reassuring the impatient. Spider and Mud sat on either side of Thorn; Spider muttered constant advice about the animals who arrived, drawing on the familiarity he'd gained in his wanderings. The weird baboon intrigued Sky; he was so well acquainted with each animal, it

was as if he had lived not with them but as them. He seemed
to understand what went on in their heads, which amused her
because she could not for the life of her understand what went
on in Spider's. Meanwhile, Mud cast his stones on a flat patch
of gritty sand, studying them and relaying their meanings to
Thorn, as the Great Father advised the latest desperate or
angry creature.

Perhaps Thorn doesn't need me at all, thought Sky with a twinge
of regret as she watched the three busy baboons. At any rate,
she would not interfere. She kept her distance and stood quietly observing, afraid of undermining Thorn or of bringing
back memories of her grandmother's time as Great Mother.
As the afternoon wore on, she found herself growing drowsy.

So it shocked her to the bone when screeching and screaming erupted from beyond the first group of animals. Starting
from her dreamlike state, she flapped her ears in alarm and
raised her trunk to give a trumpet of fear.

Three zebras and an antelope stampeded into the brush,
neighing and squealing in terror. A serval cat sprang for the
edge of the clearing, ears flat and fur bristling. Warthogs gave
a volley of terrified high grunts and trampled forward over
Thorn's hillock, almost knocking Spider flying.

Sky started forward, ears splaying in threat. *How dare some
creature disturb the Great Father's council?*

Then she froze as terror washed through her own blood.
Along the path, through the gap left by fleeing animals, three
menacing shapes waddled sinuously, their short legs moving at

a brisk pace, their thick scaly tails swaying behind them.

Crocodiles!

Nut staggered aside, abandoning his efforts to keep control. Mud gave a yelp of fright and snatched up his stones. Thorn stiffened and rose to his hind paws. Spider stared in absolute fascination, moving his paws in vague mimicry of the crocodiles' motion.

Sky herself felt tremors of terror ripple through her. These were the creatures that had killed Great Mother. Everyone knew the crocodiles did not follow the Code, let alone the Great Parents, so what in the name of the stars were they doing here?

"Thorn!" she cried, turning to him urgently. "Get into the trees! Quickly!"

Nut and Mud had needed no telling; they were already scrambling up into the branches, and they were dragging a reluctant Spider after them. But Thorn, despite Sky's pleas, did not move. He stood rock-still on his mound, watching the crocodiles calmly as they marched toward him.

"Thorn," she gasped. She reached out her trunk toward him, but he took no notice. Sky could feel her heart thudding faster in her chest, and for a moment she had an urge to snatch him up in her trunk and simply carry him away. Great Father he might be, but that would be no protection against Codeless crocodiles.

And I must stand with him! She planted her feet more firmly on the ground.

The crocodiles halted, lifting their long snouts. Their

leader opened his jaws, displaying rows of savagely sharp and huge teeth.

"Welcome," declared Thorn, in a voice that trembled only slightly. "Welcome, Sandtongue-speakers. What do you want from the Great Father?"

CHAPTER SIX

Thorn's heart pounded as if it might burst right out of his chest. He wanted nothing more than to flee, yet something deeper than fear held him fast where he stood. And he could not take his eyes off the crocodiles. Their heavy jaws looked capable of swallowing him whole—unless his hide caught on those fearsome rows of jagged teeth. Their yellow eyes, with black slashes for pupils, looked as cold as a deep river. It was odd seeing them so far from the water—their bodies were not made for land, which made them all the more terrifying.

Thorn remembered very well his first real encounter with crocodiles: the second of the Three Feats he had performed to achieve his rank in the old Brightforest Troop. He had had to swim across a crocodile-infested river, and he had never been so scared—not until that point in his life, at least.

But he was not Thorn Lowleaf now; he was Great Father,

and whether these creatures followed the Great Spirit or not, they were part of the life of Bravelands, as connected to it as he was. Despite his churning terror, he felt a duty to them.

"We are forced to turn to you, Great Father," snarled the biggest crocodile, "because we seem to have no other choice." There was a contemptuous timbre in his voice, but that might simply have been a natural crocodilian tone. Sandtongue sounded weird, thought Thorn: guttural and sibilant.

"I will try to help you." He knew that by the mystery of the Great Spirit, they would understand his own language.

"I am Rip, commander of the Muddy River Bask," the croc hissed. "These are my lieutenants, Snag and Clamp. The hippos of Plunge's pod will not leave us be. Their behavior must stop. Or there will be war, and much blood."

Thorn licked his jaws, surprise overcoming his fear for a moment. Hippos and crocodiles tended to leave one another alone. "How are they bothering you?"

"Snag can tell you best," snarled Rip, "as a target herself." He jerked his long snout at the croc on his left.

Snag lunged forward a pace, parting her jaws to show her savage teeth. "They crush our offspring," she growled. "They find our nests and stamp the eggs to splinters. No young have hatched this season."

Thorn started. Hippos could be aggressive and deadly, but this seemed like pointless vandalism. "Why would they do such a thing?"

"Because of lies!" snapped Clamp. "They call it revenge, but it is revenge for nothing. They dragged a corpse to the shore and left it for us to see: one of their offspring. It seems they accuse our bask of killing the youngster. But this was never done."

Rip and Snag nodded in agreement. "It is a lie," hissed Snag.

"It is an excuse." Rip's eyes were cold with anger. "The hippos do not like sharing the river, and they want to drive us away. They pretend to believe we killed their infant, yet it was they who killed my predecessor, Tear!"

"The hippos killed your leader?" Thorn could hardly believe his ears.

"Tear went missing not long ago," said Rip, clashing his jaws. "He had spent his whole life in the Muddy River; he had no reason to leave, and it was against his nature. Not long after that, the hippos began their vendetta."

"They crushed my clutch of eggs," said Snag, grinding her foreclaws into the earth. "And they have returned again and again to do the same to other parents. What they do is unforgivable. It must be avenged."

"It does not matter what we do to protect the eggs," said Clamp, lashing his powerful tail. "We have tried to fight the hippos. We stand guard over the nests. Our females lay their eggs in the remotest hidden places. But the hippos always find them. They drive us off and destroy our young before they have a chance to taste the air."

"So our bask will see no new young this season, or perhaps any season," snarled Rip. "You, so-called Great Father: You have the respect of the hippos. You are ruler of Bravelands. You have the power to stop them."

"Wait, now," Thorn objected, raising his paws. "I am no ruler. The Great Parent is a guide and adviser, no more than that."

"Pond-silt," growled Rip, taking a threatening pace toward him. "You have this power, Baboon. If you do not use it, we will retaliate against the hippos. They think we are young-killers? Then that is what we will become. We will hunt without mercy, tearing their infants apart as we find them. The rivers will run red with their blood, and their cries of sorrow will scare the birds from the sky."

Thorn's head reeled, and he felt a sickening sensation in his gut. It was as if he could see the vision in his mind, just as the crocodiles described it: blood, and terror, and meaningless death. He had to catch his breath before he could snarl back at Rip: "This would solve nothing! The cycle of violence would be endless, and I will not let it happen—"

"And we won't stop there," Snag interrupted. "If we lose our next generation, and if Bravelands shows us it does not care, we will make it our business to kill the young of as many creatures as we can reach. Antelope, elephant, hog, or cat: we will tear them to shreds."

"I know you don't follow the Code," said Thorn angrily, "but that would be going too far, even for crocodiles."

"We do what we must to ensure our survival," growled Clamp. "We defend our own, and only our own."

Thorn took deep breaths, trying to think. This was serious—and these crocodiles would not settle for sympathy or reassuring promises. What could he tell them that would lessen the lethal tension of this situation? For a moment he thought of calling to Sky, or to Mud where he crouched in the undergrowth. Then he set his jaw and narrowed his eyes. This was his job to do, his problem to solve. The Great Spirit was his counselor, and he must learn to do this alone.

There was one thing, though, that was not the Great Parent's job: to go into blood-soaked battle against Codebreakers.

Thorn spread his paws. "What do you suggest?" he asked seriously. "You don't believe in the Great Spirit and you don't follow the Great Parent, so what makes you think I can help you this time?"

"No, we believe in none of that hippo dung," sneered Rip. "No creature rules over us or controls our behavior. But when the last Great Parent died . . ." He glanced at his comrades. "When she died, the old elephant, we sensed something. There was a thing about her that was . . . different, even in death. It's why we did not eat her corpse." He narrowed his eyes. "So, Baboon, perhaps there's something different about you too."

"There had better be," muttered Snag.

Thorn sighed. "What the hippos are doing is wrong. It is a breach of our Code, which they do follow: they do not kill your young in self-defense, or for food. I will put this right, Rip. But I will have to think about how."

"See that you do," growled Rip, turning away with a contemptuous flick of his scaly tail. "You have until full moon, Baboon. Or there will be a war."

Thorn watched them trot away, the thud of their clawed

feet and heavy tails resounding ominously as they vanished along the path. He stood in silence as the other animals slowly emerged from their hiding places, wide-eyed and nervous.

"Phew," muttered Mud, his paws shaking as he laid out his stones once again. "I kind of hope they don't make a habit of visiting. . . ."

"What did they want?" asked Nut, staring after them.

"They want the hippos to stop smashing their eggs," said Thorn with a sigh. "So that's understandable. They think the hippos blame them for the death of one of their calves, and that this is revenge. Obviously it has to stop." He glanced up at Sky. "Did I say the right thing?"

Sky swung her trunk, looking bemused. "I can't answer that, but Great Mother once told me it's not as simple as right and wrong. The crocodiles never came to Great Mother for advice, so she never had to deal with them. But I'll do what I can to help, Thorn. We'll work this out together."

Nut shrugged. "Let's face it, those crocs probably did kill the baby hippo, so I don't blame the pod for smashing their eggs in revenge. What else could have done it?"

"Lions? A leopard? An angry buffalo?" Thorn spread his paws helplessly. "There's no way of knowing. But I agree with you, it very likely was the crocs. They share the river, after all, and they were closest to the hippos. But that doesn't justify the hippos destroying so many crocodile eggs. This quarrel cannot be allowed to become a full-blown war."

"The Great Spirit will guide us," said Sky. "Meanwhile, Thorn . . . I don't think your work is over yet for today."

He glanced at the waiting creatures. Then his eyes widened as he saw who was at the head of the queue. Another Dawntrees baboon?

"Mango!" he greeted her warmly. At least it was good to see a familiar face, after that unnerving encounter with the crocodiles. "What can I do for you?"

She came forward uncertainly and sat down on her haunches opposite him. "I'm not sure I'm doing the right thing, Thorn. I mean, Great Father."

"Please go on calling me Thorn," he begged her. "We've known each other all our lives. And it's never the wrong thing to come to the Great Parent. Another Dawntrees baboon has spoken to me already."

"Really?" Mango raised her brows thoughtfully. "That doesn't surprise me, actually."

A ripple of unease went through Thorn's fur. Were things bad in the troop? "Tell me, Mango."

"It's not just that I need the Great Father's advice," said Mango, scratching at her arm. "I also thought you'd probably want to know how things are." She took a deep breath. "This Crown Guard of Berry's—they're throwing their weight around, Thorn. I don't like to compare them to Stinger's Strongbranches, but . . . well, there are a lot of similarities."

Just as I feared, thought Thorn dejectedly. He'd been afraid of this from the moment of the Crown Guard's formation.

"There are differences, though," Mango went on dryly. "The Strongbranches never undermined Stinger, and they'd never have dared act without his say-so, or follow their own willful urges. Stinger had total control."

"And Berry?" Thorn's heart sank.

"Half the time, she doesn't even know what they're up to." Mango shrugged. "They undermine her at every turn, ruin her standing as Crownleaf. She's getting a bad reputation among the troop, for things she hasn't even ordered. The Crown Guard do as they please."

"Like what?" asked Thorn, with a rising unease.

"They've raided nearby monkey troops without her permission, for a start," said Mango. "Viper and Creeper seem to think they're the Crownleaves, and they act accordingly. They hold meetings without her, they mutter behind her back. They treat her like some sort of useless figurehead to cover for their own misdeeds, Thorn. A lot of the troop are starting to resent her for what the Crown Guard do. And the baboons who do know what's going on resent her for not being in control."

Thorn sprang to his paws. "I couldn't resolve the crocodiles' problem immediately," he growled, "but this is something I do know about. Mango, lead the way."

"Wait," said Mango nervously, "you mean now?"

"Yes. I'm coming to Dawntrees Troop. Right now."

Mango pushed aside a hanging veil of creepers and led Thorn hesitantly toward the Crown Stone glade. Around them, baboons chittered and screeched, bounding down from the branches and staring at Thorn. He was too angry to listen carefully to what they were saying, but he could detect quite a variety of moods, from excitement all the way to bitter resentment. *Fair enough*, he thought. He'd left this troop as an exile; he was returning as Great Father of Bravelands. Of course there would be different reactions. And not all these baboons had liked him much in the first place.

As Mango led him into the heart of the glade, Berry leaped down from the Crown Stone and bounded toward him. Her eyes sparked with delight, but she quickly suppressed her smile. Behind her, the Crown Guard turned as one to glare at Thorn.

"Great Father Thorn," exclaimed Berry, halting and smoothing her fur nervously. "It's good to see you, but what are you doing here?"

He nodded at her solemnly, feeling that old yearning twist his heart. But this was no time for sentiment. "I've come to help," he murmured.

"Help how?" She looked confused.

Instead of replying, Thorn padded forward to the Crown Stone and stood at its foot, gazing around at the curious troop as they gathered and muttered. Berry gave him a perplexed glance as she paced past him and leaped up to her place of honor on the Crown Stone itself.

"I have something to say to all of Dawntrees Troop," declared Thorn, rising up on his hind paws. He had to look confident, for Berry's sake, though his heart hammered in his rib cage. "Is every baboon present?"

They all exchanged looks, peering over their shoulders, calling out to latecomers. At last they seemed to settle, and a hush fell as the whole troop stared at Thorn, curious. Mango surveyed them, fingers tapping the air as he counted. Then he gave a nod.

"What I have to say," Thorn began, "it's not just because I'm Berry's mate. I speak as Great Father of Bravelands."

"And?" called Creeper. He slouched back on his haunches, chewing lazily on leaves.

Thorn bristled. That kind of behavior put more strength in his spine. It made him all the more determined to sort this out, once and for all.

"I've heard about the Crown Guard and the way they're acting." Thorn turned to focus on them. "It isn't right. The Crown Guard do not lead this troop—Berry Crownleaf does. I'm told that a little power has gone to the heads of these baboons, and it's creating friction—friction that has no place in the life of a troop. Dawntrees, we're all baboons—remember your traditions! Don't let these Crown Guards bully you. You owe your loyalty to your Crownleaf, not to her militia. Undermining your Crownleaf harms the whole troop, don't we all know that?"

There was a snort of derision from the foremost rank of the Crown Guard. "You're not even a member of Dawntrees anymore!"

Creeper again. He might have guessed. Thorn glared into his single eye, but the big baboon simply stared back, disdainful. "That's not the point," Thorn snapped.

"So what is the point?" Creeper curled his muzzle. "You did your best to undermine Stinger when he was Crownleaf, remember?"

"That was different, and you know it," growled Thorn. "Stinger was evil. That was proven many times over." He turned and nodded toward Berry. "His daughter is a fine and fair leader, and she deserves your respect and loyalty."

Some of the baboons nodded and murmured to one another, clearly in agreement with Thorn. But others, including the ones around Creeper and Viper, looked surly. There were grunts of contempt and resentment that Thorn could not exactly make out. One by one, the troop members turned away and loped back to their daytime tasks.

Feeling a sudden tug of nerves, Thorn turned to Berry. "Mango told me what they were up to. I just had to come and help."

She was watching him with an unreadable expression. She looked, thought Thorn uneasily, less than delighted.

"It's nice that you came here to stick up for me," Berry told him, her voice level, "and I appreciate your support. But I can handle Creeper and the others myself. If anything's going to undermine me, Thorn, it's the Great Father coming here to fight my battles."

Thorn started. He hadn't expected undying gratitude, but Berry sounded as if she didn't want him here at all. Surely she didn't think he'd made things worse?

He shook himself and bit back his exasperation. "I didn't mean to do anything of the sort, Berry. A baboon came to me with complaints about it, and I was simply doing my job."

She drew back, cold and formal. "Then let me do mine. Let me be Crownleaf and make my own mistakes."

Thorn stared at her for a moment, then nodded slowly. "I'm sorry, Berry. I never looked at it like that."

"No, you obviously didn't." Was that a hint of good-natured mockery in her voice? He couldn't tell.

"It won't happen again," he murmured. "You know undermining you was never my intention. Truly, I'm sorry if that's what I've done."

He desperately wanted to hug her, to feel her warmth in his arms and to melt away the indignation in her expression. Was it appropriate? He didn't care. He took a step closer, then hesitated.

Suddenly seeming less sure of herself, Berry glanced to her right and left, as if she was all too aware of the gazes of her troop. Then, as Thorn moved forward again, she yielded, leaned forward, and briefly embraced him.

Thorn could feel the stiffness in her muscles, and their eyes didn't meet. He drew away quickly and nodded to her.

I shouldn't have done that. Should I have done that? He was Great Father, she was Crownleaf. They weren't carefree young baboons anymore. *We both have responsibilities.*

Thorn turned and loped out of the Crown Glade, with a nod at Mango. It wasn't Mango's fault, he realized; Mango had done what she thought was best. It was he, as an inexperienced Great Father, who had handled it badly.

I'm still learning, he reminded himself sternly.

And from now on, he'd be a lot more careful.

CHAPTER SEVEN

Even in the blackness of the savannah night, the trunks of the Dead Forest were visible as sickly pale stalks, tinged with blue in Fearless's vision. The earth beneath his paws still had that sucking, swampy feel, and he picked his steps with caution. The stench of the wolves was strong, tangled in Fearless's nostrils with the dead and rotting reek of the forest itself.

At his side, Keen froze as another shadow shifted. Then, with a grunt, he padded on. For such a lifeless place, thought Fearless, the forest's shadows seemed to be a little too animated.

It did not help that Menace was such a distraction. Her voice was too loud, her movements too brash, and she had a bad habit of breaking her boredom by sniping at Ruthless.

"Watch out for hyenas, Useless," she taunted her brother. "It's not as if you'd be able to fight one off."

"Don't call him that," snapped Fearless in a low voice. "You couldn't fight a hyena yourself." He hated that spiteful nickname: Titan had given it to the cub when he failed to live up to *Ruthless*. That too, thought Fearless, was Titan's fault: no cub should be named too early.

"Huh," sneered Menace. "Who's Daddy's favorite? Not you, Useless. Who does our father say will be the strongest lion in Bravelands? I'll give you a clue: not y—"

"I said, stop it," snarled Fearless. He swung around.

"Fine, I'll stop hurting the poor little cubby with nasty words." Menace took a bouncing step and clamped her little jaws around Ruthless's tail.

Ruthless yelped, more in shock than pain, and jerked away. Keen gave Menace a hard swat with his paw.

"Fearless said behave!" he growled.

Ruthless trotted faster to catch up with Fearless, and Fearless shot the cub a sympathetic look. He knew all about Titan's bullying, and Menace had more than a touch of her father's nature. "Ruthless," he murmured, "you shouldn't let her speak to you the way she does. Stand up for yourself."

"I don't want to hurt her," sighed Ruthless. "She is my sister."

"Well, she doesn't seem to worry about hurting you," pointed out Fearless. Still, he couldn't imagine Ruthless ever giving as good as he got. The cub was just too gentle. With a resigned sigh, he turned his attention once more to the ghostly forest ahead of them and froze.

Pale, skinny forms moved between the trunks ahead,

stalking toward the lions. *The wolves*, he thought, peeling back his muzzle to bare his fangs, letting his claws pop from their sheaths.

Keen snarled, and Fearless heard a low, scared whimper from Menace that satisfied him more than it should have. Swinging his head around from side to side, he saw more wolves approaching from their flanks. White fangs gleamed, hungry eyes glowed, and drool dripped in silvery threads from their jaws.

The three older lions backed in a circle, keeping Menace protectively between them. Fearless lashed his tail and snarled. There were a lot of wolves, and they were advancing without a hint of nerves.

The largest, a big male, stopped in front of Fearless and curled his narrow muzzle in a sneer. "Track us, would you, Lion? How funny. How foolish! It is we who track you. The Bloodheart Pack are masters of hunting." He licked his jaws. "It is we who let you come to us. Ha!" He trotted forward, and the golden wolves bounded after him, loose-limbed and menacing. "Now we taste your plump hearts."

"Ruthless, get back!" roared Fearless, shunting the cub with his shoulder. "There are too many. Let us deal with them!"

As the wolves sprang, he spun back in time to lash his forepaws at one of the attackers.

The wolf tumbled back with a screech, but another quickly leaped in to take its place, slashing and biting at Fearless's shoulder. Another had clamped its jaws in his flank; a bolt of pain shot through his body, and he felt hot blood flow, but it only angered him. He spun and clawed at it, even as yet another sprang and clung to his neck.

Beside him he was aware of Keen, grunting with effort as he struck out at the wolves. He snatched a slower one in his jaws, shook it violently, and flung it aside. Fearless dodged it as it fell at his paws, then bucked violently to dislodge another from his spine. Teeth fastened in his shoulder again, and as he snapped at his elusive tormentor, yet another wolf bit hard into his foreleg.

They skittered back. Panting as they circled him, Fearless tried to think and plan, but his mind was too focused on survival. The wolves were small, but there were so many of them. They would harry the lions to exhaustion, Fearless knew, then close in for the kill.

And they were good at harrying. No sooner had one darted in to snap and bite than it raced back among the pale gray trunks, out of reach. As three more of them rushed from the trees, Fearless shoved Menace and Ruthless back. He could hardly keep track of the cubs. He was too panicked—and he was tiring fast.

This time, the bites were so quick and sharp that he didn't manage to lay a claw on his attackers. As the wolves bolted away yet again, and Keen and Fearless stood with heaving flanks, the big male trotted forward to laugh in their faces.

"We see you protect the little ones. Ha, you funny cats. We do not want the little hearts. For us are the big hearts, strong hearts, plump hearts."

There was a squeal of indignant rage from behind Fearless,

and before he could block her, Menace had darted between his legs to holler at the wolves.

"What do you mean, my heart isn't good enough? I'm better than any of these lions!" She lowered her shoulders and snarled a threat. "You're too scared to try, is what you mean!"

"Oh, we is? The puny lion thinks so?" The big male yapped a staccato laugh. "Maybe we try a little bite then. Maybe to whet our appetites with a snack!"

In moments, he and his cohorts had surrounded Menace in a half circle, prowling ever closer, slaver dripping from their jaws.

"Menace, you idiot!" roared Fearless, lunging forward. He reached her at the same moment the big male did, and their bodies crashed together. They thudded to the ground at Menace's side. Squirming around, flailing his paws, Fearless righted himself first and snatched the wolf's throat in his jaws.

One glowing eye was fixed on his; the wolf's tongue lolled as it fought and kicked. But Fearless barely felt the rip of its claws on his chest and shoulders. His nostrils were suffused with the scent of its hide. It was as recognizably foul as ever, but there was another odor that was instantly, horribly familiar: a bloody, earthy tang, dark and chilling.

Titan . . . This wolf stinks of Titan!

Shocked and disgusted, Fearless flung the wolf violently from side to side. He felt and heard the sickening crack of bone as its neck snapped. Then he flung its corpse aside and spun around, ready for the next wolf.

"My father's going to kill you for this!" Menace squealed. "Try to kill me, would you? Well, my father is Titan of Titan-pride, and you're doomed!"

The effect of her words was stunning. Every single wolf halted, staring, their tails quivering. They stared at the cub, not with hunger or fury but with a kind of awed fascination. For long moments, there was no movement between the trees. Then, turning as one, the wolves bounded into the darkness.

Fearless stood panting for breath, his head buzzing with confusion and anger, his flanks heaving. What had just happened?

Keen sidled against his flank. "What was that?" he muttered.

"Keen, did you smell it?"

Keen jerked his head around to stare directly at him. "Titan? Yes. I thought it was just me."

"They reeked of Titan," whispered Fearless.

"You think the wolves fought him and found out what he's like?" Keen shook his head. "Why would they back off like that?"

"Because of me," chirped Menace, prancing in a circle. "I scared them off when you cowards couldn't. I'm the daughter of Titan, and I rule."

Fearless ignored her. "Have they really gone?"

"I don't think so," murmured Keen. "I can see movement beyond those trees. But they've stopped attacking for some reason, and I don't care why." He licked at the wound on Fearless's flank.

"There!" exclaimed Fearless, and Keen jerked his head up and turned.

The biggest wolf yet prowled out of the night, her large ears pricked forward, her bushy tail twitching lazily. She halted before them, licking her narrow jaws, and she grinned.

"I am Ravage, Eater of a Thousand Hearts."

"Oh, you are, are you?" snapped Keen, but Fearless calmed him with a gentle nudge.

"What do you want, Ravage?"

"I am Alpha of the Bloodheart Pack." She lifted her head and turned it idly, her glowing eyes finding each of the lions before resting on the wolf corpse Fearless had assumed was their leader. "Which of you has killed Sever, Eater of a Hundred Hearts?"

"I did," growled Fearless, curling his muzzle.

Ravage licked her jaws again and tilted her head, studying him. "Sever was our second-in-command. Sever died with glory, as is right."

"Sever died with a broken neck," muttered Keen softly. "As was even more right."

"Hehehe." Ravage's harsh giggle made Fearless's neck fur rise. "We are the goldwolves, and we honor him, Eater of a Hundred Hearts, at his fine death."

"Fine death or not," said Fearless, forcing his voice to stay steady, "I have brought you a message from the Great Father."

"Perhaps we do not want this message," hissed Ravage, her eyes glinting with detached amusement.

"I bring it anyway," growled Fearless. "The Great Father

knows what you are doing. He summons you to explain yourself and your pack's misdeeds. You tear out hearts and spirits,
and the Great Father wants you to know it has to stop."

They stood in tense silence, as Ravage flicked her ears and
twitched her tail.

"This Great Father"—she grinned at last—"we have heard
of him, oh yes. A puny baboon, by all accounts." She glanced
over her shoulder at her pack, who were slinking out of the
shadows once more. "We have tasted baboon heart. So clever.
So cunning. So easy to kill."

The pack behind her yelped and nodded eagerly.

"This is no ordinary baboon!" roared Fearless. "He is Great
Father of Bravelands, and he possesses great power!"

"But Bravelands is ours now," said Ravage, her face open
and innocent. "It is not belonging to Great Father anymore."

"Bravelands has always belonged to the Great Spirit and it
always will," snarled Fearless. "It belongs to the Spirit, and to
the creatures who live here. You can't defeat the Great Spirit,
not by eating ten thousand hearts."

The Alpha's eyes widened with greedy delight. "The Great
Spirit, you say? We like this! Oh, how we wish to come with
you, to meet this Great Father baboon. We will do it, say I.
We answer his summons. His heart holds such a powerful
Spirit? Then we will make it ours. Such strength! It must be
ours. Pack, pack, we will have it!"

"No!" Fearless tensed, drew himself higher, and bared his
fangs. "You will do no such thing." His heart thundered hard
against his rib cage. "Great Father Thorn has many friends,

and they'll protect him to their deaths!"

"Good, good!" Ravage looked almost deliriously happy. "So good!"

"You will not get near him!" bellowed Fearless, in panicked fury.

"Goldwolves, eaters of spirit, we always find a way." She shrugged. "Now. Leave us, Cat."

Fearless stared, taken aback at her brusque dismissal, as she turned her attention to the corpse of Sever. She sniffed at the broken body. "Sever! Glorious goldwolf, beautiful in death."

More of the golden wolves were closing in behind her; their pawsteps delicate and sinister on the yielding earth.

"Sever's heart is yours, Ravage of the Thousand Hearts," yelped one. "His heart, his spirit." "You are our Alpha," barked another. "Let him run with us! Run with us forever!"

"Let him be we!" chorused the pack. "Let Sever be we!"

None of them even glanced at the lions again as, slowly, Fearless backed up, his heart still thrashing. He nodded at Keen, who shepherded Ruthless and Menace quickly away. Fearless himself hesitated and glanced back.

Ravage lifted her head, howled once, then lunged down at the limp body of the dead wolf. There was the crunch of bone and an awful ripping sound of muscle and sinew. Her head jerked up again, dangling a dripping lump of flesh. Her pack began to yammer and wail—not in grief, but in celebration.

Fearless twisted away, revolted, and ran after Keen and the others. It took far too long for the sounds of the grotesque feast to fade behind him.

That was a mistake, he thought grimly as he raced through the lifeless forest. He'd said too much, but there was no taking it back; he would simply have to fix his error. He, Keen, and the cubs had escaped with their lives, and that was all that mattered at this moment.

He had done what he could. He had wanted to scare away the golden wolves, to intimidate them with his tales of the Great Spirit. It had not worked out as he expected. He'd created a new problem. He had made them even hungrier for hearts: one heart in particular.

CHAPTER EIGHT

The sky was a hazy blue-gray, the horizon striped by a golden glow, and the almost-full moon rode low in the sky, its brilliance dimmed by the coming dawn.

"We don't have long," Sky told Thorn. "The moon will be full tomorrow night, and the crocs will carry out their threat. We can't have another war in Bravelands, not with everything else that's happening."

"No, we can't," muttered Thorn, padding across the dew-silvered grassland at her side. "But we have to investigate, find out what really happened at the Muddy River. Until we know that, there's nothing we can do."

Sky glanced once more at the glow of dawn. It was more intense by the moment, and she felt a stir of swelling anxiety. "Let's hurry. The river's just beyond those mgunga trees." She marched on faster, then realized Thorn was no longer at her side. She glanced back, seeing that he had come to a halt and was now sitting back on his haunches.

"But we're not the first," he murmured.

Sky followed his pointing finger and gasped. "Is that Dawntrees Troop?"

Thorn nodded and raised a paw to hold her back. In silence, the two of them watched the baboons through the trees. The first sunlight spilled over the horizon, lighting the bark of the trees and glowing gold on the fur of a whole troop of baboons.

"What are they doing?" whispered Sky. There was a celebratory air to the gathering. Young baboons were assembled nervously on the river's banks, despite the knobbly backs of crocodiles that drifted in the water nearby. The youngsters looked tense and overexcited, though the older baboons watching them whooped with delight and encouragement.

One of the younger baboons bounded across to a narrow log and set about dragging it closer to the river. A few friends joined in, helping him. Another youngster gave a defiant yell and plunged in, to swim furiously for the far bank.

"What in the stars are they doing?" exclaimed Sky again.

Thorn was observing the scene in what seemed like tense fascination. He didn't seem to share her horror that healthy young baboons were flinging themselves into a crocodile-infested river.

"It's the Three Feats," he said at last, shaking himself. "This is the Second Feat: crossing the crocodile river. I did it myself at their age. That's how I became a Middleleaf, Sky. I came to this very river as a Lowleaf, and when I reached the other side without being eaten, I was a rank higher in the troop."

Sky shook her head slowly. "I thought baboons were smart," she said.

"That's the whole point. This Feat—it proves you can be quick and cunning and inventive. Look at those youngsters using a log as a raft! They'll still have to be quick. And they'll have to jump off and swim for it if a croc comes at them." He peered at the scene, riveted. "Come on, young ones, you're nearly there. . . ."

"And this happens to every baboon?" Sky still couldn't quite believe her eyes.

"Every baboon who wants to rise in the hierarchy," Thorn told her proudly. "I began as a Deeproot, did you know that? I became a Lowleaf by stealing the egg of a flesh-eating bird. I'd have become a Highleaf sooner, too, if . . ."

"If what?"

He shook himself. "It doesn't matter. I'm a Highleaf now."

"You're Great Father now." She nudged him fondly with her trunk.

"Yes." Thorn scratched at his nose, looking embarrassed. "Oh, it all seems so long ago! Things were . . . simpler then. . . ."

"But look." Sky stiffened, feeling suddenly more serious. She pointed upriver with her trunk. "The hippos are arriving. This could get nasty, Thorn, especially if they start to squabble with the crocs."

Thorn drew himself up, his face solemn. "You're right. This could be chaos. It's bad enough having to focus on the crocodiles, believe me. Come on."

He led her through the trees, ducking leafy branches. Sky simply had to walk through them, and she could not do it quietly; one by one, Dawntrees Troop heard their approach and turned toward them. She felt shy all of a sudden. Despite its high-spirited atmosphere, this seemed such an important tradition.

"Splinter! Lily!" Thorn hailed the two baboons who seemed to be in charge.

One of them glanced around, rolled his eyes, and looked very deliberately away again. But the female called Lily hesitated, then turned and padded toward Thorn, her expression guarded. "Great Father Thorn," she said formally. "What can we do for you?"

Thorn gestured upstream. "As we arrived, we saw Plunge's pod. It's big. They're going to be in this spot of the river very soon, and they're in conflict with these crocodiles, so there could be a fight. It's dangerous, Lily. The troop should postpone the Second Feat."

Lily drew herself up, looking surprised. "The Three Feats are dangerous, Thorn. That's the whole point. You of all baboons know that."

"True, but they don't have to be needlessly dangerous," he insisted.

"Am I hearing this right?" A big, strong-looking female bounded toward them. "Postpone the Three Feats? That's ridiculous!"

"I agree, Viper." Another baboon approached. "These are the first Feats we've held since the days of Bark Crownleaf," she protested. "Everyone would be so disappointed." That was borne out by the groans and cries from the rest of the troop as the rumor spread from baboon to baboon.

"Better disappointed than dead, Mango," Thorn pointed out amid the growing hubbub.

"Wait." Mango raised a paw, and they all fell silent. "What are you saying, Thorn? Is this a suggestion? Or a command from the Great Father?"

Thorn looked uneasy. He glanced from Mango to Sky, but Sky found she couldn't advise him. It wasn't just that he had to learn to be Great Father, she thought; it was more that this situation felt very much none of her business. Blinking, she shook her head slightly.

Sighing, Thorn turned away and let his gaze encompass the whole troop. "Mango, of course it's not a command. It's my advice as a baboon more than anything. Sky and I saw approaching danger, and we wanted to warn you."

"He's trying to boss us around again," called the second organizer, the one called Splinter. "Don't listen to him."

"You're so busy being Great Father, Thorn," sneered Viper, "you've forgotten what it is to be a baboon."

"That's not true," snapped Thorn. "I just don't want anyone to get hurt." He looked anxiously upriver, to where the hippos were milling, circling, churning the water—and eyeing the crocodiles with overt hostility.

Sky watched them, too, her tail twitching in agitation. Maybe she was being oversensitive, but the hippos looked to her as if they were working themselves up for a fight.

"We don't have to obey the Great Father, do we?" Splinter glanced around at the Dawntrees baboons. "He's just an adviser. It's not as if he's a troop member."

"Maybe not, but I suppose he might be right about the danger." Lily sighed in obvious annoyance. "Postponing the Feats has never happened before, but we shouldn't send the youngsters into needless peril. Oh, I don't want to make the decision without talking to Berry."

"Fine," grunted Viper, with a glare at Thorn. "I'll get her. I doubt she wants to be disturbed, but I'll fetch her." She bounded off between the trees.

"This is completely unnecessary," growled Splinter.

"Let Berry Crownleaf decide that!" snapped Lily.

As Lily and Splinter began to argue ferociously, Thorn loped a little farther up the bank, closer to the water. Sky followed and saw him scramble up onto a low overhanging branch; he was peering down anxiously at the candidates for the Feats. Some of the young baboons glared up at him; others cast nervous glances at the river's surface.

Sky strode to the tree and raised her trunk to nudge Thorn reassuringly. "There's nothing we can do but wait for Berry," she told him. "Try not to worry."

Thorn pointed upriver. "Look at them, Sky."

On the far shore, crocodiles were slinking toward the water, their eyes coldly hostile. The hippos, much closer to the baboons now, wallowed in the water, muttering together as they returned the crocs' glares. A big male hippo opened his massive jaws wide in a distinct threat. Some of his comrades bellowed in anger, driving themselves to a pitch of excitement.

"Murderers!" hollered a female.

The crocs watched the hippos without speaking. A few eased silently into the river, leaving sinister ripples on its surface.

"Sky, I don't like this," muttered Thorn.

She didn't like it either. "Do you think the hippos came here for an outright battle?" Two young male hippos had begun to plunge and splash, churning the water into creamy foam. One of them submerged.

"I don't think so," murmured Thorn nervously. "If they wanted to fight, they'd have attacked straight away. I think they're just taunting the crocs. . . . But this could escalate fast."

Sky watched the place where the young hippo had disappeared. She held her breath, hoping it was not even now bounding along the riverbed toward the crocodiles.

Thorn gave a sudden, incoherent yell and sprang down from his branch. A brash young Feats competitor had waded up to his belly in the water and was gazing longingly at the opposite shore. Thorn bolted to the riverbank, seizing him by his arm and dragging him back—and at just that moment, the young male hippo surfaced right beside him.

An explosion of water drenched both Thorn and the youngster. Sky gave a trumpet of alarm, but the two baboons were already scrabbling backward, ducking the swing of the hippo's massive head. With another great eruption of spray, the hippo submerged once more.

Sky hurried to Thorn's side, reaching out her trunk, but he

was already rising shakily to his paws. The youngster sprawled on the sandy earth, panting and coughing, his eyes panicked. Thorn gazed up at Sky with fearful eyes.

She had no time to say anything to him; Berry and Viper were racing down the shore toward them. Berry's eyes, Sky noticed, blazed with indignation. Out in the water, the hippos and the crocodiles turned to watch the baboons in detached surprise, as if they had only just realized there was life going on in the river beyond their feud. The water's surface calmed, just a last few big ripples lapping against the bank as an eerie silence fell over the scene.

"What is happening here? Thorn, why are you interfering?" Berry halted and rose up on her hind paws, staring at Thorn and the bedraggled young baboon.

Thorn pointed a shaking paw at the youngster. "Something terrible almost happened! Berry, I warned them it wasn't safe. There's risk with the Crocodile River Feat, but what's the point in being drowned by a hippo?"

Berry was silent for a long time. She clenched and unclenched her paws. Her fangs were gritted. Sky sensed that the Crownleaf had come here to give Thorn a telling-off—she had looked furious as she bounded toward them—but that the ground had shifted beneath her.

"You should have come to me, Thorn," Berry snapped at last, "instead of trying to order my troop around. Then I could have handled it myself. Don't you remember our last conversation?"

"I do, but—"

"Let me lead my own troop, Thorn!" Berry spun away angrily and beckoned her troop. "To me, Dawntrees! The Great Father is rude and rash"—she shot him a glare—"but in this instance, he's right. We'll postpone for a day or two."

Thorn looked incapable of speech as he and Sky watched the troop strut away in silence. As the rustle and crack of twigs and leaves faded, he gave a great sigh. "Berry," he whispered.

His muzzle twitched in agonized frustration; his fangs chittered with distress. It was as if, thought Sky, he had far too much to say to his mate, yet he hadn't had the chance to say a word. Poor Thorn. He looked so forlorn, Sky turned to him and touched his shoulder gently with the tip of her trunk.

"Don't be despondent."

"I can't help it," he blurted. He rubbed at his head. "I don't think I can be a Great Father to these baboons and be Berry's mate. I'll just end up doing both things badly."

Sky felt a lurch of sympathy. "Maybe," she murmured, "it isn't possible at all. I do know how you feel, Thorn, and it's painful. I couldn't stay with my herd and serve the Great Spirit."

He sighed again. "That's an awful thought."

"It's an awful predicament." She lowered her eyes. "But you've done the right thing."

"I hope so," he muttered, "but it doesn't feel that way right now. Come on. We should do what we came here to do."

Dejectedly he loped to the weeds at the water's edge and began to search through them, poking and pulling at the reeds. Sky joined him, rolling branches away with her trunk and flattening the grass in search of the baby hippo. Her hide prickled; the crocodiles and Plunge's pod might have calmed down, but they were now wallowing close by in the water, observing their every move with silent hostility.

If either the crocs or the hippos attacked, Sky thought grimly, she'd defend the Great Father with her life. If they attacked together, she didn't know just how much her help would be worth. . . . But for now at least, both sides seemed content to watch.

"Sky!" Thorn called abruptly from a patch of reeds. "Here!"

She nudged a thick dead branch aside with her foot and trotted over to him. Thorn was gazing down sadly at tattered scraps of bone and smooth gray skin.

"The rot-eaters have done their work," she said softly.

"Yes," said Thorn. "But this is her. The baby hippo."

Together they stared down at the sad remains. Sky took a deep breath.

"Are you ready?" Thorn asked her, his eyes concerned.

Taking a step forward, Sky touched her trunk to the bones.

. . . *The water was cool and pleasant, buoying her up. She flailed her stubby legs, twisting in the water to look for her mother; there! She wasn't far away. Happily the little hippo made an experimental dive, bounding slowly along the riverbed through shimmering, waving weeds. Rays of sunlight flickered from above, dancing among the grass blades. She tugged at a mouthful, then paddled back toward the surface.*

Breaching it, she flared her nostrils open. Something had changed.

She was anxious now. The grown hippos were a little way away, closer to the shore. They were distracted. She should go to her mother.

But the water was moving and shifting around her, buffeting her body.

She twisted, frightened. Was it the crocodiles?

No! Snouts broke the water's surface, baring sharp and hungry teeth, and the eyes in those yellow skulls were filled with malice. What were they? Oh, Mother—

There was no time for more thought. The golden creatures swarmed her, biting and tugging and pulling her down. She fought, struggling as hard as she could, but there were so many. Claws dug and teeth bit, and the green water was turning dark with tendrils and clouds of something else. It was strange, and frightening, and she felt real pain for the first time in her short life. The world of stained water faded. And then it was black, and there was nothing left at all.

Sky staggered back, breathing hard with horror.

"What is it? What did you see?" Thorn laid his paw urgently against her trunk.

"The wolves," she rasped. "How is that possible? How could they kill a hippo, even a baby one?"

Thorn clashed his teeth in distress. "The golden wolves? It's worse than I thought, then."

"There were so many," Sky cried. "Such a big pack. And look." With her trembling trunk, she pulled aside more grass and weed from the picked-over remains. "Her rib cage."

They gazed down. A dark sadness clung to Sky, lingering from her vision. Even with so little left of the baby hippo, the damage was obvious. A hole had been smashed and torn in the rib cage, right in the place where the wolves would have found her heart.

"They killed her the way crocodiles would, dragging her down, but they had to wound her too. She'd have been able to hold her breath long enough not to drown, so they did this to her." Sky was shaking.

Thorn was silent, but she could feel his simmering rage. Abruptly he rose to his paws and padded toward the river.

"Plunge!" he cried. Then he turned to the crocodile bask. "Rip! I need to talk to you."

Plunge swam toward him and then waded closer, wary but curious. He stopped near the bank, his huge head tilted slightly. Beside him, ripples arrowed, and a knobbly head and back broke the surface. Rip lifted his narrow snout, his yellow eyes locked on Thorn.

Thorn took a deep breath and cleared his throat. "Plunge," he said. "The crocodiles didn't kill your pod's infant. She was murdered by the golden wolves."

Plunge's small eyes widened. "What?" he roared.

Rip the crocodile lifted his head in a shower of water, opening his jaws to display his fangs. Sky did not understand his sibilant hissing and snarling, but his meaning was clear enough. And it was obvious that Thorn understood his every angry word.

He was holding out his paws in a calming gesture. "It was a misunderstanding, Rip. Plunge and his pod genuinely thought your bask was responsible."

"Understandably!" bellowed Plunge. "These sand-crawlers are savages!"

Thorn twisted quickly back toward him, looking nervous. "Plunge, I promise you. Rip and his bask had nothing to do with this."

The huge crocodile was spitting his fury, and with a slight air of panic Thorn turned to him again. "Rip, you don't want a war. Neither do the hippos. Please, leave this in the past. Both of you . . ." The crocodile snapped something else. Thorn shook his head. "No, Plunge hasn't apologized. . . . No. Listen, please. I can ask him, but I can't force him."

Plunge let his jaws gape wide. "Apologize?" he boomed.

"It would be helpful," said Thorn quietly. "It's my job to give advice. So I'm giving it."

Plunge glowered at Thorn, and then at Rip. The gleam in his tiny eyes was baleful, but at last he nodded. "I'm sorry for the misunderstanding." His grunt was sullen. "And I'm sorry about the eggs. But I still don't like him, and I don't like his bask. And they need to stay a respectful distance from my pod. Or there will be more trouble."

Thorn hesitated. He nodded. Then he turned to Rip once again.

"Plunge apologizes," was all he said.

Rip gave a drawn-out, rasping growl, one that seemed to echo for a long time.

"Apology accepted," Thorn told the hippo quickly—though Sky was sure the crocodile had said more than that.

Plunge stared at Thorn for a long moment, then nodded.

Thorn glanced upriver and drew a determined breath. "Listen to me, Plunge. There will still be friction between you and the crocodiles; that can't be helped. Terrible things have been done, and terrible threats have been made in response. You must divide this territory, at least for now. The crocodiles will keep themselves upriver, beyond that red stinkwood tree; the hippos should respect that boundary and graze only in this area and downriver of it, by the Mgunga Pools."

"You judge fairly, Great Father." Plunge lowered his weighty head in acknowledgment. "The hippos will hold to this   if the crocodiles do."

Thorn turned to the croc and relayed the hippo's message. This time, Rip's grunt was swift and surly.

"Rip swears they will." Thorn gave the crocodile a nod of respect.

Without another word, and with astonishing agility, Rip twisted his huge scaly body. He submerged, heading back to his bask and leaving behind only a trail of ripples.

"Plunge," said Sky in the sudden silence, dipping her head. "If I may—I'm sorry about your little one. She didn't deserve such a death."

Plunge grunted sadly. "May she swim in silver grass in the River of Stars." With a last nod at Thorn, he turned and dived toward his pod in a shower of spray.

For long moments, Sky and Thorn stood staring out across the river.

"She won't see the silver grass," whispered Sky. "Poor little thing. The River of Stars is closed to her."

Silent, Thorn turned and padded back through the trees toward the plain. He looked troubled, Sky thought as she walked beside him, and no wonder. She too couldn't bear to think of that poor baby hippo's lost spirit, trapped with the golden wolves.

"Thank you, Sky." Thorn sighed after a long, quiet trudge. "For your guidance. I don't know how I would have coped there without you."

"It was a good judgment," she demurred, "and calmly given."

He didn't reply, and Sky felt a tremor of unease deep in her gut. Deep down and secretly, she couldn't help agreeing with him. Things would have been a great deal worse if she hadn't been there. "You'd have worked it out," she said out loud.

"No. For a start, I wouldn't have found out what happened to the hippos' baby." He sighed. "It would have been so much harder to reconcile them if I hadn't had proof of that."

Sky said nothing. Her mind was in turmoil. *I can't leave him. Not yet.*

Would there ever be a time when she could safely leave Thorn and return to a normal life with her herd? It was hard to foresee such a moment.

But Thorn was Great Father, and he had good friends at his side. He did not have only Sky to rely on, and she must remember that.

I have to do what I've always done. I must trust the Great Spirit.

CHAPTER NINE

The sun was high in the sky as Thorn padded back into the Great Father Clearing, with Sky trudging at his side; the light shone strongly between the branches and spotted the forest floor with patches of gold. His steps seemed so insubstantial against the earth compared to Sky's; he could feel tremors run through his paw pads with every footfall she took. The heavy pulse of them seemed to echo his sense of impending doom; he could not shake the thought of that baby hippo being dragged to her death by the unearthly wolfpack.

All the same, his mood lightened as Mud, Nut, and Spider came bounding toward him, their eyes shining.

"Congratulations, Thorn!" Mud wrapped him up in an embrace. "The word has spread already—you worked something out between the hippos and the crocodiles!"

Thorn returned his hug. "Yes, I suppose I did. It was hard work, though."

"I'm sure," said Nut, slapping Thorn on the shoulder. "Not renowned for their coolheaded compromise, that lot. Hippos or crocodiles."

"Spider once had a hippo friend," mused Spider. "We had a competition to see who could hold their breath longest. And Spider won."

"Of course you did," said Nut, rolling his eyes. "I'm not sure I even believe the bit about having a hippo friend."

Spider opened his mouth indignantly, but he did not get the chance to respond before the sound of clopping hooves approached. When the baboons and Sky glanced toward the noise, a group of zebras appeared, the dappled sunlight high-lighting their black-and-white stripes with gold. Two of them walked ahead of the others.

The zebra leaders halted, looking from one baboon to the other and then, at last, straight at Thorn. The bigger of the two dipped his head.

"I am Silverstripe, and this is my deputy, Bristlemane. May our herd kindly have an audience with the Great Father?"

Thorn stepped toward them. "Of course you may. How can I help you, friends?"

The leader lifted his head once more. "We used to ask Great Mother," he said, "about our migration. When the time might be right. She always gave us good and wise advice—perhaps you could do this for us also, Thorn Highleaf? The wilde-beests too have agreed to abide by your decision."

A tremor of nerves went through Thorn's stomach. This wasn't something he'd ever done before. He knew nothing about migration tracks and times.

As if sensing his uncertainty, Sky bent her head to whisper to him. "Trust the Great Spirit. . . ."

She had a point, he thought. Before the dawn, he'd known nothing about hippo-crocodile wars. "I'll do my best," he murmured.

This time, he was not looking to understand the life of one individual creature. Closing his eyes, Thorn let his mind drift upward and outward, reaching out for the whole of Bravelands: its landscape, its climate, its plains and ridges and rivers. There was an odd sense of detachment from his body as Thorn let himself soar above it all. Yet he wasn't seeing it, exactly; he was feeling it.

He detected the zebras' old migration tracks, the energy that flowed along them, born of a million journeys: hoof prints beaten on hoof prints for thousands of years. There was a sense of serenity and certainty in the paths of travel, and no angry or fearful warnings blossomed along the lines he saw. The weather was fair, promising rains and fresh grass at the zebras' destination.

Thorn blinked, and he was back in his body, gazing calmly into Silverstripe's dark eyes.

"The timing is good," Thorn told him. "I wish you and the wildebeests well on your journey."

Silverstripe and Bristlemane pricked their ears happily, nodding in respect.

"Thank you, Great Father," said Silverstripe. Turning their striped rumps and whisking their tails, they led their herd away at a canter and disappeared beyond the trees.

"You're getting good at this, Great Father Thorn," said Mud, his eyes twinkling. "I didn't know you knew so much about migration paths."

Thorn gave him a wry grin. "I didn't know anything until a moment ago. It's not me. It's all down to the Great Spirit."

Beside him, he noticed Sky give an almost imperceptible nod.

But Nut patted his back. "Don't put yourself down," he said. "I'm thinking it takes a strong baboon to host the Great Spirit at all, let alone interpret what it says."

Thorn blinked in pleasure. Nut was rarely serious in his compliments, and this one warmed Thorn's heart.

"Well done, Thorn," Sky rumbled. He shot her a grateful look.

"Yes, nice Father-work," said Spider. "Thorn-friend will make Bravelands good again, and we'll all live in harmony like creatures should. That's what Spider reckons." He tickled his lizard's throat.

Oh, Spider. That would be perfect, thought Thorn, *if only there weren't the problem of the wolves. . . .* He shuddered inwardly. The brutes had taken down a hippo, he reminded himself yet again. It wasn't just the wolves' brutality that was worrying—it was their sheer ambition and their insane conviction about their destiny.

It was a problem that must be tackled. But the zebras had

been happy with his advice, and he and Sky together had resolved the issue between the hippos and the crocodiles. Yes, thought Thorn, there were problems and friction between him and Berry and Dawntrees Troop, but surely that too could be put to rest with time and patience.

And at that moment, Fearless came padding into the clearing with his small pride.

Thorn's neck fur prickled; it was as if the Great Spirit was warning him not to be overconfident. Thorn was always glad to see his friend, but the look on Fearless's face told of bad news. The young lion's jaws were clenched tight, his amber eyes troubled, and he stalked toward Thorn with tense shoulders, his tail flicking jerkily. Behind him came his pride-mate Keen, and the younger cubs Ruthless and Menace; all but Menace looked anxious. She wore an expression of haughty indifference, and she seemed to trail after Fearless with some reluctance.

Thorn swallowed hard and stepped forward. "What's the news, old friend?"

Fearless halted. He gazed into Thorn's eyes.

"Thorn—Great Father—we found the golden wolves, and their Alpha, Ravage, was with them. She wants to meet you."

Thorn took a breath and narrowed his eyes. "I think . . . I think that's good," he murmured. "It's the only way to fix all this, stop the killing . . ."

"She wants to meet with you," Fearless repeated in a hollow voice, ". . . so that she can eat your heart."

Sky shook her ears, threw back her trunk, and gave a trumpet of indignant fury. Spider put his paws over his mouth. Nut screeched, peeling back his muzzle, and Mud cried, "Never! She can't have Thorn's heart."

"It's not going to happen," growled Nut. "We'll protect you, Thorn. Don't even think about meeting them. Ravage won't get anywhere near you."

"Wait." Mud looked from Fearless to Thorn, and he straightened his shoulders. "Thorn will find a way to make the wolves see sense," the small baboon declared. "That's what Great Parents do, and Thorn is one of the wisest. We can take precautions, make sure he's safe. He'll have to meet this Ravage, like he told the herds he would—but he'll talk her into sanity."

Those words sent a thrill of dread through Thorn's fur. *Will I really? Can anyone?*

"Well," Nut said, scratching his ear, "I suppose Thorn's smarter than a stupid wolf. But you know what? I don't think those crazy beasts will listen to him."

"Thorn," said Sky, touching his shoulder with her trunk, "I don't like this. Being Great Parent doesn't give you any special protection. You could be killed, just like Great Mother. I don't think you should do this after all. . . ."

"No. I think, perhaps, I do have to try," said Thorn. He realized his voice was shaking. "I'm Great Father. This is my role: to try to sort these problems out."

Mud was watching him solemnly. "I have confidence in you, Thorn. If anyone can get through to those wolves, it's you."

"If you do go ahead with it," growled Fearless, "we lions will come with you, to keep you safe. Right, Keen?"

"Of course we will," said Keen.

"It seems reckless," whispered Sky, "that's all."

"I think Mud's right," said Nut. "If anyone can do it, it's Thorn. I'm just not sure that even he can get any sense through their warped heads."

Thorn gulped. He stood up straighter. "It comes down to this—I'm Great Father. I'm going to have to try. Aren't I?"

Sky gave a confident toss of her trunk. "The Great Spirit will protect you."

Fearless exchanged a glance with Keen. The two lions looked apprehensive, but they turned back to Thorn, and Fearless gave a wary nod.

"We will defend you, Thorn," he growled. "But be careful. Don't drop your guard for an instant."

"Oh, I won't," said Thorn with a nervous bark of laughter. "But Mud's right, and so was my first instinct at the Great Gathering. This is my responsibility, whether it's dangerous or not. I can't avoid these situations; I have to solve them."

How much harder could golden wolves be than hippos or crocs?

Maybe a lot harder . . . Thorn had no more idea how to deal with the wolves than his friends did; that was the truth. It was all very well for Sky to say the Great Spirit would protect him. An elephant Great Parent wouldn't have to worry nearly so much about facing that murderous pack of wolves. But Thorn was a baboon. He felt, at that moment, very easy to kill.

"Let's eat," suggested Spider in the silence. "Spider will go and find something. Food makes everything better."

So long as the food wasn't him, thought Thorn dryly.

When Spider had scavenged some small figs and a couple of wizened melons, three of the baboons sat down in the shadow of a huge mahogany to eat. Thorn took his figs and sat a little apart, closer to the center of the clearing so that he could watch any petitioners approach. Sky tore at the tender lower branches of the fig tree, while the lions settled down with the two cubs for a nap. Fearless seemed fidgety and restless, but Keen snored gently, and both cubs' paws twitched in deep dreams of hunting. For a time, it seemed almost peaceful in the glade; if it hadn't been for the gnawing anxiety in the pit of his stomach, Thorn would have been content. His appetite fading, he tossed aside the remains of a fig.

Across the glade, Fearless twitched and yawned in frustration. Giving up on his unsuccessful nap, he stretched, rose, and padded over to Thorn.

"My friend," the young lion murmured, "could you do something for me?"

Thorn blinked. "Of course, Fearless. If I can."

Fearless looked very thoughtful, his eyes narrowed. "Keen and I . . . There was a particular scent on one of the wolves, and we recognized it. That meaty, dark tang—it was Titan. Could you help us find him?"

Thorn went still, feeling his heart sink. "Titan?" He didn't have time to worry about that brute on top of everything else. It wasn't as if the huge, mad lion was a problem right now; his pride, by all accounts, had been more or less wiped out.

"Yes. And—I wondered." Fearless hesitated. "You have powers. Isn't that true? Since you became Great Father? Powers that Great Mother didn't have."

Warily, Thorn nodded.

"I've heard . . . rumors." Fearless looked anxious but eager. "Some of the animals, they say you travel across Bravelands without moving. That you see through the eyes of other animals. Are they right? Is it more than gossip?"

"It is true. It's something I've been able to do since the Great Spirit entered me," Thorn explained cautiously. "I— sometimes—can enter the minds of other animals. If I'm able to find them, if I focus hard on them, I can . . . see what they see."

Fearless's eyes were wide. "Thorn, that's amazing. Can you find Titan's mind? I need to know where he is."

How could Thorn refuse his friend when it mattered so much to him? "I'll try," he said guardedly. "But I can't promise anything."

"I understand," said Fearless. "But I have faith in you, Great Father."

Thanks for the extra pressure, Fearless. Thorn took a deep breath. He closed his eyes and reached out with his mind.

The savannah spread out before him, vast and beautiful and shimmering in the heat. Dark clusters of trees dotted it, and rivers wound silver and brown through long gullies and flat plains. Birds chattered and soared in search of insects, but even they seemed far below Thorn. A horde of zebras and wildebeests and buffalo moved in what seemed a single inexorable mass to the northwest. Thorn could make out a substantial pride of lions in the long grass, keeping pace with the grass-eaters, relaxed and unhurried. A troop of baboons was moving in the eastern grassland, migrating toward new territory. In a broad stretch of river, crocodiles drifted like tiny, dry leaves.

In wonder at it all, a wonder he knew he would never lose, Thorn let his gaze drift toward the foothills of the far blue mountains.

The cliffs, white and sheer, were broken only by dry scrub and twisted trees. A ledge of flat rock jutted over a shallow gully. Crouched on that rock, alone, Thorn found what he was looking for.

Titan's jaws tore at a huge bone between his paws; shifting its position a little, he rasped his tongue across it, cleaning it of a last few tatters of flesh. Thorn focused on that arrogant, solitary figure, and let himself sink into its mad mind.

Thorn was Titan.

No!

Thorn was a giraffe, out of place and afraid on this lonely rock above a dry gully. He was a hyena, surly and hostile. He was a buffalo, his slow mind confused. He was a cheetah that seemed to dart back and forth, captive and angry. He was an impala. He was a leopard. He was a python.

A creeping terror snaked into Thorn's consciousness. This was not possible. All these animals, in a single small place. He had seen none of them as he homed in on Titan; how could he be in their minds now?

It was too much to take in, too much to understand. With a gasp of confusion, Thorn pulled his mind back, and he sat in the clearing once more, meeting Fearless's concerned gaze.

"I'm sorry." Thorn shook his head, dispelling the unsettling trance. "I can't find him, Fearless. What I felt just then—it was more like a dream than a true vision."

Fearless's expression fell. "You haven't had these powers for long, have you?" His ears perked up. "You could try again! Thorn, one more try, and I think you could find him! I have faith in you!" His eyes were bright and eager again.

The hair on Thorn's spine bristled. Anger stirred inside him. Fearless had no idea what he was asking him to do, no idea how unsettling Thorn's powers could be.

"I know this matters to you, Fearless," he said through clenched teeth, "but I want you to take my word for him. I cannot find Titan, not right now. Don't ask me again!"

Fearless blinked, shocked. His ears flattened a little. "I'm sorry. All right, Thorn, I understand. Thank you for trying, anyway." He turned and padded back to the sleeping lions, his tail drooping.

Thorn watched him go, feeling a little remorseful but mostly relieved. He hadn't meant to scold, but he had had to make Fearless understand—because whatever it was that he'd seen in his search for Titan's mind, it wasn't an experience he wanted to repeat—at least, not now.

Regaining his composure, Thorn turned with a sigh and bounded over to the other baboons.

Mud smiled up at him, his teeth stained with fig juice. He picked at them. "Hello, Thorn!"

"We've been talking about Dawntrees Troop," Nut told Thorn, frowning. "Mud and I went over there to check on them—discreetly, of course. It's not good, Thorn."

Mud cast his eyes downward. "Berry must regret ever forming the Crown Guard," he said. "They're still throwing their weight around when Berry's not watching. You won't believe what Creeper did."

"What?" asked Thorn, though he wasn't sure he wanted to know.

"Climbed up on the Crown Stone and perched there!" Mud looked utterly indignant. "Right there, where only his leader ought to sit!"

"It was only for a moment," added Nut. "But it wasn't right. He sat there smirking, and the rest of the Crown Guard just laughed."

"I think you should go to them again, as Great Father," said Mud. "Put those arrogant baboons in their place. They're not just defying Berry Crownleaf, they're defying you!"

It was horrible news, and it made his heart sink like a stone, but Thorn shook his head firmly. Much as he longed to sort everything out for Berry, he couldn't interfere.

"No," he told them sadly. "No, Mud, I can't. You know what Berry said, and she has a point. Every time I get involved, it chips away another bit of her authority. She doesn't want my input, and she's made that very clear."

"But you're Great Father!" exclaimed Mud.

"I'm sorry." Thorn shook his head. "I hate what's happening in Dawntrees, you know I do. But I don't have a choice. Until she tells me otherwise, Berry's on her own."

CHAPTER TEN

Fearless was not looking forward to returning to the Dead Forest, with its unsettling stench and its eerie, lifeless vegetation, but the journey was unavoidable. Now that Thorn had failed to locate Titan, the scent on the wolves they'd fought here was still his only clue. He and Keen, Ruthless, and Menace padded back toward the pale line of sagging trees in the distance.

Menace was the only one who seemed excited. She trotted along beside the three of them, her tail high, her nostrils eagerly snuffling at the faint breeze, and she kept babbling pointless comments in that arrogant voice of hers. Keen kept shooting her irritated looks and occasionally growling, but nothing could dampen her high spirits.

"I can't wait to see my father again," she mewled. "He's a really important lion. It's going to be great being in Titanpride.

He's the best lion, the fiercest lion, and he loves me. I'm his best cub, he said so."

"That's enough, Menace." Fearless shot a sympathetic glance at Ruthless, but the cub was silent, staring straight ahead as he plodded on.

Menace wasn't to be silenced. "My father's going to be so happy to see me! It's going to be really exciting being a Titan-pride lioness. I'll be able to hunt and kill who I like, when I like." She curled her muzzle in a sneer at Fearless. "This pride is boring. You never let me do anything. I don't know why you even want to find my father. He won't let you join him. He'll just tell you how weak you are. There's no point in you finding him, then. So why do you keep looking?"

"Well . . ." Annoyed as he was with the little lioness, Fearless couldn't bring himself to tell her the truth. "Look, I don't want to join his pride, Menace, so don't worry. I just want to . . . settle an old argument with him."

"Well, if you're having an argument with Daddy, you'll lose." Menace pranced ahead, her tail twitching from side to side.

Keen rolled his eyes at Fearless.

"I can hardly tell her what I really want, can I?" Fearless whispered.

Keen huffed and padded on.

They slowed as they reached the edge of the pale, sparse forest. Fearless halted, flaring his nostrils. There was a familiar dankness and foulness; but there was also another scent: muskier, meatier . . .

"The wolves," he growled. "They're still around. But so are hyenas."

"I smell them too," rumbled Keen. "Lots of them."

"Ruthless. Menace." Fearless turned to them. "Be quiet, and be on your guard."

"Hyenas don't scare me," muttered Menace, but she had finally lowered her voice.

Fearless and Keen began to pace ahead through the trees, setting each paw down with caution. Afraid to make too much noise, but scared too of missing any clues, Fearless halted at every root, every fallen branch. He flared his nostrils, inhaling the mingled odors smeared on them. Hyena-territory spray was one he recognized, with a disgusted curl of his muzzle. Beneath it were slight, sweet traces of shrew, and hints of lizard and snake that were like sun-warmed stone. The smells of grass and leaves were faint; over everything hung the dank, bloody stink of the wolfpack.

But he could catch no lingering scent of Titan.

"What happens if we do find him?" murmured Keen. "We fended him off together at the Misty Ravine—but Fearless, you know as well as I do it was a close call. Titan could easily have killed you."

Fearless grunted. He was reluctant to admit it, but Keen was right. He had made his move too soon.

"I'm not telling you to back off," Keen went on quietly. "I'm just saying that we need a plan."

"We're both getting bigger every day." Fearless flexed his shoulders; they were sturdy and solidly muscled. "We're almost fully grown. Together we can take him. And it's together that we should take him. He killed both our fathers."

Keen grunted skeptically. He opened his jaws to reply, when Fearless heard a high yelp and felt something soft and heavy hit his back. Tiny claws dug through his fur. He reared back, growling and shaking himself, trying to dislodge the attacker.

"Menace!" With a low snarl, Keen bounded over and seized the cub's scruff in his jaws, tugging her off Fearless. "What are you playing at, you young fool?"

"Hunting," she snapped as he dropped her unceremoniously to the ground. "I'm practicing hunting, the way I'm supposed to."

"I told you to be quiet!" snarled Fearless. "We don't want to alert the—"

"Too late for that," Keen interrupted grimly. He turned toward the trees, his tail lashing.

Fearless turned with him. A pack of snarling hyenas advanced toward them on three sides, jaws dripping. Ten or more, Fearless reckoned, his heart pounding. The stench of them was powerful now, even among the stinking trees of the Dead Forest and the reek of the golden wolves.

"Stay behind us," he growled to the cubs.

Ruthless gaped at the hyenas, his gentle eyes wide with fear, but Menace peeled back her muzzle and snarled. "Hyenas don't scare me!"

"No, Menace, do not get involved," warned Fearless. "Keen and I will try to fight the hyenas off. But if you have to run— run!"

The hyenas watched them with angry yellow eyes. Hackles high, muzzles peeled back, they stalked stiffly forward. One by one, they opened their jaws in menacing grins, slaver dripping from their muzzles. Fearless felt Ruthless press against his hindquarters; the cub was trembling. But he could still hear Menace's snarls.

"Come on then," she yipped, though Fearless doubted the hyenas could hear her through their own violent snarling. "You can't take me down, you dirty brutes, I'm the daughter of Titan! Just try!"

Fearless really hoped the hyenas kept up their threatening racket, just to drown out her angry squeaks. But their leader took a single pace forward, and the hyenas quieted.

She was a huge creature, her long yellow teeth deeply stained with old gore. Across her muzzle ran three hideous claw scars, and there was another deep slash across her face where some enemy had barely missed her left eye. Somehow, Fearless doubted the enemy had lived to try again. As all four lions stared at her, even Menace mercifully shut up.

The leader swung her head to her second-in-command.

"Can we be bothered?" she snarled.

"It'd be a waste of energy," growled her lieutenant, licking his jaws. "And the wolves could be back at any moment."

"The wolves?" Fearless was surprised enough by their hesitation to take a pace toward them.

The leader jerked her head at him. "The golden wolves. You must know them."

"Every creature in Bravelands knows the wolves," added

her lieutenant. "Even the dumbest of lions."

"We were attacked by them too," said Fearless, ignoring the insult. "What happened to you?"

The leader gave her pack a questioning look, and they nodded sourly. She stepped forward from the line.

"My name is Skulldrinker," she growled. "I am the matriarch of this pack, and I have led it well for many moons. The wolves wanted me for that reason. They told me they wanted to eat my heart."

"We lost the fiends in the trees," added her lieutenant.

"But we're sure they'll come back," put in another, smaller hyena. "They don't give up."

"When the golden wolves want something, they keep coming till they've taken it," said another.

"And they're close," snarled Skulldrinker. "Even through the stench of you lions, we can smell them."

Fearless stared in silence, lashing his tail. He did not want to fight these hyenas; it would be as much a waste of his strength as it was of theirs. What was more, a hunt for Titan was going to be impossible while the golden wolves still lurked in the shadows of these woods. Their stench overlaid every clue that might lead to Titan; and besides, they could strike at any moment, ruining any careful plan or well-prepared stalk.

"I want rid of those wolves just as you do," he told Skulldrinker. "For once it looks as if lions and hyenas might be on the same side." He drew himself taller, tossing his head. "We need to get those creatures off our lands, and so do you. Our best chance lies in working together. You hyenas have the numbers, and I have a plan." He looked from Skulldrinker to her lieutenant and back again. "Will you take me to your den?"

For a moment there was silence, and his heart rose in hope.

Then Skulldrinker lifted a paw arrogantly, stalked toward him, and tossed her neck.

"I have a plan." Her voice had grown oddly deeper, and Fearless frowned in confusion. "Teamwork is the thing. The liony thing. Oh, so very liony. This is what I want, and this is what I shall achieve, because I am the Great One. See my magnificent mane." Pompously she shook her shoulders again, making the bristly fur shudder. "I am beautiful, am I not? So splendid and golden and ever so clever. Also, I have neck hair." She tossed her scarred head high, wrinkling her nose with a superior air. "Oh no, wait—I don't."

The hyenas of the pack erupted, howling and shrieking with laughter, and suddenly Fearless's confusion cleared. *She's mimicking me!*

Menace sniggered, and even Keen seemed to be stifling laughter. Only Ruthless stared at the ground, looking mortified for him.

"She's not bad at that," muttered Keen, "you've got to admit."

"She sounds nothing like me," protested Fearless, and there was another snort from Menace.

The hyenas' hilarity was dying down, and only a few of them still hiccupped and giggled. Skulldrinker curled the corner of her muzzle and eyed Fearless.

"Cheer up, your splendidness. We'll try your plan, whatever it is. Follow us, and we'll take you to our den."

She seemed entirely unafraid of leading lions to the heart of her territory, and Fearless was more offended by that than he was by the impersonation. *One day*, he thought, *I'll have a pride that other animals respect.*

But, he supposed, that day was not now. He sighed and turned to Keen, Ruthless, and Menace.

"Be careful," he warned. "We're allies for now, but they're still hyenas."

"I can see that," sneered Menace, bouncing after them. "And they still don't scare me."

Fearless hated walking behind Skulldrinker, watching her and her lieutenants stalk on unafraid despite having lions at their tails. Her arrogance was maddening—and besides, it sent shivers of fear along his spine that he couldn't suppress. *They could turn and rip us to pieces, any time they chose.* For his own sense of honor, he was determined not to glance back at the hyenas who padded behind him—he would not show nerves, even if it killed him—but he could feel their yellow gazes, and it made his rump itch.

He glanced sideways for reassurance at Keen, but his friend looked every bit as on edge as he felt. At that moment a bony young male crashed into Fearless's flank; he'd been shoved by one of his pack-mates, fat-bellied and broad-faced. The two were quarreling.

"You couldn't bring down a shrew on your own, and you know it," sniped Bony.

"Ha-ha. That's rot-flesh coming from you," growled Fat-Belly. "I reckon the golden wolves would be putting you out of your misery if they caught you. Except they won't, because who wants the heart of such a terrible hunter?"

"Shut up, you two," barked a hyena just ahead. "I swear I'll eat your eyeballs if you don't."

"Yeah, Bloodfang, I'd like to see you try," Bony snapped at her. "Eater-of-Beetles."

"Hey, Bloodfang! I doubt you could catch our eyeballs if they were rolling loose on the ground," yapped Fat-Belly, and he and Bony sniggered together.

Fearless shot a surprised look at Keen, who shook his head in bemusement. How, he wondered, did hyenas ever coordinate a hunt? This lot never seemed to stop sniping and squabbling.

"Lions are so much better at teamwork," he murmured to Keen. "I'm amazed the hyenas don't end up eating one another."

"All the same, they're efficient killers," Keen pointed out in a soft voice. "We should stay on our guard." Just as he said it, Fearless saw his friend's rangy muscles tense. "There's the den."

Beyond the sparse and stunted acacias lay a pale cliff of stone, craggy and uneven and slashed with dark shadows. Fearless narrowed his eyes, tensing. Some of the hyenas were already ducking and squirming into a ragged gash at the foot of the escarpment, vanishing into the darkness beyond.

"Wait, cubs." He turned to Ruthless and Menace. "I'll go

in first, and you come after me. Keen will come last to protect
your rumps."

"I," squealed Menace for the hundredth time, "am not
scared. I should go first!"

"And I," gritted Fearless, "don't care if you're scared or not.
Wait. Here."

"You're not my pride leader." Menace jammed her forefeet
firmly on the ground, her hackles springing up. "I don't have
to do what you say!"

"Fine." Fearless hunched his broad shoulders and pushed
past her to enter the den.

The tunnel was dank and musty, and its darkness was a
cool contrast with the heat of the forest. Its roof was high, and
Fearless stood up straight. Glancing back at the entrance, he
resisted the temptation to laugh at Menace, who still quiv-
ered indignantly in the sunlight. For once, she seemed lost for
words.

"I could have gone in first," he heard her yelp, finally.

Beyond her, Keen gave a snort of amusement. "Now you
can go inside."

With no possible comeback, she squirmed sulkily after
Fearless, and Ruthless and Keen followed on her heels. Menace shot Fearless a murderous look, her eyes glowing in the
darkness.

As they padded on down the tunnel, there was silence; the
hyenas had stopped their squabbling. Fearless felt a tug of
uncertainty in his gut. This wasn't the first time he'd entered
a hyena den, and his earlier venture hadn't ended well; his

sister Valor had had to come to his rescue as he fled from a vengeful pack. But he swallowed his fears and followed these hyenas as they slunk into a broader cavern.

They all turned in the shadows to watch him, their eyes burning with a pale glow. The hyenas behind him pushed past and formed a circle around the lions with their clan-mates. Fearless couldn't watch them all at once, and his tail itched again.

"All right, Lion," growled Skulldrinker. "What's your great plan?"

Fearless took a deep breath. "The wolves are already stalking us," he began. "You must be able to smell them?"

Skulldrinker barked a scornful laugh. "Of course we can."

"They don't realize that we know they're close," Fearless said. "Or at least, they can't be certain. They probably reckon you've withdrawn to hide in your den—they're arrogant enough to think you're scared. And they don't know that we're working together."

"We hope they think all that," said Skulldrinker's lieutenant.

"I believe the wolves are smart, but they're not as smart as they think they are," said Fearless. He raised his head and flared his nostrils, then glanced around at the den. His night vision had kicked in swiftly, and he could make out dark recesses within the den and smaller tunnels leading from the main cavern. It looked like a good place to hide, and an even better place to lay an ambush.

He turned to Skulldrinker's second-in-command. "What's your name?"

The hyena peeled back his muzzle. "Bonesnapper. For good reason."

Fearless ignored the implied threat. "Bonesnapper, you take your fastest clan-mates. Circle round outside and lay a scent trail toward your den. We want to be sure the wolves come, but not too soon. Can you lead them a roundabout way?"

"What do I look like, a hyrax?" sneered Bonesnapper. "Of course we can." Jerking his head at some of the others to beckon them, he turned and bounded away.

Fearless nodded in relief. The hyenas might be snide and aggressive creatures, but they were cooperating for now. "Skulldrinker, you know the tunnels in this den. Can you assemble half of your best fighters and wait with me, in the one that faces the acacia plain?" He jerked his head back at the entrance tunnel.

"Only half? Ah . . . I see what you're thinking." Skulldrinker nodded, wrinkling her scarred muzzle. "Then your friend can go with Bloodreaver and the rest of my pack and hide in a different passageway? There's a cavern that opens on the south face of the cliff."

"That would be perfect!" Fearless nodded, his hide prickling with excitement. "When the wolves arrive, they'll attack our group. Once we've got their attention, Keen and the other half of your pack can ambush them from the other direction. We'll catch those wolves like the pincers of a scorpion."

Skulldrinker gazed thoughtfully at the acacias, then at the rock face. "That might work. It won't be unlike a normal hunt."

"Except that the wolves aren't grass-eaters, and they can't be aware that we're there. A gazelle could see us coming, at a certain distance—in this case, our second group has to take the wolves by complete surprise, and they have to be on them almost before the wolves know it."

Skulldrinker licked her jaws thoughtfully. "The south tunnel should work; if you and I are engaging the wolves at the entrance, the others will be able to come out almost right behind them." She jerked her head at some of her clan. "Right: you lot come with me and the chunkiest lion. Bloodreaver! Did you hear all that?"

A big, muscular male stalked to her side and nodded, as Fearless bristled with indignation. Chunky? He was well muscled!

"Yes, Skulldrinker," said Bloodreaver. "I heard."

"Take the rest of the clan. You know the tunnel I'm talking about: wait there with the lion's lanky friend. Keen, his name is." Skulldrinker peeled back her muzzle and stared at the assembled hyenas. "Was everyone paying attention? You all know what to do?"

The hyenas nodded eagerly, yowling and yapping.

"We do, we do!"

"Yes, Skulldrinker, we were listening! We were!"

"That makes a pleasant change," growled Skulldrinker. "And shut up with your noise." She stared at their guilty faces, curling her lip. "Why are you all still here?"

The hyenas twisted and shot off after Bloodreaver. Keen gave Fearless a last wry look and prowled off after them.

"Menace, Ruthless?" said Fearless. "You are staying in the den. No argument." He glared at Menace, baring his fangs.

She glowered back at him, but slumped into a crouch and said nothing. He realized she was still sulking about his maneuver at the entrance tunnel; that was fine with him.

The rest of the hyenas trooped after Skulldrinker and Fearless as they stalked back toward the entrance tunnel.

"This had better work," growled Skulldrinker quietly to Fearless, "or I'll have questions you're not going to want to answer."

"It'll work," Fearless assured her, with more confidence than he felt.

He crouched beside Skulldrinker to wait just inside the tunnel entrance; the other hyenas crowded behind him. There was no squabbling or snapping; the clan was suddenly, unnervingly quiet and disciplined. Beyond the gash of the entrance, no breeze stirred the stunted grass; no cry of a hyena tore the still air, and there was not even a whistle of birdsong. Fearless could feel his heart thudding hard in his rib cage. He hoped Keen was all right, back there in the darkness with Bloodreaver and half of the hyenas.

Don't be silly. If Keen was in trouble, you'd hear it soon enough.

He took a deep breath; it caught in his throat. The scent of more hyenas drifted to his nostrils; he already recognized Bonesnapper's musky odor. Fearless couldn't see them yet, but the advance party was back, and they must have set their lure. Between the dark twisted trunks of the acacias, quick shadows flickered.

"The wolves are here," he murmured.

Skulldrinker's hackles sprang up, and her shoulders tensed. She placed a paw carefully forward, curling her muzzle with a look of vicious glee. Out on the grassland, the narrow snouts of wolves appeared, questing eagerly for blood. The whole pack emerged into view, bounding after Bonesnapper and his gang.

"Now!" roared Fearless.

As he sprang out of the tunnel, he caught a fleeting glimpse of Skulldrinker at his side. She and the other hyenas were outpacing him already, racing toward the wolves. The wolves started, hesitated, and spun around, baring their fangs, then flew to meet them. For just a moment, Fearless's heart quailed.

Then, beyond the wolves, he saw the shapes of Keen and the other hyenas racing out of the darkness of another tunnel. Some of the wolves noticed them, and skidded and twisted.

But Fearless had no more time to watch. Skulldrinker was already among the first wolves, snapping and biting, and Fearless himself collided with a big female, bowling her over.

He felt sharp fangs bite into his foreleg. Slamming her down with his forepaws, he lunged for her throat. He sank his fangs into warm, bitter flesh and felt the gush of blood in his mouth.

He tossed her limp corpse aside and turned to the next wolf, clamping his jaws around its spine. It yelped, flailing its legs as he lifted it clear of the ground. From the corner of his eye, Fearless was aware of Keen, snarling as he clamped his jaws around a wolf's throat and suffocated it to death. But he couldn't let himself be distracted.

The wolves seemed completely taken by surprise; they were darting and spinning in shocked chaos, while the hyenas seemed to be in a frenzy, ripping and tearing at skinny bodies.

Ravage's shrill howl cut through the noise of battle. "Blood-heart Pack, regroup!"

Fearless swung his head, searching frantically for the wolf leader, but when he caught sight of her she was already flee-ing toward the trees. Other wolves scrambled up, disengaging from battle and scampering after their leader. A few tried to drag themselves, bleeding, after their comrades, but hyenas pounced and lunged to finish them off.

"Take my heart! My pack!" The squeal of one wolf chilled Fearless's nerves. "Let me be we—!"

But he was instantly buried under two hyenas, who cut off his high begging screams with satisfied grunts and tearing fangs.

Catching his breath, Fearless stared around the battlefield. A last few wolves eluded the pursuing hyenas and scuttled after their pack, but more lay torn and lifeless, their blood soaking the dry earth. Through the carnage stalked Skulldrinker, her muzzle curled in a delighted grin. Some of her clan bounded off in pursuit of the fleeing wolves, but she herself halted in front of Fearless.

"Not a bad plan," she growled. "Not bad at all, for a lion."

"And you're not bad fighters," he retorted. "For hyenas."

Grinning, she turned and raced after her clan. He heard her warlike yammering, fading in the distance as she too chased the stragglers.

Fearless stood very still in the new and dreadful silence. Keen padded over to him and licked his bloodied muzzle.

"It worked," he growled softly. "For now."

Two small shapes were scrabbling out of the dark slash of the den's entrance. Menace trotted ahead of Ruthless, her snub nose cocky, her tail high.

"Well, that took you long enough," she sniffed. "I'm just glad to get out of that stinking hole."

"That was brilliant, Fearless," murmured Ruthless behind her. "Menace and I watched from the entrance tunnel."

"Thank you," Fearless told him, with a pointed glare at Menace. "And now we can hun—I mean, search for Titan without worrying about the wolves being on our tails. Come on, let's get going."

"Yes," warned Keen, "but let's not get too confident, eh? That battle could have gone very differently."

"But it didn't," said Ruthless loyally.

"No, it didn't, but we risked a lot," said Keen, twitching his tail. "We were lucky. We may not always be." Softly, to Fearless, he added, "This may not end well, my friend."

"Oh, don't worry," Fearless told him. He rubbed his head against Keen's. "I'm even more certain now. It'll all work out perfectly—you'll see."

CHAPTER ELEVEN

There was something so unusual about the dawn. Instead of glowing golden and violet, it was a red and angry glare. Sky raised her head, an unnamable fear running through her bones.

Around her, the herd stirred and milled as panic began to spread from elephant to elephant. They too, she realized, were afraid of this extraordinary light. Turning back to face the horizon, Sky saw that despite the harsh glow, the sun was not rising; just like the elephants, it seemed to huddle in fear, and its light did not spill over the mountains as it always did.

Sky looked up, raising her trunk. There was a shining ball in the sky that was not the sun and was not a star. It was a fiery streak of white, approaching too fast to see clearly.

A comet? It was like one she had witnessed before, but it did not hang in the sky, its tail apparently motionless—this one streaked toward the herd, growing larger and more terrifying by the moment, and it seemed to home in directly on her family.

With trumpets of alarm, the herd stampeded. Blaring, squealing in panic, they fled, their great feet raising clouds of dust that glowed eerily red in the strange light. But Sky could not move. Her feet felt rooted to the spot, her legs heavy.

Above her, the comet was huge now, aflame with lethal streamers of fire. Its heat bathed her skin. Sky knew it would be the last thing she saw. . . .

She jerked awake. The sky was dark above her, the earth cool beneath her feet. No comet turned the sky to a flaming scarlet, and only a pale purple dawn edged the fractured horizon beyond the trees.

Sky let out a juddering breath as she stood blinking into wakefulness in the Great Father Clearing. A dream. It had been only a dream.

Her limbs felt weak and unsteady. Closing her eyes for a moment, Sky gathered herself, letting her heartbeat settle into a normal rhythm. She opened them again. On the far side of the clearing, a shadow was moving and stretching in the twisted branches of a fig tree.

As soon as her legs felt strong again, Sky walked over to Thorn. "Great Father," she murmured. "Good morning."

"Sky." Thorn gave a great yawn that bared all his teeth. "Is everything quiet?"

"In the real world, yes." She smiled ruefully. "In my dreams, less so."

He sat up straight, looking suddenly much more alert. "What happened?"

Sky pulled at a branch with her trunk, taking a moment to order her thoughts. The dream had been so chaotic, so violent, the clearing seemed almost unnaturally peaceful. "I saw . . . a comet, Thorn. But it wasn't like the one I saw when I was small: unmoving in the sky, just hanging there. It was fierce and fast, and it had come to destroy my whole herd."

"That's a terrifying dream," he said, shaking his head, "but still just a dream. Don't worry, Sky. There's no comet, see?" He pointed upward through the branches. "And no stone has dropped from the sky. I think that, now, were a star-rock to fall anywhere on Bravelands, I would feel its impact."

"I know," she said, "but it seemed real, Thorn: more like a vision than a dream. I'm worried . . . worried that it means something. That there is a danger to my family. And a comet, of all things? Perhaps it means Comet herself will come to harm. Or that she is leading the Strider family into terrible danger . . ." She swallowed.

Thorn was watching her, solemn and quiet, as her voice trailed off. He reached out a paw and stroked her trunk.

"What do you want to do, Sky?"

"I don't know," she said helplessly. "I want to stay and help you. I have a duty to the Great Spirit. But—"

"The Great Spirit understands loyalty and family," Thorn told her gently. "It knows the fear you must have for your herd, Sky. You must go and make sure they're safe."

"But—"

"Sky, you have been more help to me than I can ever describe, but I'm getting used to it now—to making decisions, to being Great Father. The Great Spirit is with me." He smiled at her. "How can I fail?"

She bowed her head. "Thank you, Great Father. Thank you. I will return, I promise—it's just . . ."

"I know. Your family is important to you, Sky, and I know you won't rest until you know they're all right. Your visions aren't something to be taken lightly."

Sky nodded. "The bull elephants should be starting their migration, too. I'll travel with them till I catch up with my own herd. Wherever they are . . ."

"That I can help with." Thorn patted her trunk and sat back. "I'll find them for you, Sky, so at least you'll know in which direction you must walk."

Her heart in her throat, Sky watched Thorn as he closed his eyes. Would he start out of his trance, horrified, and tell her that her family was in terrible danger? But no flicker of fear or shock crossed his face, and in a moment he opened his eyes once more and smiled.

"They seem to be safe. They are waking right at this moment, in the shadow of a mountain shaped like a crouching baboon, and the morning is peaceful. But I can't know if danger is on its way. You must go to them. I've told you, I'll be fine."

Was that a trace of anxiety she heard in his voice? He was

trying so hard to be strong and calm, but . . . She peered down at him.

There was something different about him these days, something in his eyes and posture. Thorn was small, and he did not have the strength of an elephant. But she couldn't help noticing that a quiet confidence had been growing inside him. Perhaps her worries about him were groundless? With every passing day, the role of Great Father seemed to fit him more easily.

It was odd, the small stir of melancholy she was feeling. Had she overestimated his need of her? *Yet nothing changes the fact that he's vulnerable in a way Great Mother wasn't. . . .*

"The Great Spirit chose you, Thorn," she murmured at last. "You really will be fine. I'm sure there will be challenges while I'm gone, but I know you'll meet them like a lio—no." She smiled. "Like the courageous baboon you are."

In their nearby nests, the other three baboons were stirring, stretching and yawning. Sky turned to them, touching Mud's arm with the tip of her trunk.

"I have to go away for a while," she murmured. "Will you look out for Thorn?"

Mud rubbed his eyes, startled, and scrambled down from the tree to stand beside Thorn. "Of course I will. We all will. Right?" He glanced at Nut and Spider.

"Always," said Nut. He looked wide-awake instantly.

"Good," said Sky. She stroked Mud's head. "I know he needs and values your advice, Mud, even more than mine.

And Nut and Spider, you are strong and brave defenders of our Great Father."

Nut looked vaguely awkward but pleased. He scratched his jaw. "And we'll go on defending him. We promise."

"Spider too," put in Spider. His lizard peeped out from his armpit, and he tickled its throat.

"Thank you," said Sky softly. "I know I can count on you. And so can Thorn."

Ahead of Sky, the male elephants marched implacably along their migration track, their bulk raising clouds of shimmering yellow dust. Over the baboon-shaped mountain in the far distance, the sun that rose was dazzling, and Sky was happy to stride along in the bulls' long shadows. She walked alongside Flint in an easy, comfortable silence, the cheetah cubs Nimble and Lively trotting at her heels.

"You don't have to stay beside me, young one," Flint told her at last in his rumbling voice.

"But I want to," she said. His company was quiet and restful, much more so than Forest's—the young bull had a habit of sidling close to her and trying to talk. She liked him, but sometimes she liked silence and solitude, too.

The cheetah cubs had helped lighten everyone's mood on the journey. Nimble and Lively were growing fast, she thought as she glanced at them. They were losing their fluffy crowns, growing sleeker and more long-limbed by the day. They seemed excited to be on the march, and they often startled her by sprinting away. But they would always return, some small prey-creature grasped in their jaws. The bull elephants watched their antics, clearly amused by the distraction. It must be a pleasant change for the males, Sky realized, traveling with youngsters in tow; the baby elephants, of course, would always migrate with their mothers and aunts. The youngest bull here was Forest.

She found her mind drifting back to the days, not so very long ago, when she would travel with Great Mother and the other females: happy to trudge in their wake, confident that her grandmother knew every path and trail, that she had anticipated every danger. Great Mother must have traveled the elephant tracks for so many seasons.

"Flint," she said suddenly, "can you tell me about Great Mother when she was younger? When she was just Sun?"

Flint cast her an amused glance. "When she was Sun? She was a lot like Sky, if you must know. Always . . . curious."

Sky felt a little rush of embarrassment mixed with pleasure. "I'm nothing like Great Mother," she told him. "She was always so calm, so decisive. So much in control! I seem to blunder from crisis to crisis." Shaking her ears, she gave a rueful laugh.

"Great Mother was far older and more experienced," Flint told her kindly. "And that's not what I meant. I was talking about your kindness, your instinct for understanding others." He halted, turning to her. "You know, the Great Spirit did not choose Sun because she always made the right decision. It chose her because she knew something more important: that there is not always a correct decision to be made. Sun always understood that some questions don't have an answer. Sometimes there's simply a choice of paths, and all an animal can do is follow its instinct."

Sky opened her mouth, trying to find a reply, but she was distracted by a slight commotion ahead. Forest had broken into a skipping jog, trying not to step on the cheetah cubs who gamboled carelessly between his legs.

"Nimble, Lively!" called Sky, alarmed. "Be careful!"

Forest glanced back, slowing to a regular stride. "It's all right, Sky," he called. "I don't mind, and I can avoid them." Reaching out his trunk, he swept them both up and settled the cubs on his head. Nimble and Lively squealed with delight.

Sky smiled. "Thank you, Forest. You're so good with those two."

Forest's eyes shone; he looked as if he might burst with pleasure. Sky felt a nudge on her left shoulder; her brother had fallen back to walk alongside her.

"Oh! Hello, Boulder." She butted him gently with her trunk.

"You know, it isn't the cubs Forest is fond of," he told her, a mischievous spark in his eye. "He likes you a lot, Sky."

"Oh!" Sky glanced ahead at the young bull, her heart clenching with anxiety. "Do you really think he's that interested?"

"Yes, I do think so." Boulder laughed. "Haven't you noticed the way he looks at you? How he's always trying to talk to you?"

"I . . . well, I didn't think . . ." Sky struggled to find the words. "Do you think he's that serious?"

"Don't be surprised if he asks you to be his life-mate," Boulder murmured. "That's all I'm saying."

"But that can't happen!" exclaimed Sky. "I'm betrothed to Rock, remember? That's irrevocable. I can never take another mate."

"Well, I've been thinking." Boulder stirred and blew at the dust with his trunk as he walked. "Surely we could all bend the rules, Sky? Just this once. Rock was a mistake, and the Great Spirit understands mistakes—so do all elephants." He hesitated. "You know one of our stopping points will be the Plain of Hearts?"

Silent, Sky nodded. Yes, she knew; and she dreaded that moment. The Plain of Hearts was the place where couples reunited, where elephants without a mate would often find one.

"So . . . couldn't you open your heart to Forest there?" Boulder glanced at her. "He would be a good mate, don't you think?"

Sky set her jaw. "Yes. Yes, he would, Boulder, but not for me. I can't even consider another mate—and it's not about tradition." Losing Rock had broken her heart, after all. It was not so long ago that Boulder had told her about Rock killing River Marcher. The pain of rejecting the love of her life—though she had had no choice, given what he'd done—was still fresh. "Can you please stop talking about it?"

Her brother took a breath as if to argue, but seemed to change his mind. He nodded reluctantly.

And I hope he keeps to that, thought Sky. It was bad enough missing Rock as she did, without Boulder spending this whole migration trying to pair her off with Forest.

She plodded after the bulls as the sun rose high in the sky, and as the afternoon lengthened into dusk. At least the herd kept up a good pace, and the effort helped keep Sky's mind off her unhappiness.

One day melted into another, hot and cloudless, as the trek continued, and Sky pushed Rock to the back of her mind. The baboon-shaped mountain that shimmered in the distance drew closer; its hazy blueness became greener, more distinct, till she could make out crags and hollows and shadows of forest. Not far now. *One foot in front of another,* she told herself constantly. *One foot in front of another . . .*

Besides, there were other things for her to worry about: more important matters. How was Thorn getting on without her? She hoped he was gaining confidence all the time. Trust the Great Spirit. . . .

And there were Nimble and Lively. The young cheetahs were still her responsibility, although their hunting skills were developing by the day and they seemed almost perfectly self-sufficient. The cubs brought back lizards and rats and ground squirrels, proudly showing them off to Sky before they ate.

Forest brought gifts to her too, though, and that didn't help her deep sense of unease. Once it was a branch of freshly sprouted young green leaves; once it was a jackfruit that she simply could not resist. The young bull was still taking every opportunity to walk beside her, asking questions about her earlier life, and telling her funny stories of the herd's previous migrations.

"Oh! I don't think I've ever told you about the time your brother pulled down a branch, and there was a snake on it. You've never heard such a high-pitched squeal from a grown bull elephant! The snake would have squealed too, if it could. You couldn't see Boulder for dust. . . ."

Forest could make her laugh all too easily, Sky realized. *I always knew he would make a good mate, though*, she told herself for the umpteenth time. *But as I told Boulder: not mine.*

The days were such a blur of relentless marching, it came as a jolt when, one late afternoon, the bull at the head of the herd gave a resounding trumpet of declaration. Sky halted, startled, and lifted her head to gaze toward the horizon.

The savannah still stretched out before them, hazy with golden heat. But beyond the plain, she saw it clearly now: that enticing mountain, green with forest and mottled with rock shadows, hunched over the plains like a crouching baboon.

Filled with renewed energy, Sky strode on, her pace quickening with each step, her trunk swinging. Between mountain and plain there was a barely discernible dark line that gradually resolved into vague shapes. In time, as they drew closer, those shapes became distinct: Sky could make out a herd of elephants. And she was soon close enough to recognize them.

My family! She was trotting now, outpacing even the biggest of the bulls, breathlessly eager to join her herd. But as she approached them, her steps faltered for a moment, and she gasped.

Something was wrong. Sky felt a chill ripple through her hide despite the late afternoon heat. Her aunts and cousins milled anxiously around a single female: one who looked frantic, distressed. As Comet and Star paced and shifted aside in agitation, Sky realized the elephant in trouble was Breeze.

Sky broke into a thundering canter, and at last the elephants around Breeze glanced up in alarm. Comet the matriarch scooped up chunks of earth in her trunk, ready to fling them in warning.

Then she dropped them. Her ears flapped forward, and she raised her trunk to blare a joyful greeting. "Sky!"

The others, too, were relaxing their hostile postures, moving forward as one to greet her.

"Sky? Is it really you?"

"She's back!"

Sky slowed to a halt, pressing her head to Comet's, greeting the elephants who gathered around her with touches of her trunk. "Oh, it's good to see you," she cried. "But I don't understand. What's wrong? What's happened to Breeze? Is she hurt?"

"Not hurt." Comet drew back, solemn again, as her herd murmured and rumbled in distress. "But yes, Sky, something is wrong. The calf is ready to be born—but Breeze? She won't accept it, she can't submit. She won't let the baby come."

CHAPTER TWELVE

There was only one thing Sky could do, only one urge that gripped her; she joined her herd, supporting them, protectively huddling around Breeze. The short-tusked mother swayed and rocked, raising her trunk and blaring her unhappiness.

"It's all wrong, Comet! It's wrong!"

Beyond the circle of females, one bull paced and trumpeted, but Comet turned and shooed him away, flapping her ears. "Get away, Branch. This is not your business!"

He withdrew a few reluctant paces, but would go no farther, and Sky realized that he must be the baby's father. But Comet was ignoring him now, reaching out with her trunk to comfort Breeze.

"Let the baby come, Breeze! Let it come, it's ready."

"It's not the right time!" blared Breeze. "Night hasn't fallen! Our babies should not come in daylight!"

"We're with you," Comet soothed her. "No harm will come to your baby, we swear it!"

"Breeze," cried Star, "my baby Moon came in the afternoon, and all was well with his birth. Let your baby be born!"

Sky had seen few births, and all had been in the hours of darkness. Confused, she reached out to hesitantly stroke Breeze's rump.

"Let it be, Breeze," rumbled Comet. "Let it be as the Great Spirit ordains."

Breeze lifted her head and gave an incoherent trumpet of fear. Her hindquarters began to rock, rhythmically, forward and back, forward and back.

Sky gasped. The thin sac that encased the baby bulged between Breeze's hind legs.

"You cannot stop it," murmured Comet, rubbing Breeze's ears as the young mother flinched. "Let your baby be born into Bravelands."

Breeze's hindquarters lurched forward, and she sank almost to her back knees, her forelegs jutting into the ground. With a suddenness that made Sky's heart trip and thunder, the baby dropped to the ground, its fall cushioned by its fluid sac.

A great chorus of cries rose from the female herd: relieved, ecstatic, welcoming. Breeze twisted with a look of vague shock in her eyes and gave a cry of happiness. Gently she caressed the baby that even now was trying to struggle to its feet. Part of the sac still enveloped its head; Sky darted her trunk forward and broke the membrane, and the baby gasped.

A surge of happiness filled Sky that for a moment

obliterated all her dull worry, all her misery about Rock. Breeze too seemed to have forgotten all her concerns about the daylight; she stroked and fondled her infant, urging it to its unsteady feet.

"A female!" trumpeted Comet in ecstasy. "Sisters, daughters, we welcome a new calf to our herd!"

The sounds of celebration around Sky were deafening, and she joined in with a happy heart, raising her trunk to holler her thanks to the Great Spirit. The baby was staggering to her feet, fumbling with her tiny trunk for her mother's milk as Breeze gently guided her.

Breeze closed her eyes in delight as the baby found what she was looking for. "You were born in the day, little one," she cried, "and you could see the far border of Bravelands from the moment you opened your eyes. I name you Horizon."

"That's a beautiful name," murmured Sky.

An urgent instinct overcame Sky, one she could not resist. Reaching out with tusks and trunk, she began to scoop up clod after clod of earth, dumping them over the remains of the birth. The other females felt it too; Sky saw them working at her side, raking up earth and dust with their tusks, flinging it across the discarded sac and the streaks of blood that remained on the ground. It had to be done thoroughly, Sky knew in the deepest part of her. The lions she'd spotted still lurked beyond the shimmering haze of heat—two old and prideless males—and now there were jackals too, pacing in excitement as they stared toward the elephants.

Those flesh-eaters already knew about the birth, but more

would come, their nostrils hungrily sniffing the air. The work
the female elephants did was age-old, Sky knew, and very necessary. Deep inside her she felt a powerful connection, not
only to her own family but to all the female herds that had
come before them, protecting mother and baby, masking their
vulnerable scents.

This is my family, she thought. *This is where I belong.* She should
never have stayed away so long. This was natural, this was
right, this was the way of Bravelands.

Cautiously, some of the males were edging closer, and
despite Comet's threats, Branch trudged nearer still, gazing
longingly at Breeze, his trunk questing for the scent of his
infant. Even the cheetah cubs crept forward, their dark eyes
burning with curiosity.

"She's beautiful," mewled Lively.

"Horizon is a good name," declared Nimble.

The female elephants still looked wary, but as the tiny new
baby drank and tested her wobbly legs, they began to relax.
Some of the Strider family had begun to notice and recognize
their mates in Boulder's herd, and they greeted one another
with rumbles of affection and touching of trunks.

Sky noticed a sadness in Star's eyes as she watched the new
baby. No wonder; Star's own little son had died at the jaws
of Titanpride only recently, and this must be a bittersweet
moment for her. Sky hoisted her trunk over the bereaved
mother's shoulders and let it rest there, comforting.

"Well, look at these sweet cubs!" exclaimed Comet, who
was peering down at the young cheetahs.

"Oh!" Star seemed glad of the distraction. "They're adorable! Sky, are they yours?"

"In a way," said Sky wryly.

"Sky's our mother," chirped Lively. "Sort of. In a way."

Sky felt a gush of warmth in her chest, and she caressed the cub's head with the tip of her trunk. "I do what I can, little one. For your true mother's sake. For Rush."

For a while the male and female elephants mingled, exchanging greetings and endearments and snippets of gossip, but gradually, as little Horizon became steadier on her feet, they began to move again, trudging relentlessly toward the foothills of the baboon-shaped mountain.

Sky found her heart much lighter as she walked with them. Horizon's birth seemed to have changed everything. Surely such a moment of joy signaled hope for Bravelands, and even for Sky? The Plain of Hearts no longer seemed a place to dread. Sky's steps were far lighter than she had expected as she followed her aunts toward the mountain.

It was Boulder who now seemed morose. His head sagged a little as he walked at her side, and she nudged him gently.

"What's wrong, brother?"

He sighed. "Nothing, Sky. It's just that I haven't returned to the Plain of Hearts since it happened."

Sky took a breath. *Of course: his lost love, River.*

"She died close to here," Boulder murmured. "In the ravine on the edge of the plain."

"Oh," whispered Sky. "I'm sorry."

Boulder straightened his shoulders a little and marched on.

"Don't worry. It's an old sadness, but it still hurts."

"I know that feeling," she told him softly.

"I know you do. We'll face the terrors of the Plain of Hearts together," he rumbled, touching her shoulder.

At that moment, Comet the matriarch halted, trumpeting a joyful declaration of arrival. Sky took a breath, peering ahead. Elephants of other herds already milled on the plain, looking expectant and excited, and they turned to greet the newcomers.

Sky gazed around as she walked on. This place was almost too beautiful to make her sad, despite its painful meaning for her. Rippling golden grass extended in a great arc to the foot of the mountain; the plain rose in a shallow slope to white cliffs that bordered it on three sides. Loose rocks from the mountain had tumbled down, and they gleamed in the sunlit grass among the long shadows of the late afternoon.

She was so busy admiring the landscape, it took Sky long moments to realize that elephants were turning to stare at her. Trunks were raised, ears flapped forward, and voices rose from inaudible murmurs to distinct bellows of happiness.

"Sky Strider! It's her!"

"The elephant who led the Great Herd! She carried the Great Spirit, did you know?"

"Is that her, Mama?"

"Yes! That's the young elephant who defeated the False Parent!"

"Sky Strider! Moon and starlight, what a wonderful surprise!"

Sky halted, shocked and a little embarrassed, as from all sides elephants ambled eagerly toward her. Some came close enough to greet her by touch, dipping their heads in respect.

"Thank you, Sky Strider," said an old and long-tusked matriarch.

"For all you've done for Bravelands, we thank you!" That was a bright-eyed young bull.

"This is my little son, Stone." A young mother approached Sky, drawing her baby forward. "You made Bravelands safe for him, and I am forever grateful."

Overwhelmed, Sky could only mutter her gratitude and give her admirers shy nods. This was unexpected, and it gave her a warm sense of belonging, but beneath it all was a prickling urgency. Although she was humbled and delighted, it felt oddly frustrating to be surrounded. Through the crowd, it was so hard to see the other elephants who filled the valley. . . .

Yet why was she even looking? Did she still hope that somewhere on this plain, Rock was waiting for her?

Yes.

No, she mustn't think that way. Sky shook herself. Rock wasn't here. And even if he was, she could never be with him, knowing what he had done.

Her own aunts had dispersed, seeking and finding their own life-mates. Pulling herself together, Sky nodded to a young bull who had come to introduce himself.

"You're Sky Strider, aren't you?" he said, a little breathlessly. "I just want to tell you how much I admire you. Are you fond of acacia leaves? Fever trees are my favorites. Perhaps I might bring you some later? I'd love to. Did you have a long trek to get here? My brothers and I had to cross the Shadow Canyon."

It was hard to focus on his small talk. Sky settled for nodding and murmuring noncommittal replies. "Yes, indeed . . . Oh, very much . . . Thank you, that's kind. . . ."

As the young male at last gave up, excused himself politely, and wandered away, Sky watched him approach a dark-hided female; other bulls and females were shyly introducing themselves and pairing off. At the edge of the valley she could make out Boulder, conversing hesitantly with a creamy-tusked female. The female's eyelashes fluttered. *Perhaps Boulder might begin to move on from his grief for River?* Sky hoped so. Her brother deserved happiness.

She gave a deep, quiet sigh. She couldn't be part of all this, and there was no point wishing for the stars.

Just as she thought that, she felt a presence at her shoulder and scented the strong musk of a male elephant. She turned.

"Sky," said Forest softly. He looked so nervous, and her heart sank.

"Forest," she murmured. She knew what he had come to say—Boulder had warned her, after all—and she felt a wrench of regret.

"I . . . I like you, Sky, a lot." He swallowed. "I think you like me, too. Is there any hope—I mean, may I ask you—Sky." Forest gulped again and closed his eyes. "Would you be my life-mate?"

Sky hesitated for a moment, gathering her courage. She couldn't deny how touched she was. She knew how flattering

it was, to be asked this by such a fine and strong young elephant. If only . . .

It was her turn to swallow over the lump in her throat.
"Forest, I'm honored. You've no idea how deeply. And I'm
sorry, truly sorry—but I'm betrothed to Rock. I cannot break
that bond. I'm sorry," she said again, her voice fading.

"But I think—no, I'm sure—an exception could be made.
You're so widely admired, Sky. Others would understand
that your betrothal was made under a misleading impression.
Mistakes happen, Sky." He gulped. "You deserve to be happy.
And I know I could make you happy."

Oh, Forest. She didn't think she could bear to refuse. Yet she
had to. "I'm sorry, Forest. I . . . I just can't. It wouldn't be fair
to you."

The pain in his eyes was almost unbearable. Slowly, Forest
nodded.

"I understand." He seemed about to say more, but instead
he gave a slight shake of his ears and turned away.

Sky watched him go, her heart aching with remorse.

"I couldn't help overhearing." The voice at Sky's ear was
gentle. She turned to look into Comet's sympathetic eyes.

"I don't have a choice, Comet," Sky whispered.

"Is that really true?" Comet hesitated, raking the grass with
a forefoot. "Sky, you have done such extraordinary things in
your young life. You've broken tradition—you've befriended
lions and baboons, you've adopted a dead cheetah's cubs as
your own. If any elephant can change tradition, it's you. You're
still so young. If you wanted to forget your hasty betrothal

and be with Forest, I know that—"

Sky shook her head quickly. "Thank you, Comet. I mean it, I'm grateful. But I can't. I do like Forest, it's true, but . . . I can't forget Rock, however much I wish I could."

"Rock did a terrible thing," Comet reminded her. "Any elephant would understand if you changed your mind."

"But I can't. I can't change my mind or my heart." Sky sighed. "Maybe one day I could be ready to find a new love, Comet. But not yet. I just can't bear to do it."

Slowly, Comet nodded. "Very well, Sky. But remember that a broken heart will mend. It always does, even though you may not believe that right now. I . . . I would hate to see you miss the greatest opportunity of all."

"To be with Forest?" Sky tilted her head and half closed one eye.

"No, Sky. To bear infants. I watch you with Nimble and Lively, and I watched you with little Moon when he was alive. It's clear you would be a wonderful mother."

"Oh." There was a painful twinge in Sky's chest. Comet had not needed to say it; she already knew it was one of the things she would regret most.

"Sky," sighed Comet, "I really hope you will rejoin the herd now. You belong with us. And we miss you so much."

"I miss all of you too," Sky told her with feeling. "More than ever, since I saw Horizon being born."

"So what's stopping you?" whispered Comet. "You know we'd welcome you back. Don't worry about Mirage and her sharp tongue."

"I don't mind her, truly, and I'm fond of Mirage," admitted Sky. "I know the Strider family is where I belong, and I ache to come back, but—"

"But what?"

Sky swung her trunk in agitation. It was so hard to put into words. She could barely explain it to herself. But she vividly recalled Flint's words: *Some questions don't have an answer. Sometimes there's simply a choice of paths.*

"I don't know, Comet," she said at last, honestly. "But it's an instinct. A deep-down instinct, in my blood and my bones." Sky drew a determined breath.

"And if Great Mother taught me anything, it's that I have to heed it."

CHAPTER THIRTEEN

"I've got a plan," said Thorn. "You may not like it, my friends, but hear me out."

He sat in the Great Father Clearing as the evening shadows lengthened, casting golden stripes through the trees across the exposed sandy ground. Nut, Mud, and Spider had gathered in a semicircle facing Thorn. They exchanged apprehensive glances, and Nut chewed his lower lip, narrowing his eyes.

"Go on," he said.

"I can't think how to deal with the wolves, and believe me, I've thought hard." Thorn eyed each of his friends in turn. "It's not possible to make a plan. So all I can do is go to meet with them, think on my paws, and hope for the best."

"Just hang on." Nut sprang to his feet, his eyes widening. "Mud and Spider and I have thought this over, and we've talked about it, and we've decided that that was a silly proposal.

Even the Great Father can't be expected to make those brutes see reason. Don't even think about going."

"Thorn, you can't," agreed Mud firmly. "I was wrong. Sometimes you shouldn't listen to me; I shouldn't have encouraged you. It's far too dangerous."

"Spider likes to talk to other animals," remarked Spider thoughtfully, "and even he thinks this is a crazy idea."

"Spider knows," said Thorn with a touch of irritation, "that talking to other animals is the only way to really get to know them."

"You're not going to get to know those wolves," remarked Nut, "before they're spitting out your finger bones."

"No, listen," said Thorn. He did not want to hear any prophecies of doom; he was already terrified enough of his own proposal "It's just possible that I can get them to explain to me why they're doing this. And if I understand why, then there's a chance I can persuade them to stop."

"Just possible," echoed Nut. "A chance. This is your worst idea yet, Thorn Highleaf, and I've heard a few."

"It's better than staying here and doing nothing," cried Thorn. "That's not even an option!"

"Of course it's an option," snapped Nut, thumping the ground with a fist, "if the alternative is being eaten on the spot!"

"I've got to agree with Nut," said Mud, fiddling anxiously with his stones. "Thorn, this is a bad plan. It may seem like a reasonable idea—it did to me at first—but those wolves are not the kind of animals who listen."

"Not like lizards," said Spider fondly, tapping his own lizard's head. It gave him an indignant look and nipped his finger. "Lizards listen. Wolves, no they don't."

"Wait. What about Big Talk?" asked Nut suddenly. "That lion's one of your best friends, Thorn. What's the point of having a lion friend if you can't ask him a favor? He could round up some more enormous lions and take the wolves out."

"That would be breaking the Code," Thorn told him. "And I'm Great Father. I'm not doing that."

As his friends stared at him, Thorn clenched his jaw to stop it trembling. Oh, he wished they weren't here to give such good advice. The fact was, he was terrified. But he could not think of a single other way to solve the problem.

"Someone's coming." Mud rose to his paws and turned toward the crackling sound of twigs on the path.

As Spider and Nut turned to follow Mud's gaze, Thorn's shoulders sagged with tiredness. *Oh, please, Great Spirit, don't let it be another zebra, or some warthog who's involved in a crazy feud. I've got enough real worries of my own right now.* . . .

Mud was loping toward the approaching creature, but he halted, staring, as a baboon stumbled from the trees: a filthy, bedraggled, limping creature.

"Tendril?" Mud blurted. "Tendril Crownleaf?"

Thorn gasped. The former Crownleaf was almost unrecognizable, but this was Tendril all right. Nut growled, and Spider tilted his head curiously, but Thorn could only gape in horror.

Tendril had once been a sleek and strong baboon, so

confident in her power she was unbearably arrogant. Now she was a lurching, sorry mess. She looked half starved, her rangy limbs reduced to nothing more than bone and stringy sinew, but that was nothing compared to her scars. Half her fur was gone, and the bare patches of skin were a raw and angry red, edged with blackened, stubbly hair. With shock, Thorn caught sight of something moving on her belly. Huge, frightened eyes peeped around Tendril's foreleg, and Thorn realized it was a baby.

He bounded forward, reaching out to help Tendril but drawing back his paw at the last moment; she looked as if the slightest touch would cause unbearable agony. Eyeing him sidelong, she flinched away and clutched at her baby with a defensive paw. It was a bug-eyed, scrawny little thing, with a splayed patch of black fur, like a dried baobab leaf, on the crown of its head.

"Not Tendril Crownleaf," she rasped almost inaudibly. "Tendril Deeproot."

Thorn stared at her. This once impossibly proud baboon had accepted Berry's punishing demotion, even when Berry wasn't here to enforce it.

"Your baby." Thorn ducked to stare at it. "Is it hurt? His head—"

"It's a birth pattern, not a wound," whispered Tendril. "He's unharmed, thank the Great Spirit. But I am not."

"What happened to you?" Mud set down his stones on the ground and wrung his paws together.

Tendril gave Thorn a pleading look, and he felt a lurch of

dread. Berry had wanted Tendril killed for her crimes against Dawntrees Troop, but as Great Father, Thorn had insisted Tendril be spared and exiled. Had Berry gone so far as to disobey him and try to carry out her threat?

"Did Dawntrees—" he began hoarsely.

Tendril shook her head, shutting her eyes at the pain the slight movement caused her. "No. I found my own, Crookedtree Troop. What was left of them." She coughed. "We found a place to live quietly. We abided by Berry Crownleaf's demands."

"So who hurt you?" Thorn asked, bewildered.

"Not who." She coughed again and spat dark saliva. "What. A plant grew in our home, a deadly, terrible thing. It grew so fast. In moments. Its flowers burned and bit and killed. It ate the other plants, it ate the trees, it ate my friends and troopmates. They died screaming, swallowed by the flowers."

Nut and Mud looked at each other in disbelief. Thorn stared at Tendril, his mind a turmoil of confusion. "What?"

But Spider stepped forward, opening his palms to display them. He nodded eagerly.

"Fire!" he exclaimed. "Beautiful fire!"

Thorn sucked in a breath. Spider's palms had that same raw, naked look as Tendril's exposed and wounded flesh. And now he remembered how Spider had made the fire-flower grow with his splinter of clear stone. It had been a small thing, flickering red and gold, but it had terrified Thorn. The idea that it could swell large enough to kill baboons and trees? It did not bear thinking about.

"I escaped," rasped Tendril in the silence. "I alone, with my baby. But I wandered too close to Dawntrees, and their sentries spotted me. I am afraid, Thorn Highleaf. I am afraid they will come after me again, and this time they will kill me. Look at me. Can I defend myself? Can I protect my baby?"

He shook his head No words would come.

"I came to you, Great Father Thorn, because I have nowhere else to go." Tendril dipped her head; Thorn knew what it must cost her to beg from her old enemy. "I know I have hurt you and threatened you in the past, but you are Great Father, and I throw myself and my infant on your mercy. I broke the Code, I know this. Perhaps I am being punished for that, but Seedling here does not deserve my punishment. He is innocent. I am a Deeproot now and forever, and I ask for your help and protection."

"Of course I will help you," Thorn blurted, horrified at the state of her. "Of course we will protect you!"

Nut glanced at him. "Dawntrees won't like that," he said. "They'll come for her, now that they know she's alive."

"True," said Thorn grimly. He doubted Berry would be vindictive enough to come after Tendril—at least, he hoped not—but Viper and Creeper undoubtedly would. "Dawntrees will still pose a threat, to Tendril and Seedling both. But I think I know the solution."

"Whatever you suggest, Great Father, we will obey." Tendril's head sagged.

Tentatively, Thorn touched her arm. "You should go and live on the mountain with the vultures," he said. "You'll be safe there. It's no habitat for a baboon, but you'll survive, and I believe the vultures there will protect you. And I suppose the strangeness of it will be your penance for breaking the Code."

"I will obey, Great Father." Tendril's humility was painful to watch. "Let me rest here for a short time, and then I give you my vow I will go to the mountain and never return."

"Of course you must rest first," said Mud, his eyes still wide with horror. Loping forward, he led Tendril gently to his own nest, the one on the lowest branch of the fig tree. Even climbing that far seemed to be agony for her—she grimaced with pain as she reached for a pawhold, and her breath came in short gasps—but she clutched her baby tightly with one paw to keep him secure.

Thorn could barely take his eyes off the wretched baboon as he withdrew to his own favorite tree. He was glad he had been able to help her, the poor wounded shadow of the proud baboon she had been. But news of the fire-flower was one more worry to add to the rest. What had caused it to bloom in Bravelands and bring such death and destruction?

Closing his eyes, he lay back against a stout branch and let his mind drift across Bravelands. He had done this more and more often in the last few days, searching desperately for answers, for understanding. It brought him neither, but the act itself was becoming easier every time.

He let his mind sink into that of a rhino, chewing lazily on withered acacia leaves. He felt the tingle of leaf against his upper lip. His body felt strong and stolid, his brain troubled only by simple thoughts. His three-toed hoof pawed the dry earth beneath him; he raised his horned head and noticed a herd of impalas. At once, with barely a thought, he made the leap; suddenly he was heavy no more, but so light and agile he felt he could fly. Something moved in the long grass, and he sprang away, fleeing on delicate hooves from the thundering paws of a lion pride. . . .

. . . And he was back in the rhino. It was as if he had made only a trembling, fragile connection that had snapped as he ran. His ability was not perfect, then, but he knew with quiet confidence that one day he would be able to leap from one mind to another with barely a conscious urge.

Somehow, too, he was more than the rhino: He was the hard, dry ground beneath its heavy feet, parched and longing for the rains. He was the grass that moved as the stalking lions did. He was the warm air that hung heavy on the savannah, crackling with sunlight, waiting motionless for the clouds that lay beyond the horizon. He was the relentless movement of the herds, wildebeest and zebra and buffalo, as they followed their migration trails like single-minded flocks of starlings.

Something jolted his drifting mind, something dark and malevolent. Instantly he knew the mind he had fallen into. It was the mind of a golden wolf.

Oh, the hunger and the glee, and the delight of terror! He and his pack were one—*I am we*—and they trotted together toward the silver glisten of a watering hole. Before him, before them, animals scattered, stampeding and panicking. *We are the goldwolves. We are fear. We are death.* Tipping back his head, he opened his slender jaws and howled in horrible joy.

Reeling back, Thorn felt the rough bark of the tree at his spine, and he was back in himself. He was breathing hard and fast, and the skin beneath his fur tingled with revulsion. He had to blink furiously to be sure he was fully back in his own forest, with his own friends busy at the clearing's edge and Tendril curled asleep in Mud's nest. He found himself breathing hard.

Those wolves. They took such delight in evil. Yet they were not the only thing that terrified Thorn, and his head still swam with the enormous scope of his vision.

He was one small baboon, and quick thinking was the only weapon he had ever possessed. How could he possibly protect and defend the sprawling, living vastness that was Bravelands?

CHAPTER FOURTEEN

In the bright light of morning, elephants milled and drifted and browsed in the shadow of the great white cliffs, their movements slow and unthreatened; all of them, it seemed to Sky, had formed into pairs. Here, in the Plain of Hearts, the elephants felt secure and happy, and very much part of a place where they belonged. In the air, bee-eaters darted, their colors flashing in the sun; high in the blue arc of the sky, a couple of vultures soared.

Sky stood alone, pulling idly at the lower branches of an acacia, watching the couples with a sad but peaceful heart. She would have liked to be part of it all, but really this place was nothing to do with her, not anymore. So long as she remembered that, she could be content; she could even be happy for the couples who renewed their affection for each other in the shelter of the valley.

The trouble was, her own gaze kept betraying her. Almost against her will, her eyes would drift to the far side of the valley, seeking someone she knew would not be coming. Each time she caught sight of a dark-hided elephant, her heart would give a small, unwelcome jolt.

There beside the trees, right now, half hidden by a small group of young elephants—could it be? Sky knew how improbable it was, but that young bull was the right size, and his tusks were creamy. Her jaws went still around a leafy branch, and something inside her lurched. But when the dark-skinned bull turned in her direction, his eyes were not green, and they didn't seem to look into the depths of her being. *He's not Rock. None of them are.*

Sky sighed, lowering her gaze firmly to the ground, as the strange bull ambled off, flirting with his new mate. If only her heart would stop yearning for her beloved Rock, she could concentrate on the work that mattered: looking after little Horizon and the two cheetah cubs who were entertaining the baby elephant with play-fights and harmless, funny ambushes. Horizon was flailing her tiny trunk at Nimble and Lively as they tumbled around her feet, and all three of them were giggling with delight.

She caught the scent of another bull close by, and this time it was one she recognized. But he wasn't a threat, and she was glad of some adult company. Sky turned to him.

"Hello, Flint."

"Sky." The old elephant butted her head with his own. "You

look thoughtful. This must be difficult for you."

She did not want to talk about it, not even with Flint. Brightly she asked, "Do you have a partner you'll meet here?"

"What?" His mouth twisted in amusement. "I'm too old, Sky. No female would see me as a good prospect for a mate, and besides, I haven't got the energy for flirting. I have plenty of descendants, and I'm proud of all of them. That's more than enough for me." He gave a rumbling laugh. "Age takes away many urges, Sky, but it does give one a bit of perspective. All that running around bellowing, charging other males, getting into fights? It seems silly to me now."

Sky watched him, curious. He seemed quite sincere and not at all regretful. "I suppose it all makes sense at the time. What do you call it—the Rage?"

"Yes, that's right." Flint laughed again. "A lot of nonsense, in retrospect. But as I said, it did provide me with many calves and grandcalves. There's a time for everything, Sky."

Sky wondered if, one day, Rock and Boulder would look back on the fight that had caused River's death and think it was all a lot of fuss over nothing. It seemed so strange and unjust. "You don't suffer the Rage at all, now?"

"I feel it sometimes—or an aftershock of it, like the echo of a wild trumpet from the rocks. But it's not a flaming inferno, Sky, burning everything before it. It's more like the dying embers of a grass fire."

"I've heard of this grass fire, but I've never seen it." She furrowed her brow.

"And I hope you never do, but it happens occasionally in the dry seasons. Then you'll understand what I'm saying. Roaring flame that devours everything before it, leaving nothing but a thing called ash that's all that remains of trees and bush and grass. Well, that's how the Rage is, Sky. A memory of it is still within me, ash and smoke that smolder away, but it will never ignite again."

She did not really understand his talk of the thing called fire. "What's the Rage like? Describe it for me, Flint, won't you? I so want to understand what Boulder goes through. . . ." She swallowed hard and added to herself: *What Rock went through.*

"It's a madness. Almost like a bloodlust. You don't know fire, but—imagine a storm coming. You feel a pressure in the air, an almost unbearable heat and density. You know that until the storm breaks, there will be no peace; terrible as the wild weather will be, it must be endured."

Sky could not imagine this noble, calm old elephant in the grip of such a tempest of fury. Hesitantly, she asked, "Have you ever heard of an elephant called Rock?"

"Rock?" Flint narrowed his eyes. "The name is familiar. . . . Did something happen to him?"

"Not so much to him," said Sky quietly. "He was driven out from his herd of brothers, because he killed a female when he was in the grip of the Rage."

Flint glanced at her in surprise, his ears flapping forward. "That sounds unlikely. Bulls in the Rage attack other males, not their prospective mates."

"But I know it happened," protested Sky. "My brother told me so."

"Boulder?" Flint looked thoughtful. "But how can even he be sure? No elephant remembers clearly what happens in the Rage. Everything is . . . blurred."

Sky stiffened with surprise. Flint's words felt as if they were tearing her in two directions. It was reassuring to think that things might not have been exactly as Boulder described, but . . . Sky was only just coming to terms with Rock's actions, at least as her brother had described them. Could Boulder really have been mistaken? "If there was a way to know for sure . . ."

"But there isn't." Flint shook his ears. "We can only imagine, or guess. The Rage is a mystery, Sky."

As she watched him plod away, Sky's heart was in turmoil. She tensed her muscles and raised her head. She might never know what had happened on that dreadful day, but she knew one thing for sure: she couldn't leave things like this. And besides, perhaps there was a way to know for sure. . . .

An older female was chatting amiably to a matriarch from the desert lands in the north; Sky had talked to both of them earlier, and now she turned and trotted over. "Crag. Sandstorm. May I ask you something?"

They turned to her together, craning their ears forward. "Sky Strider!" said the matriarch. "Of course you can."

"Whether we can help you is another matter." Crag chuckled.

Sky took a deep breath. "River of the Marcher herd was

killed in a ravine near here," she said.

"Ah, a sad day." Sandstorm's expression darkened, and she shook her head.

"Can you tell me where the ravine is?"

"You don't want to go there," warned Crag. "It's a treacherous place."

"But I must," persisted Sky. "There's something I'm curious about. I promise to be careful."

"You'd better," said Crag. "I don't want to have to explain to Comet that you're not coming back." The two exchanged a hesitant glance, and Sandstorm nodded.

"All right, young one. Past that baobab, then make a direct line toward that cleft in the mountaintop. You'll come across the ravine very suddenly, after a hundred paces or so. Be cautious."

"Yes," added Crag. "You'll come across it much sooner than you think. Stay alert."

Dipping her head in thanks, Sky turned and trudged toward the baobab tree. Two small shadows darted at her feet, and she paused and glanced down.

"Can we come?" called Nimble, batting at a dry tussock of grass. "We're bored."

Sky laughed softly. "All right. But it's a dangerous place, cubs. You have to stay with me. No running ahead!"

The cleft in the mountain ridge was easy to make out, and Sky kept her eyes on it at first. But the more distance she put between herself and the other elephants, the more conscious she became of Crag and Sandstorm's warnings. There were fissures in the dry ground, some of them deep; she took large strides over them as the cheetah cubs crouched and jumped. But none were deep or wide enough to trouble a grown elephant.

Crag and Sandstorm had been right: the ravine appeared very suddenly, just beyond a long, low ridge. She saw the shadow of it in time, and she halted, her heart giving a little jolt. The cubs crept forward with her as she edged closer, peering over.

A shudder went through her bones, and her head swam. It was a precipitous drop, and a long one. No elephant could climb down there, and no elephant could survive a fall to those faraway, broken rocks at the bottom. She could make out the path of a streambed, with ripples etched in sand as a memory of water, but right now it was as dry as a seed husk.

"Nimble," she said quietly, "Lively. Could you do something for me? It's dangerous."

"Good!" announced Lively. "We told you we were bored!"

"But you have to be careful," insisted Sky.

"We promise," said Nimble, all solemnity.

Sky drew a breath. "Can you scramble down to the foot of the cliff?" she asked. "And can you look for elephant bones there? If you find any, bring one up for me. Can you do that without hurting yourselves?"

"Of course we can." Lively strutted toward the edge, tail high, and her brother bounded after her. In less than a moment they had vanished over the edge, and Sky's gut clenched. But she could still hear them mewling and chirping in excitement.

"Don't shove, Nimble!"

"Well, leave me space! Oh, watch that rock, it's loose."

Their voices grew quieter until at last they faded altogether, but there was no squeal of terror, no sound of crashing rocks. Waiting as patiently as she could, Sky let herself breathe more easily.

The day was very still, the air peaceful, so Sky's ears twitched at the sound of a distant commotion behind her. Frustrated, she looked away from the ravine and back toward the elephants on the plain.

Beyond the herds, beyond the cliffs that flanked the Plain of Hearts, an ocher dust cloud was rising from the savannah. Sky's brow furrowed. With a last anxious glance after the cheetah cubs, she turned and took a few paces back toward the herds, peering hard at the cloud. Something was on the move, but she could not make out what.

The movement became suddenly recognizable: a black mass of buffalo, stampeding toward the Plain of Hearts. They were a shapeless, narrow line at that moment, obscured by dust and distance, but they were coming fast. Horns tossing, eyes rolling, they bellowed as they pounded closer; even from far away, they sounded panicked. The thunder of their huge hooves made the earth vibrate beneath Sky's feet.

For long moments she hesitated, torn. She looked toward the ravine. When she turned back to stare at the buffalo herd, they seemed suddenly much closer. Her heart thumped faster. Soon they would reach the edge of the plain.

The cubs would be fine, Sky decided. The herds' need was

more urgent. She trotted back hastily to the elephants, finding Flint on the edge of them. He stood staring at the oncoming buffalo, his massive ears spread wide in warning and alarm. Behind him, elephants blew and flapped their ears and stirred the dust in agitation with trunks and feet.

"What spooked those buffalo?" he wondered aloud as Sky trotted to his side.

"I don't know, but they're not stopping," said Sky.

"Higher ground!" bellowed a matriarch between them and the buffalo. "Everyone, get to higher ground!"

Her words galvanized the elephants. They turned and began to shamble away from the stampeding buffalo; mate found mate and leaders found herds, shepherding one another out of danger. Peering around for her own family, Sky at last caught sight of Comet, hurrying toward the mountain's lower slopes with Rain and the others. But Breeze had hesitated, raising her tusks and frantically scanning the chaos.

Breeze is looking for her baby. And at that moment, Sky caught sight of little Horizon, cantering wildly first one way, then the other. The baby stopped, then trotted in a circle, squealing in panic. *Horizon must be unable to see her mother in all the dust and turmoil.*

Sky raised her trunk. "Breeze!" she blared. "Horizon's here!"

Breeze spun toward her. "Horizon! Daughter, wait, I'm here!"

Horizon halted, confused. She stared at Sky, then twisted to look for her mother. Both Sky and Breeze cantered toward her; suddenly, Horizon seemed to make a decision and lurched into a canter towards her mother—

But in that instant, the buffalo herd was on them. An onrush of powerful black bodies, a maelstrom of thundering legs and heavy swinging horns; the noise was like a sudden breaking storm. Sky flinched back, shocked, as the buffalo herd surged across her vision, right where the baby elephant had been standing.

"Horizon!" she shouted.

Sky swung left and right, raising her tusks and trunk, staring desperately into the commotion. She reared onto her hind legs, trying to balance as she peered over the thundering mass. There was something there, she was sure, besides the buffalo: streaks of quick gold, agile and sly.

"The golden wolves!" she cried in horror. They weren't attacking the buffalo; of course they weren't. The stampede was a distraction. Sky's heart lurched. If the buffalo weren't the target, then the wolves must be after—

"Horizon!" Setting her jaw, Sky flung herself into the waves of buffalo. Some veered around her, squealing and bellowing; others crashed against her with grunts of surprise. She felt a shoulder strike her leg, then another. One buffalo skidded to a halt, then tumbled heels over horns before scrambling back to its feet and galloping away.

There was no sign of Horizon. Desperately, Sky forced her way through the chaos, closing her eyes against the dust.

She halted, still buffeted by running bodies. She reeled as another buffalo struck her, but kept her balance. This spot

was where she had last seen the calf, she was sure. But among
the stampeding black mass, there was no sign of Horizon, not
even a trace of footprint. Scents and tracks were all obliterated by the trampling horde. Spinning, twisting, Sky bellowed
Horizon's name, but her cries were lost in the din.

Horrible flashes of memory assailed her: little Moon, sav-
aged by lions, helpless and terrified. Cold horror gripped her
gut: she hadn't been able to reach Moon. She had to reach
Horizon!

It can't happen again. It can't. Horizon can't die!

But there was nothing she could do. This tide of buffalo
would never end, the herd would keep running till even Sky
was crushed beneath their combined weight—

No. There were gaps now, as the main herd charged on
toward the hills, and smaller groups of buffalo thundered
after them. Sky took a breath, hopeful, as a space opened up
around her; then she flinched aside as a dozen more stragglers
charged past her. After a moment, another single buffalo pursued its comrades, bellowing.

The herd was thinning. Gasping, blinking, Sky watched as
a last few individuals galloped in the wake of the herd. The
dust cloud was lifting, and she scanned the emptying plain,
daring to hope. The wolves could not have picked Horizon
out in that chaos; however skillfully they hunted, they could
not have driven and harried her through the storm of bodies.
Horizon must be here somewhere, she must be. . . .

"Horizon! Horizon!" Breeze's terrified, desperate trumpet
resounded across the sudden quietness.

Trotting back and forth, Sky stared at the churned and dusty plain till her eyes watered. Anguish rose in her throat as she finally realized the horrible truth: Horizon was nowhere to be seen. With a half-stifled cry of despair, she turned at last and ran toward the baby's mother. "Breeze!"

The mother was wild-eyed with panic. "Sky, they took my baby! They took Horizon! The wolves, I saw them!"

"No. No." Sky was trying to convince herself as much as Breeze, but she clung to one faint hope: "There's no blood. This was where I last saw Horizon, and there's no blood on the earth. They haven't killed her."

"Not yet, perhaps. But they've taken her!"

Coming up against the cliffs and foothills, the vast herd of buffalo were veering, cantering out of the valley once more. Even their headlong gallop was slowing as they realized they were no longer being pursued. Sky watched them trot out into the dusty savannah again. Around Breeze, the other elephants were returning, gathering, stroking her with consoling trunks. The bulls trotted to join the females, their broad ears still flapping wide in agitation.

Sky turned to Flint. "The wolves have taken Breeze's baby!"

"What?" he rumbled in horror.

"My calf?" Branch thundered forward, reaching out his trunk to comfort Breeze. "They've taken my baby! Horizon!"

Flint's old eyes sparked with determination. "We'll find her, Branch. We'll get her back!"

"We'll search the whole of Bravelands if we have to," agreed Boulder, his ears flaring wide with anger.

"I'll come, Boulder," declared Forest, with a glance at Sky. "I want to help."

"So do we." Half a dozen more young bulls trotted up.

"Thank you," Branch told them all. His gaze was agonized as he scanned the savannah. "Let's go now!"

"Cover all the gullies, all the riverbeds near the cliffs," commanded Flint. He suddenly looked vigorous again, like the young and powerful herd-leader he had once been. "The wolves must be near the foothills—they can't have left the plain. They wouldn't take Horizon that far without—" He shook his head, as if he didn't want to follow his own thought process. "We'll find her. We'll find Breeze and Branch's calf."

Each elephant set off, keen and anxious, to search the crannies of the cliffs that edged the eastern plain. The dust was gradually clearing, but it still hung thickly in the air, obscuring the hillsides. *I wish Thorn were here*, thought Sky desperately. *He could find those wolves in moments.*

But so could she. Gritting her teeth in determination, she raised her trunk, then swung her head toward the ravine. She paused. *The cubs. They might be able to cover ground faster than any elephant*, Sky thought.

No other searcher seemed to be heading for the ravine; its shadow slashed the landscape in the direction of the desert, and the other elephants were focused on the foothills. Making her decision, Sky set off toward the ravine.

The air was clearing by the moment; the buffalo were long gone, leaving only confusion behind them. Sky sneezed out dust and scented the air again. Looking to her left, she peered harder into the murky distance. Could the wolves have left this part of the plain after all? Flint hadn't thought so; why would they bother?

Yet Sky was sure she saw something moving, out toward the open desert where the grassland had been parched to yellow barrenness. That movement wasn't the buffalo, Sky knew. These running figures were far smaller, and there were fewer of them. Breaking into a run, Sky thundered after them, leaving the baboon mountain's flanks behind her.

She was panting harshly by the time she had left the Plain of Hearts behind, but at last she could make them out: sleek golden shapes, viciously prodding a larger creature between them. Horizon!

The wolves nipped at the calf's heels and bit at her hindquarters, driving her on though she squealed in terror. One of the wolves glanced over his shoulder, and his muzzle peeled back from his fangs as he caught sight of Sky.

He yelped something, and the rest of his pack picked up speed, but Horizon was at the limit of her endurance. Clearly the baby could not go faster, whether the wolves threatened to kill her or not. As Sky charged on, furious and petrified, a wolf leaped into the air and snapped at the baby's trunk, forcing her to a stumbling halt. The calf collapsed to her knees.

All the golden wolves turned on Sky, snarling as she thundered closer. She thudded to a stop in front of them and glared down, flaring out her ears and brandishing her tusks.

"Get away from her!" Sky trumpeted. "Leave her alone!"

Lowering her tusks, she lunged. The wolves scattered at the

attack, dodging Sky easily, yelping and howling in mockery. Skidding to a halt, Sky swung her tusks at a female wolf, who skipped nimbly away with a taunting bark.

"We take the tender little elephant heart. Pity it's so small!"

"Bigger than an impala heart!" yipped another.

"True true!"

"You leave her alone!" The baby's hindquarters were bitten and bleeding, Sky noticed with fury, and she was shaking with terror. Sky trotted to stand over her, protecting the baby with her body and glaring a deadly threat at the wolves.

They were circling now, wary but eager. Sky snorted in threat, twisting her head as she tried to keep her eyes on all of them at once.

They were small, but there were so many of them, and their eyes flickered with a murderous light. A shudder of unease rippled through Sky's gut.

"Ha, we don't want the little elephant," yelped the female leader. "Too little, not plump!"

"Scrawny!" agreed her lieutenant.

"Your heart, though . . ." The leader licked her jaws, and drool spattered on the dry earth.

Sky's breath rasped in her throat, and her heart pounded so painfully she thought it might break through her ribs. The dust burned her eyes, and she blinked hard. It must be some trick of the eerie light, combined with her exhaustion, but she imagined for a moment she saw not wolves but lions. Shadowy lions, prowling alongside the shapes of wolves.

Sky squeezed her eyes shut as long as she dared, then glared at the pack once more. The ghostly lions were gone; there were only the savage faces of hungry golden wolves.

"Come and try, if you think you can take my heart," she growled.

She'd been paying too much attention to the wolves in front of her. With a shock of realization, she felt claws rake at her haunches, and she twisted around to lash out at the wolves who had crept up behind. One of them leaped impossibly high, landing on her back, and she felt claws dig deep into her spine.

Panicking, Sky gave a violent shudder. One wolf was dislodged, falling with a yelp, only to be replaced by another two. Terror surged through Sky. As she struck out with her tusks, yet another wolf sprang and clung to her trunk, biting so hard she felt dizzy with pain.

Clouds and dazzling sunlight spun around her. Losing her balance, Sky stumbled to her knees. This wasn't possible—it couldn't be possible. These wolves were so small, so skinny. They couldn't take her down, a grown young elephant!

Except that they didn't seem like wolves at all. Memories sparked and flashed through Sky's panic. They were attacking like lions, she realized. Was that what her vision had warned her of? That these wolves had the strength and brutality of lions? *No, that can't happen—*

With one massive shake of her shoulders, she flung off the wolves that clung to her and managed to twist her head around to find Horizon. The calf was staggering to her feet, and their eyes locked for a moment.

A huge wolf was prowling toward Sky, his eyes dazzling gold in the dusty light, his teeth glinting. Sky gritted her jaws, then swung back to the calf.

"Run!" she blared at Horizon. "Run!"

The last thing she saw, before the wolf sprang at her face and its claws raked deep, was the tiny calf bolting for the open desert. Horizon was getting away. Even as her vision blurred with streaming blood, Sky felt a rush of relief.

Thank you, Great Spirit. Thank you. And now, you can take me.

CHAPTER FIFTEEN

Fearless's paws ached. He didn't like to think how it was for Ruthless and Menace, so much younger and smaller; their little pride had wandered for what seemed like forever, but now that they had left the Dead Forest far behind them, the ground underfoot was dry and hot enough to burn sensitive paw pads. There was barely even a blade of grass to break the sandy waste.

Fearless paused, picking up each paw in turn for relief, and sniffed at a barren patch of rock. Stunted, fleshy plants clung to it. He gnawed at one, but it did not taste good. Its moistness was bitter. He shook his mane and spat.

"No scent of Titan," he growled, with a glance at Keen.

But Keen was not paying attention. He stood and stared listlessly ahead, his tail twitching.

"Keen!" Fearless tried again. "Can you catch a whiff of Titan anywhere?"

Keen swung his head, blinking. "There's no point, Fearless. We could search forever and never find a hair of him. Look at these cubs." He nodded at Ruthless and Menace, who stood hunched and panting. "They're exhausted. They can't keep going for much longer. We can't expect them to."

"But we must be close to him now!" objected Fearless. "He cannot be far away!"

With a glance at Menace, Keen lowered his voice. "Even if we find Titan, we're in no state to fight him."

Eyeing the cubs, with their sagging heads and drooping eyes, Fearless knew with grim certainty that his friend had a point. "Just a little farther?" he pleaded. "Let's make more ground."

Keen heaved a sigh of resignation. "Fine."

The four lions plodded on across hard, hot earth. Fearless tried to ignore the beating of the glaring sun on his back. This terrain was a setback, but what kind of lion would he be if he let this little discomfort dissuade him?

A sensible lion, said a small voice inside him, *because it's more than a little discomfort for those cubs.*

Fearless tossed his neck briskly and ignored the voice.

Something scuttled between rocks, and for an instant Fearless felt a surge of renewed vigor. He pounced, stuck one paw between the rocks, and felt one claw dig into something soft and yielding.

He yanked out his paw. Brandishing a writhing lizard at Ruthless and Menace, he gave a growl of triumph. "There. Something to eat. We'll stop here for a rest."

Menace still had the energy to wrinkle her muzzle in a sneer as she flopped down. "Big deal," she rasped.

It didn't stop her snatching the lizard, with a sidelong snarl of warning at Ruthless.

"I eat first, Useless." Menace lashed out a small paw, catching his nose, and Ruthless flinched back.

"Hey!" growled Fearless angrily. He grabbed the now-dead lizard back. "For that, you can go hungry. You're not the precious heir of Titan around here." He tossed the lizard to Ruthless, who fell on it gratefully.

Turning away from Menace's glower of hungry rage, Fearless stalked over to lie beside Keen. "She's more of a problem with every passing day," he rumbled.

Keen nodded, resting his head on his forepaws. "I don't know how much more of her I can take. When we're back on the plains, and she has a chance of surviving alone, I say we cut the brat loose. She's nothing but trouble. And she's making Ruthless miserable."

Fearless licked Keen's ear. "I . . . don't agree," he said softly. "I still think Menace could be useful. We should keep her with us." For a moment he hesitated, wondering if he should say it. Then he growled, "It's what Stinger would have done."

"Stinger?" Keen's head jerked up in disbelief.

"Sure. Stinger was evil, I know that. But he was smart, too. He knew how to turn situations to his advantage."

"The last creature you should be trying to emulate," snarled Keen, his eyes dark, "is Stinger Crownleaf."

"I'm not. Keen, I promise." Fearless gazed at his friend. "But defeating Titan is going to be hard enough. Stinger would know how to do it, and I just . . . I just think, if I can imagine what he might do, it could help. . . ."

Keen got to his paws, glaring at him. "You know something, Fearless? You care more about what Stinger would think than about what I think. And I'm the one who's living and breathing, right here with you!"

"No!" Fearless protested, sitting up. "I do care about your opinion, Keen, truly I do! But I . . . I swore an oath. Don't you understand? I swore an oath to kill Titan, and I don't have any choice but to see it through. I need all the help I can get."

"Even imaginary help from a dead baboon?" Keen curled his muzzle.

"Stinger isn't even here!" exploded Fearless, rising to his paws to face his friend. "I'm not asking him for help, I can't! All I'm doing is trying to imagine what he might do. That's not so bad, Keen! If it helps me kill Titan, what's the harm?"

"That you'd be emulating a Codebreaker?" Keen gave a snort. "You know what you forget too easily, Fearless? You're not the only one Titan wronged. Don't you even remember how we met? You were with Titanpride when that brute came to murder my father too!"

"I know that—"

"Do you? Do you? Because I often think it slips your mind." Keen's eyes blazed with fury. "I hated Titan for killing Dauntless. But what good did that do? So I've let it go. Because I knew if I didn't, I'd spend the rest of my life obsessing about revenge! I'd care so much about the past, I would never look to the future!" He glared at Fearless, his breath coming hard and fast. "And that's you now, Fearless. You think of nothing but the past. Right at this moment, Titan means more to you than I do."

Fearless stepped back, stunned. "That isn't true," he growled.

"Yes, it is. You should admit it to yourself. It might be the start of you finding your purpose again."

"I have a purpose!" roared Fearless, feeling hot rage burn his throat. "I'm going to find Titan, and I'm going to fulfill my oath. As any decent lion should! I'm going to kill Titan—and that's when I'll be able to look to the future. What future is worthwhile if I break an oath?"

Keen stared at him for a long, silent time. For once, Fearless couldn't read his friend's eyes—or perhaps, he admitted to himself, he was afraid to.

In the tense and motionless standoff, a scent drifted to Fearless's nostrils, and he sniffed reflexively. Buffalo.

It wasn't just hunger that sparked inside him; it was relief. It might be the most ordinary of interruptions, but at least he and Keen would not have to glare in contempt at each other anymore.

"Can you smell that? We should hunt."

"Two of us," scoffed Keen, "and two cubs. Going after buffalo?"

"We can try," growled Fearless. "You don't have to be so negative." *About everything*, he wanted to add, but didn't. "Come on!"

Despite Keen's misgivings, Fearless noticed his friend had found new reserves of energy as they loped in the direction of the thick grassy scent. *He'd enjoy some buffalo meat as much as I would.* The barren plain was obscured by a layer of dust cloud, but that was good news. *It must be a big herd*, Fearless thought. Perhaps they had calves running with them, newborn calves that might lag behind the adult buffalo, the ones who could break every bone in a lion's body. . . .

A despairing blare of pain rang through the air, and Fearless gasped and halted. He raised his head, snuffling at the faint breeze. The scent tickled his nostrils, familiar. But it couldn't be . . . could it . . . ?

"It's . . ." He sniffed again, frowning. "It's Sky!"

"Sky Strider?" Keen halted beside him, his ears twitching in frustration. He gave a yearning glance toward the buffalo-scent trail.

"Yes!" Fearless shook his head as the trumpet of distress resounded again. "Keep Ruthless and Menace here, Keen. I need to go to her!"

"You need to wha—" But Keen's exasperated exclamation faded behind him as Fearless sprang into a run.

Sky was not far away. Fearless could hear her frantic cries more clearly, and as he sprinted closer through the ocher haze, he could make out a bloody tussle on the ground. He narrowed his eyes against the dust. The young elephant lay on her flank on the ground, still trying to raise her head and lash at her tormentors. Fearless sucked in an angry breath.

The wolves. The golden wolves!

A dozen or more of the creatures were crawling across Sky's prone body, biting and tearing, clinging on with sharp claws, scrabbling with their hind legs. One big wolf had its jaws clamped around Sky's bulky throat, as if it was a far bigger predator trying to suffocate a much younger elephant.

Who do these vicious brutes think they are? thought Fearless in disbelief. *Lions?*

He did not even take a moment to pause. As soon as he was in range, he sprang, cannoning into the big wolf and tumbling it off Sky. Fearless clamped his jaws around its skinny neck and tore, breaking its neck and savaging its throat at the same time. He flung the wolf's limp corpse from his bloodied jaws and spun to face the others.

They cringed in wild-eyed surprise. With a snarl, Fearless rose up and slashed with his paws, feeling his claws catch deep in flesh. With yelps and high howls, the wolves turned tail and fled, their wounded comrades dragging themselves at the rear.

Fearless did not deign to give chase; their leader Ravage, he had noticed, was not even among them. He gave one contemptuous, full-throated roar of warning at their fleeing rumps, then turned back to Sky.

"Sky," he murmured fearfully. "Sky Strider!"

The young elephant was trembling violently, but she

struggled to get upright, jamming her forefeet into the ground. For a moment she paused, panting, and Fearless peered anxiously at her many wounds. She was scored and gashed across her hindquarters and neck and back. A great slash in her shoulder leaked dark blood onto the dry earth. Her injuries looked painful, but not, Fearless realized with relief, life-threatening.

"Sky, what happened?"

At last she stumbled to all four feet and stood there, swaying and shuddering. "They'd have killed me," she rasped, dazed. "It would have taken a long time, Fearless, but they'd have finished me. Thank you."

"Don't thank me," he growled. "They may believe they're lions, but they're vermin. It was nothing."

"It was everything." Closing her eyes, she stroked his mane with her trunk-tip. Then her eyes started open. "Horizon! Is she safe?"

Fearless furrowed his brow and glanced around. "Horizon?" Then the dust drifted away a little more, and he saw a shape a little distance away. Small ears flapped in distress, and a tiny, spindly trunk waved desperately in the air. "Is that her? If so, she's fine. Terrified, but fine."

Sky turned to see. She staggered to her feet, then limped awkwardly to the baby elephant, Fearless padding at her side.

"The wolves spoke the truth, then," she murmured as she reached for the baby with her trunk. "They didn't want her. They wanted me."

"Forget those savages," snarled Fearless.

Horizon was staring at him with wide, white-rimmed eyes, and her little ears trembled. She edged closer to Sky and huddled against her legs.

"This is Fearless, little one," whispered Sky. "Don't be afraid. He's my friend."

"I am." Fearless tried to look as amiable and unthreatening as he could, but the baby only widened her eyes even more and pressed tighter against Sky. "I'll get you both back to your herd. Where are they, Sky?"

Sky nodded exhaustedly toward an outcrop of rocky cliff. "The Plain of Hearts, across the desert that way. Look, they're coming now. We were all searching for Horizon. I guess I was the lucky one who found her. . . ." She gave a shaky, breathless laugh.

Elephants were trotting in an urgent, dust-raising mass toward them—males and females together, Fearless registered with mild surprise. Their leader was a big gray male; Fearless thought he looked familiar. As the herd crowded around Sky and Horizon, and a female with wide, scared eyes pushed through, Sky pushed the baby gently toward her.

"Horizon!" exclaimed the mother, hugging the little elephant against her with her trunk. "My calf! You're safe. Thank you, Sky."

"Thank Fearless," said Sky in a weak voice. "He saved both of us."

The big male leader was caressing Sky with his trunk, touching her wounds with tremendous gentleness. "Sky, my sister," he rumbled. "You're hurt. Badly hurt."

"I'm fine, Boulder," she told him. "The wounds look bad, but they're shallow."

Boulder raised his head, stretching out his ears in warning as he gazed beyond Fearless. His eyes blazed. "Who's this now?"

Fearless looked around. Keen looked surprisingly small as he paced toward the elephants, the cubs beside him tiny, and it occurred to Fearless for the first time that he himself was standing in the middle of a crowd of dangerous animals who were a lot bigger than he was—big enough to squash him beneath their hooves. He felt suddenly as if his skin was shrinking against his bones, but he shook off his nerves and straightened, trying to look both dignified and fierce.

"That's Keen," he growled in the deepest voice he could manage. "Don't worry, he's a friend."

He'd known Keen thought he was being ridiculous, dashing off to save an elephant. He'd known Keen was angry with him about his obsession with Titan. Still, there was something else in his friend's dark and somber expression, in his deliberate, slow stride. Keen halted in front of the elephants, and Fearless studied him curiously. Ruthless and Menace waited farther back—even Titan's she-cub couldn't hide the tremble in her fur at the sight of the elephants.

"Fearless, there's something bad back there," he said quietly. He glanced up. "You elephants should know what we found. But I'm going to make it clear: what's happened to one of your friends had nothing to do with us."

There was a rumble of angry curiosity through the elephant

herd. Boulder snorted in bewilderment and raked the ground with one foot.

Fearless pricked his ears forward, frowning. "What is it, Keen?"

"An elephant, like I said." Keen jerked his head to gesture behind him. "A dead one."

CHAPTER SIXTEEN

"Definitely wolves," said Nut. "Definitely."

The four baboons stood staring down at the leaf-littered ground of the Great Father Clearing. In the remaining patches of sandy earth, where the soil had been scraped bare by the elephants' work and hadn't yet grown over, there were distinct slim paw marks.

Spider crouched, his forepaws splayed over the tracks, and bent his muzzle to inhale deeply. "Yep," he said. "Wolves for sure."

Thorn stared at the spoor with a sinking feeling in his gut. The paw marks were fresh—the wolves had come right into his home while they all slept. Yet no baboon had heard a thing; they could all have been killed before they even woke.

"At least Tendril had already left," Thorn murmured. "A

baby like Seedling might have been too easy a target for them to resist."

"Look over here," called Mud. He was pointing at a big old mahogany on the western edge of the clearing. "They've been here too. See the claw marks?"

"They weren't exactly trying to hide their visit, were they?" remarked Nut. He loped over to join Mud and peered at the scratches. "No, this isn't right. These aren't made by wolves, Mud. Whoever this was, they climbed the tree."

Spider shambled over, his lizard peeking nervously over his shoulder. He pressed his face to the bark. "Nope. Wolves all right. Spider knows the smell."

"But that's crazy." Nut's eyes widened. "It's not possible. Wolves can't climb trees."

"These ones can." Thorn stood behind the three of them, staring at the tree trunk. "I told you about Sky's vision, remember? Of the little hippo's death? That baby saw the wolves approaching like crocodiles, under the surface." He swallowed hard. "If they can swim like crocs, they can climb like leopards."

"That . . ." Nut touched the claw marks with a shaking paw. "That doesn't bear thinking about, Thorn. It would mean . . ."

"It means they're taking on the abilities of the animals they kill," said Thorn. "Sky said so. Along with their hearts, they take their spirits and their power."

The four baboons stared at one another in silence. They might have stayed immobile for far longer, lost in horror and disbelief, but the clop of hoofbeats disturbed them, echoing through the forest.

Thorn turned to see half a dozen zebras trot into the clearing, their eyes white-rimmed, their hides sweaty. With a lurch of anxiety, he realized they looked familiar. He bounded to meet them.

"Bristlemane! Has something happened? Why aren't you on your migration?"

The foremost zebra stumbled to a halt, looking exhausted, and nodded respectfully. "Great Father. We thought you should know."

"What?" asked Mud, bounding to Thorn's side. He shot his friend an apprehensive look.

"The migration . . . It went badly." Bristlemane's head drooped. "An ambush . . . They killed Silverstripe and took his . . . his heart. His spirit. We panicked."

"Who wouldn't?" muttered Nut angrily.

Thorn's throat constricted. "They killed your leader?"

"The wolves drove our whole herd into a swamp. Many of our number drowned there."

Spider scratched his ear. "Ah. An old hyena tactic, if Spider isn't mistaken."

Thorn's throat felt dry and tight. He gazed at Bristlemane. "I'm—I'm sorry. I should never have told you it was safe to migrate."

"It isn't your fault, Great Father!" Another zebra took an urgent pace forward to stand at Bristlemane's side.

"Of course we don't blame you!" added Bristlemane. "Who could have foreseen those horrors? They don't belong in Bravelands—they're an . . . an abomination!"

"We only thought," said a third zebra humbly, "that it was our duty to inform you, Great Father. We had to report such a terrible breach of the Code."

Thorn stared at them in silence, shaking his head. With the Great Spirit guiding him, how could he have got this so disastrously wrong? "No, my friends," he said quietly. "I do blame myself. And I'm sorry for what happened. I swear to you—I will do everything in my power to stop these golden wolves."

The zebras exchanged glances. Bristlemane nodded sadly.

"We know you will, Great Father. We have faith in you."

They turned, dejected and weary, and plodded away. As he watched them go, Thorn felt his heart clench.

I'm lying to them. What am I doing about the wolves? Nothing!

"Thorn." He felt Mud's gentle paw on his shoulder. "Thorn, I know you're upset, but . . . there are more creatures here. More petitioners."

"Already?" whispered Thorn. He looked up to see a small mob of meerkats scuttle into the clearing. They rose onto their hind feet expectantly, tails stiff and high.

Well, this was his job now. It was his calling. He needed to fulfill it. "Greetings," he told them, trying to look energetic and authoritative. "What can I do for you, friends?"

"Great Father," piped their leader, "Great Father, we came to tell you—"

"Tell you what we saw," another interrupted.

"Something bad," squeaked a third, pushing forward.

"Something awful." A fourth meerkat pranced forward for his share of the attention.

The leader glared at his mob, then turned back to Thorn, dusting leaf fragments from his chest fur.

"A baboon," he announced. "We saw a baboon being attacked by another baboon. The first baboon was a mother baboon, and she had a baby! But the bad baboon killed her!"

Thorn rose up on his hind paws. "What?" he whispered. He felt sick.

The meerkat took a deep patient breath and started again. "A baboon. We saw a baboon being attacked by another baboon. The first baboon was a mothe—"

"It's all right, I heard," interrupted Thorn, holding up his paws. "No, you don't need to explain anymore." A fearful rage rose in his throat. "Show me."

"Poor Tendril," Thorn whispered.

The four baboons stood staring down at the former Crownleaf's lifeless body, scrawny and scarred with those old raw burns. Tendril's eyes were wide and blank; there was no sign of a fresh wound. But for those dead staring eyes, and the dried blood that lay in a dark pool beneath her head, she might have been asleep. Around them, the meerkats stood, finally hushed.

Crouching, Thorn turned the corpse gently over. The back of Tendril's skull was a mess, splintered and bloody. He let out his breath in a shaky sigh.

"There's no sign of her baby," said Nut darkly. "Whatever killed her must have taken him too. Or some other flesh-eater."

"Or he simply ran away." Thorn shivered with pity. "He won't survive the forest without his mother."

"Poor little Seedling-sprout," murmured Spider. "Running is never good, Spider knows. He'll fall out of a tree. Or get eaten."

Thorn didn't want to imagine all the things that might happen to Seedling. "That wound." His voice was harsh in his throat as he pointed at Tendril's head. "Only a baboon kills that way."

"Indeed," said Mud grimly. He picked up a jagged chunk of stone that lay near the body and held it out to show them. It was clotted with blood and fur.

Thorn could not take his eyes off the weapon. He half expected Stinger to step out triumphantly from behind a tree, his jaws stretched wide in a mocking grin. A rock to the skull was how Stinger had killed Bark Crownleaf; it was how he had tried to kill Thorn himself. And who were the natural heirs of Stinger's malevolence?

"The Crown Guard," Thorn whispered. "This has to be their doing."

Mud nodded grimly. "Berry Crownleaf accepted your rul-ing about Tendril," he said, "but Creeper and Viper and the rest never did."

Rage filled Thorn, threatening to choke him. "I will deal with this." He spun around to face the meerkats. "Thank you for letting me know about this terrible breach of our Code. I promise you, I'll find the perpetrators, and I'll give Tendril and Seedling justice somehow. Mud, Nut, Spider? Stay with the body. I will handle this alone."

He had turned and bounded away before the meerkats could even reply. He did not even glance back to ensure that the other three baboons were obeying him; he simply raced on, heart seething for justice. To disobey the Great Father was one thing; but to murder a nursing mother—a mother who was already injured and weak? It was too much to bear. Thorn had to clench his jaws to stop himself howling in fury as he ran toward Tall Trees.

As he burst into the Crown Stone Clearing, a troop meeting was in session, but he didn't care. He shoved through the crowd of indignant baboons.

"Hey!" cried Petal Goodleaf. "No need to push!"

"Thorn?" said Lily, as other baboons turned to stare.

"What are you doing here?" demanded Splinter.

"We're having a meeting!" exclaimed old Twig. "This is most irregular!"

Ignoring their protests and complaints, Thorn bounded to the foot of the Crown Stone itself. The disciplined ranks of the Crown Guard stood there between him and Berry Crownleaf, glaring at him with contempt. Thorn halted, rose up, and returned their stares without blinking.

Berry too rose to her hind paws and glared down at him from the Crown Stone.

"What is this?" she asked coldly. "My troop and I were

discussing the resumption of the Three Feats—the Feats that you interrupted, Great Father Thorn. What is the meaning of this new interference?"

"This interference," gritted Thorn through clenched fangs, "is on behalf of Tendril Deeproot, a murdered mother, and her helpless infant, Seedling." He glared at Berry over the heads of her Crown Guard. "The Code has been broken, openly and contemptuously. It has been broken by your Crown Guard: the ones who killed Tendril."

There was silence in the glade. Every baboon gaped at him, but none spoke. Some of them glanced up nervously at Berry, who looked speechless.

"How dare you!" she blurted at last, peeling back her muzzle from her fangs. "How dare you, Thorn Highleaf! My Crown Guard had nothing to do with this death. How can you suggest such a thing? Where is your proof?"

Thorn stared at her, and for an instant he felt an inward qualm of doubt. Where was his proof?

He had none. *I just know it.* He clenched his fangs.

"Tendril was killed by a baboon," he snapped. "That's not in doubt. And the only baboons with reason to do it are your Crown Guard!"

"So," hissed Berry, "no proof at all!"

As the two mates glowered at each other, there was movement in the lines of the Crown Guard. Two of the front rank shifted aside, glancing over their shoulders with surprise. Between them stalked Creeper, his single eye alight with cold loathing as he smirked at Thorn.

"He needs no proof, my Crownleaf." Creeper didn't look at Berry, but at Thorn. "I killed Tendril, and I confess it with pride. I killed her for the good of this troop." At last he swung his head around and fixed his eye on Berry. "As you should have done."

The troop broke into gasps of shock and astonished muttering.

"Be quiet! All of you!" Berry silenced them, but there was panic and disbelief in her eyes as she turned back to her Crown Guard captain.

"Creeper." Her voice trembled. "This can't be true!"

He shrugged. "Why else would I admit it? Not that it's a confession as such, since that implies guilt. I feel no guilt. Smashing that baboon's skull was one of the proudest moments of my life."

Berry could only gape at him, her jaw wide. She swallowed hard at last and shook herself. "A nursing mother," she grated. "How could you, Creeper?"

"I told you how." He tilted his head insolently. "With pride. I did it for revenge for all her insults and disrespect. For the honor of our troop. Tendril deserved to die."

Berry drew herself up, eyes flashing. "Then you are no longer a member of my Crown Guard!" she cried. "You are no longer a Highleaf. From this moment you are a Deeproot once more. And a Deeproot you will remain till the end of your days!"

Creeper picked at his teeth, then examined the seed he'd withdrawn. He looked far from disturbed, Thorn thought with a prickle of unease in his fur; there was cool contempt in his face. The one-eyed baboon glanced at his fellow guards and shrugged again before turning back to Berry.

"Sorry, Berry," he sneered, "but you no longer have the authority to demote me."

Thorn sucked in a breath. Shocked murmurings ran around the glade, and there were a few cries of protest and outrage. But not many, Thorn realized. Not enough.

Deep in his gut, dread stirred. It was as if he could sense the disintegration of everything he'd ever known, every certainty. *It's all falling apart*, he thought with a cold rush of foreboding.

"Crown Guard!" cried Berry. "Seize Creeper!"

Thorn watched the Guards as they exchanged looks and nodded. A few of them turned and stalked toward Creeper; one by one, other Guards followed. Good, thought Thorn. The other Guards were going to deal with him. Creeper had at last gone too far.

Then all the Guards turned to face the Crown Stone. Standing defiantly at Creeper's side, they stared up at Berry.

Creeper smiled.

The silence felt as if it could crush the forest. Thorn could not believe what he was seeing, and there was a weight like a stone in his belly. Behind him, from the troop, came a couple of shocked sobs, a gasp or two . . . and a few hoots of muted approval. His skin crawled.

"A Crownleaf," declared Creeper, "is an outdated concept. This has been proven. Let us remember what has happened over these last few seasons." Cockily, he leaned a paw against the Crown Stone and stuck out his lip as if in deep thought. "Bark and Grub—they were weak, to put it kindly. It was those two Crownleaves who allowed and enabled the rise of Stinger. The less said about him—about your father—the better . . ." Creeper paused. He glanced up at Berry. "And now . . . ?"

Creeper paused, spat, and continued in that silky, menacing voice: "Now we have Berry Crownleaf: a baboon who has let her mate interfere with the running of this troop. She lets Thorn dictate how Dawntrees Troop behaves, how we live. But then . . . Berry is Stinger's daughter. We should not have expected better."

"These are lies!" shouted Berry, her eyes brilliant with rage.

And at last, some of her troop began to holler loudly in protest.

"Berry is not Stinger!" yelled Mango angrily.

"She's been a wise Crownleaf!" shouted one of the Goodleaves. "How can you say such things, Creeper?"

"Because they are true," snapped Creeper. "All our Crownleaves have let us down, Dawntrees Troop. They have not worked for the good of the troop, but for themselves. This has gone on too long, and we, the Crown Guard, say: it stops now! We do not need a single flawed leader. From today, the Crown Guard will pool its wisdom and represent every baboon. We will rule this troop for the good of all!"

"No!" shouted Mango in fury, bounding forward. Petal and Twig were at her back, their faces grim with determination.

But Creeper gave a flick of one paw, and six of the Crown Guard rushed forward to stop Mango and her friends in their tracks. The Guards fell on the three rebels, wrestling and beating them to the ground.

"Stop!" screamed Berry. "Creeper, stop this!"

He ignored her. Mango, Petal, and Twig fought back, snarling, but they were outnumbered, and they were soon almost invisible beneath a furious pile-on of powerful baboons. In the hush from the rest of the troop, the sound of thudding paws on flesh was sickening. Berry gave a single, angry sob.

"Have I—have we made ourselves clear?" asked Creeper, coldly surveying the troop.

No more baboons dashed forward to defend the Crownleaf, and Thorn swallowed hard against the bile that rose in his throat. He knew that if he didn't do something, Berry could be in real physical danger.

He pushed his way back to the front, past the maimed and bleeding figures of the three rebels. Turning, he faced the troop, his fangs bared.

"Listen to me! Berry is your leader! You know this, all of you. You elected her Crownleaf yourselves—she didn't take the Crown Stone by herself. You voted! She is your rightful leader—not these thugs!"

Viper bounded to his side and pushed him, lightly and contemptuously, with one paw. "This? You'd take notice of this?" she demanded of the troop. "Is this your Great Father? Seriously? The Great Spirit does not live within this pathetic monkey." Her lip curled in disdain. "Ever since he rose to be Great Parent, he has done nothing but harm this troop.

He has used his position to undermine us at every turn, to weaken us."

"Indeed, Viper—and even Stinger did not stoop so low." Creeper nodded. "He was evil, yes, but when he was Great Father, Stinger made this troop powerful. He promoted baboons to be Driftleaves! He gave us authority over every animal in Bravelands! What has Thorn ever done for us?"

"Nothing!" cried a baboon from the back. Thorn glanced in shock at Bud's face. He looked genuinely resentful and bitter.

Viper smiled at Thorn, then faced the troop once more. "Do you, wise baboons, truly believe that the Great Spirit would do this to us? That the Great Spirit would choose a Parent who would attack his own kind at every opportunity?"

The air crackled with tension. No baboon spoke to defend Thorn. Some gazes rested guiltily on the ground; others flickered to him with the same resentment Thorn had seen in Bud.

"He is a False Parent," declared Viper, nodding with satisfaction. "Thorn Highleaf: you are not our Great Father."

Thorn was too hurt, too shocked, even to speak. He felt as if all the breath had been sucked from his body, and he was afraid he might collapse. So when the low chanting began, he heard it very clearly.

"False Parent. False Parent."

It started as a low murmur, then swelled, and other voices threw in new insults.

"False Great Father."

"False Crownleaf."

"False Parent."

The Crown Guard led the chorus, but every baboon in the troop was joining in.

"False Parent. False Parent."

The noise beat against his ears now, making his head swim. If there were any voices raised in Thorn's defense, they were drowned in the racket of condemnation.

"False Parent. False Parent! FALSE PARENT!"

Creeper raised a paw, and the noise stopped instantly.

"I declare," he said solemnly, "that Thorn and Berry are now exiles, reviled and rejected. Neither of you two may ever return to Tall Trees. You are not welcome here. Take your treachery and your scheming and go." He drew a triumphant breath. "And never come back."

For a horrible moment, Thorn thought he and Berry were both about to be killed; baboons sprang forward in a mass, chittering and screaming. But they were focused on the Crown Stone. They slapped droppings and rotten fruit on its surface from top to bottom, smearing and defiling it until it was unrecognizable. Berry dodged and gasped, staggering and sliding down from the Stone. Backing away, she put her paws over her mouth as she watched her former troop dishonor the symbol of her authority.

Suddenly more afraid than ever, Thorn glanced at the Crown Guard. Their eyes burned as one with a malice that was terrifying.

"Berry," he urged her, "we have to get out of here!"

BRAVELANDS #5: THE SPIRIT-EATERS   211

He seized her arm and dragged her away as the Crown Guard stalked forward, picking up rocks and tossing them in their paws. At last she gave a cry of despair and turned to flee at his side.

Thorn bounded through the trees, leaping rocks and dead branches, retreating as far and as fast as he could from the riot at the Crown Stone. Occasionally he glanced over his shoulder, but Berry was still there, fleeing as urgently as he did, though her eyes were wide with distress and bewilderment. Thorn did not stop running until he was sure there were no sounds of pursuit, until they were far from the Crown Stone Clearing and its mob of rebellious baboons.

He sprang onto a rotting tree trunk and caught his breath, panting. His heart pounded painfully in his rib cage. From a great distance, he heard hollering, whooping, and cheers; birds scattered into the sky, alarmed. But no baboon pursued them. They didn't have to, Thorn thought with a lurch of his gut. To Dawntrees Troop, he and Berry were already dead.

His heart ached for his mate. He reached out a paw to help Berry onto the log, but she slapped it away, her eyes blazing.

"This is your fault," she snarled. "Yours!"

"Berry, try to calm down. Please." Stunned and desperate, he reached out for her.

"Get away from me," she growled. "This would never have happened if you hadn't tried to boss Dawntrees around. You were never our Crownleaf—I was! But in you came with your clumsy lectures and your pompous judgments. All you ever did was undermine me, Thorn."

"No, Berry! I never meant to cause you harm. I—"

"You never meant it, but it still happened!"

Anger swelled in his own chest. "And maybe it wouldn't have happened if you hadn't taken all the strongest and most powerful baboons and given them the authority of the Crown Guard. Look how that turned out . . . look what they've done! Weren't your father's Strongbranches warning enough?"

Her eyes widened. "How dare you bring up my father!" she spat. "I did my best for Dawntrees!" Her voice rose to a scream. "Are you saying I'm like Stinger? Are you?"

"I warned you not to form the Crown Guard!" Thorn shouted. "And no wonder they thought they had permission to kill Tendril. You said yourself you wanted her dead. Right in front of them!"

"I did not kill Tendril! I am not responsible for Creeper's actions! Creeper thought he could do as he liked because you undermined my authority! You, Thorn!"

The rage in her golden eyes was almost unbearable. Thorn flinched and fell silent. *What are we doing?* He'd gone too far with that accusation about Tendril, he knew it suddenly and sickeningly.

Berry bared her teeth and hissed. "You may be a true Great Father—I'll give the Great Spirit the benefit of the doubt, though I don't know what it was thinking—but you are a terrible one." Deep in her throat, she gave a growl. "And you're an even worse mate. How can you claim you ever loved me? When have you actually shown it?"

Thorn tried to speak. The words formed in his throat: the

words that would reassure her, bring her back to him, make everything all right between them again. But he couldn't speak them. His throat was too hot and tight, his heart in too much pain.

"I never want to see you again, Thorn. You've ruined my life. Stay away from me, for what's left of it."

Berry shook her head violently, spun away from him, and ran into the depths of the forest.

CHAPTER SEVENTEEN

As Sky and the small party of elephants trudged across the parched plain after Fearless, her throat was tight, her heart pounding. She did not want to see what Keen and the cubs had seen, but she knew she must.

The dead elephant lay in plain view, a huddled smudge of shadow against the paleness of the dry grass. Boulder halted over the lifeless shape. He turned to raise his trunk in warning, but suddenly she did not need him to say it: Sky knew who was lying there dead. She broke into a run, a shard of pain searing her heart.

"Forest." She came to a halt beside his corpse, sucking an anguished breath.

Fearless padded around the body, staring and sniffing. "You know this elephant, then?"

"Yes." It came out in a sob.

"There's a wound in his chest." Boulder touched the broken rib cage gently with the tip of his trunk and eased it open. The chest beneath was an empty cavity. "They . . . took his heart."

"That isn't possible," said Flint, swinging his trunk in agitation. "It shouldn't be!"

"Yet they have," rumbled Boulder grimly. "Somehow."

"Evil," breathed Comet, her eyes wide with horror. "How can even a big pack of wolves bring down a grown male elephant? It's as Flint says—it can't be done!"

"The golden wolves are capable of anything," growled Fearless.

Sky could hardly bear to look at Forest's body, but she set her jaws and forced herself to do it. She owed it to him, she thought. If she'd been less dismissive, if she'd given him even a hint of hope that she might agree to his courtship, poor Forest wouldn't have been out here on the exposed plain in the first place. "Oh, Forest," she whispered under her aching breath. "I'm sorry."

Beside her, Boulder stroked her flank gently with his trunk. "It's not your fault, Sky. You can't blame yourself."

"He was so . . . so kind," murmured Sky. "Such a noble elephant, and so gentle."

"But he fought hard." Flint gestured with his tusks at a couple of broken wolf corpses that lay a little distance away.

Sky recalled again the myth of the wolves' power. Could it really be true that they gained the strength of the animals they killed? This seemed to prove it, because she could think of no animal other than a lion—and a pack of lions at that—that could take down a full-grown male elephant.

"There's a trail of blood, too," said Fearless, nodding at dark streaks on the ground leading toward the open desert. "Your friend wounded at least one more of them." He pawed the wolf corpses, shuddering. The rib cages had been torn wide, cannibalized by their own kind. "They're twisted creatures."

"We have to do something!" Sky raised her trunk, suddenly furious. She turned from one elephant to the other. "They can't get away with this, Boulder! Comet! We need to confront those wolves and put a stop to this carnage."

"I can't argue with that," growled Boulder, raking the dry earth with a foot.

Flint's usually kind eyes were hard and angry. "I've been alive for longer than any of you, but I've never seen anything like this before. These wolves are a curse on Bravelands, and they must be driven out."

"I'm with you elephants," said Fearless, padding back to them. "The golden wolves are a threat to every animal in Bravelands. I've met them, and they don't listen to reason. They kill and kill without need or hunger, and they devour spirits and discard the flesh. That's against the Code in itself, isn't it?"

"I agree," announced Comet, nodding. "There would be no Code-breach in killing these wolves. Am I right, Sky?"

Sky nodded, blinking. "Yes. I'm sure of it, Comet."

"Then we should track them down before they get much farther away," declared the matriarch.

"Go, then," said Flint gruffly. "I'm not too old for a fight, especially with these Codebreakers, but I would slow you down in the chase. I'll stay here and look after the cheetah cubs, Sky. That'll give you one less thing to worry about, at least."

"Thank you, Flint." Sky butted his head, grateful. "Comet, you should stay, too. Our family needs you. Boulder and Fearless and I can deal with these cowards, if we catch them."

"Very well, Sky." Comet dipped her head a little, as if Sky were her matriarch rather than the other way around. "But be careful!"

Boulder swung his head suddenly and stared across the savannah. One ear flapped out, and he angled it upward a little.

"The wolves aren't far away," he said. "Listen."

They stood in silence for a moment, craning toward the plain. Sky tensed. Her brother was right: on the still air drifted a faint howling.

Fearless flicked his ears forward and scowled. "I hear them too." He broke into a loping run, and Boulder and Sky thundered after him.

It was as if the golden wolves did not care about being followed, thought Sky. Their tracks were obvious, their scent pervasive, and they had not even bothered to run on hard ground. Was it arrogance, wondered Sky, or some warped kind of death wish?

Yet she realized she wasn't afraid of them right now; she was too angry. Poor Forest—the wolves had taken not only his life, but his spirit. He would never linger in the sunlight and sweet grass of the Plain of Our Ancestors.

And the wolves would pay for that, she promised Forest in her heart.

Ahead of the two elephants, Fearless slackened his pace. He raised his head, sniffing the wind that stirred the dust.

"They're close," he snarled. "And listen to that!"

The eerie, crazed howling drifted on the breeze, tinged with ecstatic excitement. It chilled Sky's gut, but she still wasn't afraid. Creatures so murderous and mad could not be allowed to destroy Bravelands.

Fearless slowed to sniff the ground, his ears pricked forward and his muzzle curled back from his teeth. He looked to Sky as if he was searching for another scent altogether.

But as Sky spotted a patch of stained sand ahead, Fearless seemed to notice it too. He jerked his head up and broke into a sprint.

Sky cantered after him, the other elephants behind her. It was obvious at once what had happened here; the dark smears were blood, already drying in the wind and the sun, and the breadth of the splatter told of a fight. A chaos of bloody pawprints led in several directions away from the stained sand.

"They've taken another creature!" bellowed Boulder angrily.

Sky went quite still, raising her trunk to scent the air. Her ears twitched. "There!" she cried.

She trotted toward a corpse that was already half buried in blown sand. Brindled black-and-gold fur stirred in the breeze, and as Sky approached, she saw the head: yellow eyes open but quite dead, and a thin muzzle drawn back in a frozen snarl.

Her head spun with confusion. *That's a wolf!*

"It's Ravage," blurted Fearless as he came to Sky's side. He stiffened and pinned his ears back. "This wolf was their leader!"

"Their leader?" Boulder looked startled. "You're sure? But what killed her?"

"I think the wolves did," growled Fearless, drawing back a pace from the horrible sight. His hackles were erect. "Her own pack!"

"I'm guessing she was holding them back," rumbled Boulder. He blew away some of the sand that had drifted over Ravage. "Look—she's the one Forest wounded." A vicious gash had been ripped down her hind leg, deep enough to expose the bone.

"She kept them in line." Fearless shook his head and twisted his muzzle. "There's no limit to what they'll do now."

As Sky and Boulder stared, Fearless dug at the sand around Ravage's rib cage with a paw. He stepped back and nodded at the hollow chest beneath ragged tatters of hide.

"They've taken her heart," he said in a low voice.

Sky shuddered.

"So they must have a new Alpha," rumbled Boulder.

"Ravage was bad enough," said Fearless. "I dread to think what kind of wolf this new leader is."

For long moments they all stood without speaking, gazing down at the mutilated corpse.

"I should tell you." Fearless looked up at Sky and Boulder.

"Though you may find it hard to believe. The wolves massacred Titanpride."

"Titanpride?" gasped Sky. But they'd been the most feared and deadly lion pride in all of Bravelands! She'd witnessed their ruthlessness herself, when they'd killed little Moon.

Fearless nodded. "We came across their remains, Keen and the cubs and I. The wolves took their hearts."

Sky swallowed hard. "When the wolves attacked me," she murmured, "I saw something. I thought it was a . . . a mirage, or that my eyes were playing tricks because I was so scared. I saw the wolves clearly enough, but I also saw . . . I saw the shapes of lions around them."

Fearless nodded slowly. "The spirits of Titanpride. They really are taking on their victims' power."

"It would explain how they managed to bring down Forest," said Boulder grimly.

Sky nodded. "The wolves grow more powerful with every death." Suddenly her fear returned, making her gut clench. She looked out across the plain. "I think we're being rash," she admitted, "and I think, too, that the wolves are long gone. Now that they've killed Ravage, they've nothing left to delay them."

"I agree," said Boulder. "There's no point chasing them further, and even if we catch them, it might not end the way we want it to. I suggest we leave our vengeance for another day."

"That's elephant wisdom," said Fearless dryly, "and I think you're right. Besides, it's time I got back to Keen and the cubs."

"We won't forget what the wolves did," added Boulder as they turned back the way they'd come. "This is unfinished business, and we will finish it."

Fearless nodded. "But for now, farewell."

The two elephants watched him as he sniffed the air, then loped away with a steady stride toward the northwest. Sky sighed and nodded to Boulder, and they both set out on the long trek back to the Plain of Hearts.

The sky had darkened almost to black, and only a violet glow remained on the horizon as Sky and Boulder trudged back to the herds. Above them, stars twinkled into life, and a half-moon rose over the distant hills.

A few of the elephants acknowledged them, but apart from some muted murmurs and a stroke of greeting from two or three trunks, the herds were subdued. Already they were mourning Forest, whose body would remain where he had fallen until his bones could be transported back to his final resting place, on the Plain of Our Ancestors.

Sky could make out Breeze, the mother's silhouette almost lost in the deepening night as she held her new baby close at her side. She recognized Comet and Star, talking softly, their heads pressed close together.

But one female detached herself from her quiet herd and ambled toward Sky and Boulder. She had long, creamy tusks.

"There's your prospective new mate, brother," murmured Sky.

"Baobab." There was a catch in his throat.

He really likes her, thought Sky. *I'm glad.* "A lovely name. You should go to her."

Boulder hesitated for only a moment, then gave Sky a slow nod. As he strode toward Baobab, Sky released a long breath. As reassuring as Boulder's company was, she needed some time alone to think.

Turning, she walked a little away from the other elephants, watching the sky darken to full night. The silver path of the spirits was clearly visible now, arching above Bravelands.

There was the brush of soft fur against Sky's forefoot, and a soft mewling. Sky glanced down.

"Nimble," she murmured. "Lively."

"Hello, Sky," purred Nimble. He sounded much quieter than usual; clearly the cubs had heard about the day's terrible events. Gently, he set down a bone at Sky's feet.

"We found something in that gully," he whispered. "I hope it helps, Sky."

Sky stared down at the bone. "It came from an elephant skeleton?"

Lively nodded. "Just where you said we should look, at the foot of the slope. Some of the smaller bones were broken. That's how we managed to carry this one. I think it's a piece of a rib."

Poor River, thought Sky with a wrench of pity. River's herd must have hated leaving her there, but they could never have negotiated that steep precipice to find her body; it had been brave of the little cheetahs to attempt it.

"Thank you," she whispered.

Sky found herself strangely reluctant to touch the bone, afraid of what she might discover. But at last she took a deep breath and curled her trunk around its smooth bleached surface.

She felt herself give a gasp of shock—but she did not seem to be in her own body anymore. The night and the stars had vanished, and the sun was high and bright and hot over the plain. She was River Marcher, bolting across the Plain of Hearts toward the ravine, her heart aching with fear and remorse.

"Stop! Please, stop!" she cried.

The two bull elephants at the cliff edge took no notice. They had only burning eyes for each other as they repeatedly clashed their heads and trunks. Boulder drew back, twisted, and lunged with his long tusks, trying to stab past Rock's defenses; Rock dodged and thrust back. Once again, their heads smashed together, with a thunder that made the earth shake.

"Stop fighting! I don't want this!"

Some elephants called River lucky, to have two fine bulls battling for her affections. Perhaps, before this had happened, she would have thought the same herself. But the reality was horrible. The Rage was horrible. These two would kill each other if they could: River felt it in the crackling air, she smelled it in the blood that spattered the earth. And she saw it in their blazing, maddened eyes.

"Boulder! Rock! You're too close to the edge. Oh, please step back!"

It was no use. They would not, could not listen. It was as if their fight had nothing to do with her. The stench of rage and hatred filled River's trunk until she felt faint.

I have to stop them, she thought desperately. *They'll fall. I have to stop them!*

Charging on through clouds of dust, she raised her trunk and blared her misery. "Stop it! Both of you, please. Listen to me!"

Through her blurred vision, she saw Boulder lunge suddenly, his tusk catching Rock's shoulder and digging into his hide. Rock roared with pain and stumbled backward, and Boulder staggered sideways.

River was cantering too fast: she couldn't avoid Rock, she couldn't stop. His rump slammed hard into her shoulder, and she reeled sideways. Her feet slithered beneath her. She felt a hind leg slide over the edge into thin air.

Panic surged in her chest. Her foot scrabbled at the edge of the drop, finding a tenuous, crumbling hold.

"Boulder! Rock! Help me!"

Her foot slipped back over the edge. Her other hind leg followed it, and she felt her underbelly hit sharp stone. Terror coursed through her, turning her blood cold. The ridge scraped her belly as she slid slowly backward.

"Help!"

The desperation in her voice must have filtered through Rock's fog of Rage. He staggered back from Boulder, twisting toward River, his eyes widening in horror. He lurched toward her, stretching out his trunk, curling it desperately around hers.

It all felt so slow. His trunk sliding through River's, unable to get a grip. The Rage dying in his eyes, replaced by terror and an awful hopelessness. To River, he and Boulder already seemed distant, unreachable. And then the tip of her trunk lost its final contact with his.

There was a moment, a tiny one, as the air itself seemed to hold its breath. Just for that instant of stillness, River thought the Great Spirit held her safe in its grasp.

Then the cliff edge receded, hurtling away from her. Sick despair washed through her, chasing out even the fear, as her body plummeted. Her flank struck an outcrop, but she didn't feel pain; then she was falling again, toward the onrushing ground that would kill her—

Sky gave a cry of fear and jerked away from the vision.

It was no longer daylight. In the blackness of the hot night, Sky stood trembling, her breath coming hard and fast. Her hide shivered violently.

Oh, River. Poor River.

But she knew the truth. At last, she understood.

Rock hadn't killed River. Neither had Boulder. It had been a terrible, lethal accident.

"Sky? Sky, are you all right?" Nimble and Lively prowled around her feet, anxious, their furry tails tickling her hide.

"Cubs. Thank you." Sky's voice was hoarse. She shook her ears. "You found what I needed. Please, will you do one more thing for me?" She glanced down with sorrow at the broken bone.

"Take this to where Forest's body is, over there near the

bulls. At least part of her should go to the Plain of Our Ancestors. River Marcher deserves to be at peace."

As Sky watched the cubs pad away, she felt a familiar dull
pain growing once more, and sharpening inside her.

She had made the worst mistake of her life when she drove
Rock away. And now it was too late to do anything about it.

CHAPTER EIGHTEEN

The Great Father Clearing lay in silence, but for the whir of crickets and the piping of an occasional tree frog. Soft starlight threw pale shadows over Mud as he crouched, intently studying his moonstones. Thorn watched him, trying to focus on what Mud was deducing from them, but it was hard to concentrate when so many doubts and regrets jostled for space in his head.

He had been a failure as Great Father: that was the only conclusion he could come to. He'd sent Tendril to her violent death, and the zebras too. He had tried to help Berry, only to see his efforts end in her overthrow. He had not protected a single Bravelands creature from the golden wolves.

He had to put all this right. Somehow, Thorn knew, he had to make up for all his mistakes, all his catastrophic decisions. And he'd thought and thought, but there was only one way to do that. It was a terrible conclusion, the worst decision he had ever had to make, but it was the only possible option. The only thing left for him to do now was to go through with it—

"Thorn!" Mud twisted and stared up at him, his eyes glowing with alarm. "The stones. They say something terrible is coming to Bravelands!"

Thorn stifled a groan. "Another 'something'?"

"It's true. I know there've been so many awful things lately." Mud's shoulders slumped. "But Thorn, this looks worse than the rest. Please listen. . . . Listen to what the stones are telling us!"

Thorn rested a paw on his friend's shoulder. "Try not to worry, Mud. I think I know what the stones are saying. Never forget—Bravelands is strong. It is forever. It will cope."

Mud rose to his paws, turning to stare into Thorn's eyes. "Thorn? What's wrong? You seem distracted. Are you all right?"

Thorn shook himself. He must not alert Mud or the others to what he was about to do. "I'm fine. Don't worry, Mud, I've just been moping too much, overthinking things." He paused. "Mud, can you do something for me? Will you find Berry? I know she's made a camp for herself in that acacia grove on the edge of the forest, beside the Starshine River. Could you go there, make sure she's all right? Help her if she needs help? That would reassure me."

"You don't want to go yourself?" Mud frowned.

Thorn couldn't quite meet his friend's eyes. "There's something else that I need to do."

Mud crinkled his brow, puzzled, but he nodded. "Of course

I'll do that, Thorn. Berry may not want me around for long, but I'll at least make sure she has everything she needs and that she's safe."

"Thank you, my friend," murmured Thorn. "That means a lot to me."

Mud gave him a last, perplexed stare before gathering up his stones and loping off into the bush. Spider and Nut were busy on the far side of the clearing, chewing on nuts and arguing lightheartedly about the various qualities of different lizards.

"Oh, come on, Spider, they can change color and everything," Nut was teasing.

"Nut-friend cannot compare a chameleon with an agama lizard," Spider retorted. "Why would Spider's beautiful lizard want to change his colors?"

Allowing himself a small, regretful smile, Thorn slipped away.

The night was a beautiful one, cool and quiet and alive with stars. In the distance, a jackal barked, and he could hear muted hoofsteps from the sentries of a herd of dozing gazelles. Thorn stayed in the shadows and the deeper darkness, not wanting to talk to anyone or deal with more problems. He kept his eyes fixed on the plain until he made out the shimmer of water in the distance.

Picking up his pace, Thorn bounded toward the watering hole. It was clear how much had changed in Bravelands; no herds milled on the banks of the lake, and there was no muted hum of conversation, no splash of animals cooling off in the shallows. Only one group of creatures loitered on its banks, and that was the pack of pale, skinny wolves who sprawled there as if they owned the watering hole and the whole savannah beyond. Everyone else, they had scared away.

At Thorn's approach, the wolves jumped up, rising simultaneously on their hind legs like meerkats. They peered at him, blinking their pale glowing eyes. Their jaws opened wide in malicious grins as they glanced at one another. Then they dropped back onto all fours.

Suddenly, they looked a lot less like meerkats, Thorn thought. They looked like what they truly were: a pack of vicious wolves who had devoured the hearts of some poor meerkat mob.

For a long moment, Thorn paused, his paws locked to the ground with fear. Then, taking a deep breath, he strode forward.

"You're hunting for the Great Father," he said through clenched fangs.

The wolves exchanged sly looks, and the biggest of them stalked forward.

"We are," he growled. "Tell us where he is, and you may live, Baboon."

Thorn swallowed hard. He could not let his fear stop him, even though every nerve in his body screamed at him to run.

"The Great Father is with you now," he told them. "I am the Great Father of Bravelands. I'm here, and I'm defenseless. No other creature is with me." Thorn shut his eyes for a moment, feeling his heart thud painfully in his rib cage. But he wanted to feel every precious beat: there were not many left to him now.

Sucking in a breath, he snapped: "Eat my heart, if you must. And let that be enough for you."

The big wolf stared at him as if he couldn't believe his luck. He turned to his comrades, tail twitching gleefully, then looked back at Thorn with a delighted grin.

"This is unexpected, such an unexpected pleasure," he sneered. "We take your heart back to our new leader. Oh, he will so enjoy eating it! Plump and full of Spirit!"

"He will be so very pleased with us," added another wolf, flicking her big ears. "Let we not tell him the baboon surrendered? Let we tell our Alpha we caught him by ourselves!"

"Tell your leader what you want," said Thorn dully. "Just get it over with."

"Oh, we will," growled the big wolf silkily. "All of we. It won't be over with soon enough for you. But console your tasty heart, Great Father! You make Bloodheart Pack happy, very happy!"

Thorn knew he couldn't run away now even if he wanted to. And anyway, he wouldn't do that, couldn't do that. His mind was made up; this was all he could do. For Bravelands.

Images flashed through Thorn's mind as the wolves prowled in a circle around him: his friends, Mud, Nut, and Spider. His former troop, some of whom he'd liked very much. Fearless and Sky. And Berry, of course: whatever she thought of him now, she was still the love of his life and always would be.

I'll miss you so much, Berry.

He hoped that when it left him, the Great Spirit would find a new Great Parent quickly: one who would do a better job than he had managed. For he knew one thing certainly, the heart the wolves ate would not be that of a Great Parent, but one of a middle-ranking baboon who should never have risen above his station.

Still, the attack when it came was shocking. A pale blur, bristling with teeth and claws, sprang at him. For an instant Thorn froze in terrified shock; then he felt a hard blow to his chest. It flung him backward, and in the moment it took for the pain to kick in, he didn't understand.

Then he felt it. Sharp agony shot through his chest and rib cage, a burning point of torment. The wolf that stood over him dug its fangs into his chest, tearing at the flesh. Its teeth scraped against bone, and Thorn howled in pain.

The other wolves leaped to join the first; he saw nothing but their white, savage teeth and the darkness of their open throats. *Oh please, Great Spirit, let it be quick, let it be over soon—*

Through the blood and pain, Thorn heard the colossal eruption of what sounded like a river in sudden spate. Time seemed to stand still; then a cascading wave from the lake drenched him and the wolves alike. It was water, real water.

The wolves sprang back, shocked, their hackles prickling. They were soaked. Thorn tried to shake himself, but it hurt too much and all he could do was give a feeble cry of agony.

What happened—

Crocodiles: a whole bask of them, ten or more. They

lurched up onto the shore with astonishing speed. The foremost of them opened its terrifying jaws wide and clamped them around the biggest wolf, tearing him away from Thorn. Then the croc retreated, plunging under the lake's surface with the wolf in its teeth.

Thorn's vision was blurred; he could barely make out the bloody scene unfolding in front of him. The crocodiles were swarming all over the wolves, that much he knew. The rest was a chaos of snapping jaws, ripping teeth, and yelping, howling wolves. One by one, Thorn's attackers were dragged away, screaming and fighting, to be pulled beneath the water.

Thorn staggered to his paws, reeling, barely able to stand but managing somehow to stay upright. His eyes were full of blood and wolf slaver, and he wiped them frantically. When the crocodiles came to attack him in turn, he needed to be able to defend himself.

With a last squeal from a wolf, and the thudding slam of a croc's tail on the shoreline, silence fell. Water lapped and rippled up the sand, the waves dwindling at last.

Thorn stared at the watering hole. The drowned corpses of wolves floated one by one to the surface, torn and ragged.

Scaly backs surfaced in the water once more, and Thorn gave an exhausted hoot of terror as he stumbled backward. But as the crocodiles emerged from the bloodstained lake and ambled toward him on their stubby legs, they suddenly seemed much less threatening.

Thorn's whole body sagged. He swayed. "What did you— why—why did you—?"

"A debt," snarled the biggest and oldest croc. His Sand-tongue was guttural and harsh, and his glowing eyes were locked on Thorn. "No Great Parent ever helped the crocodiles. None was ever interested in us. Until you. You helped Rip's bask at the Muddy River, and that is known now by all crocodiles." As he walked forward, his long snout almost touched Thorn's chest. "We have no belief in the Great Spirit. Or, we didn't—till now. Perhaps, if it exists at all, it lives in you."

Without another word, the crocodiles turned and slid back into the watering hole. Wolf corpses began to disappear again, with bubbling plops as the crocodiles retrieved them. Thorn knew he'd never see those wolves again. He shuddered, relieved he couldn't make out anything that was happening beneath the surface.

Helpless disappointment overtook him, and he sank to his haunches, shaking.

He couldn't even sacrifice himself properly. That was how effective a Great Parent he was. He could give himself to the golden wolves, bare his chest to them, offer his heart, and still fail.

And it hurt. His sacrifice might have been unsuccessful, but the pain was still atrocious. Blood soaked his chest fur, and a burning agony gripped his whole rib cage. In despair, Thorn collapsed miserably onto the ground. Maybe the rest of the golden wolves would come, maybe they'd finish him off. Maybe, just maybe, they'd leave Bravelands alone—

In his blurred sight, two baboons were sprinting toward him down the shore. One was small and scrawny, one beautiful and golden-furred. *No, they're not even spirits. I can't even die right.*

As Mud and Berry reached him, chattering their distress, Thorn felt all the strength go out of his body. Letting merciful darkness swamp him and drown all his misery, he blacked out.

Thorn blinked. He lay on his back, staring up at the purple dawn beyond the canopy. He was in the Great Father Clearing, he realized, but he felt no relief, and no gratitude to the two baboons who had found him. He felt nothing but emptiness and a ragged, almost unbearable pain.

He saw Berry's beloved face lean over him. She pressed a wad of damp leaves to the wound in his chest.

"I hope this will help, Thorn," she murmured. "I'm no Goodleaf, but I learned some things from my mother. I think jackalberry leaves and honey stop the wound going bad. I hope so. It's deep."

One of her paws stroked his head, very gently. Her touch made Thorn's heart ache worse than ever.

"I'm sorry, Berry," he choked hoarsely. "I'm so sorry about everything. How it turned out. The troop. Everything."

"Hush, Thorn," she soothed him. "I'm sorry too, but all that matters now is that you heal. You have to live, Thorn. I can't bear to lose you." Her voice faded to a whisper. "And neither can Bravelands."

That sent a new shard of despair and pain through Thorn's body. *I tried . . . I tried to save Bravelands.*

"Berry, I—" But the effort of speaking now sent fresh waves of pain rolling through his body, and he felt blackness

creeping over him once more. Almost gratefully, Thorn sank
back into unconsciousness, with Berry's lingering touch the
last thing he felt.

"Get away! Get away from him, you rot-eating brutes!"

Thorn blinked as hazy awareness returned to him. The
pain was a dull, thudding ache now, but as he struggled to sit
up, a shard of agony jolted through his chest.

Wincing, Thorn managed to make out a little of what was
happening. The air of the clearing was a flurry of black beating wings, and Nut was jumping frantically up and down,
trying to drive the huge birds away with a stick.

"I said, get away!" screeched Nut. "He's not dead yet!"

"Nut, no!" gasped Thorn, his throat raw. "Mud . . . Mud,
stop him. . . ."

Mud nodded and rushed toward Nut.

"Nut, stop!" cried Mud, pulling at the arm that held the
stick. "The vultures are here to help Thorn!"

Nut hesitated, the stick still brandished in a paw. With a
last warning glare at the birds, he threw it down and stalked
sulkily out of their way.

Giving Nut a cold look, Windrider hopped and flapped
over to where Thorn lay. Her flock hurried to flank her, their
wings protectively hunched.

Thorn stared up at Windrider. He didn't know for sure
that she was here to help him, but the truth was, it didn't matter anymore.

She might as well eat me as heal me.

Windrider was so huge, her shape blotted out the dappled sunlight, but Thorn didn't mind that either; the glare had been dazzling. With vague surprise, he realized the bird's feathers were glossy with water. Tilting her head, the great vulture spread her wings and shook them out over him.

Droplets spattered Thorn's face and body. *They are deliciously cool* was his first thought; then some of it trickled into his jaws, and he instantly recognized the sweet taste. Windrider had brought water from the sacred pool that lay high on her mountain, the pool where Thorn had finally accepted his destiny.

"Rest, Great Father," croaked the vulture. "Rest and heal."

For a fleeting moment, Thorn thought her command was impossible to obey; he hurt too much. Then, with gratitude, he felt himself slip back once more into a silent, blank darkness.

The sun was high over the canopy when Thorn woke again. It glittered and flashed between the branches, dazzling white. Dark shapes perched above him in the trees, wings spread, and he realized the vultures were still here, still watching over him.

Propping himself up, testing the strength of his shoulders, Thorn realized the pain had ebbed a lot. His muscles felt as if they would work again. Taking a deep breath, he sat up fully, blinking as he looked around.

Beside him, Berry smiled, her eyes alight with relief and love. "Thorn! You're awake!"

Nut punched the air. "Yes!"

Spider grinned, and Mud lunged forward to hug Thorn. Thorn winced and drew back, nodding and smiling at his friend. He didn't want Mud to think he didn't appreciate his affection, but oh, that had hurt.

"Welcome back to the land of the living," said Mud, clasping his paws tightly together, as if to stop himself attempting another embrace.

"The vultures' water worked," said Spider happily, picking at his teeth. "Spider had a feeling it would."

Thorn glanced up at the vultures and nodded his thanks. His sacrifice may have been thwarted—but he had to admit, it was good to be alive.

Windrider gave him a nod of acknowledgment, then jerked her head suddenly upward to study the sky. Above her, with frantic flashes of red and a tumult of beating blue wings, a flock of turacos swooped down toward the clearing.

"Great Father!" A male turaco landed on a branch near Thorn, craning his crested head urgently toward him. "You must come, come fast! The sky is disappearing!"

"Yes! Yes! Come fast!" echoed his flock. Red flight-feathers flickered above Thorn as he turned to watch the turacos in astonishment. "It's eating the sky, Great Father!"

"What's wrong? What do you mean?" Thorn lurched up onto his hind paws. "What is eating the sky?"

"Come! Come!" The bird took off again, soaring with his flock in agitation.

Windrider stared down silently at Thorn.

"I have no idea what they're saying," murmured Berry, "but it sounds as if those birds need your help." She gave Thorn a wry smile and the gentlest of touches with her forepaw.

"What are you waiting for . . . Great Father?"

CHAPTER NINETEEN

He had to forget about Titan for the moment, Fearless told himself. He would soon be back on the tyrant's trail and hunting him down to do justice—but for now he had a more important job to do. He had to find Thorn and warn him about the golden wolves' new leader. If this new Alpha wolf was even more pitilessly brutal than Ravage had been, it was very bad news for Bravelands. And the Great Father had to know.

Leading Keen, Menace, and Ruthless, Fearless bounded rapidly across the yellow plain toward the watering hole. Perhaps Thorn wasn't there. Perhaps he was at the Great Father Clearing. Perhaps he'd gone to see Berry Crownleaf in Tall Trees. The fact was, Thorn could be anywhere. Yet Fearless had to track him down and pass on this news, however long it took. Gritting his jaws, Fearless stretched out his forelegs in an even faster sprint.

"Slow down, Fearless!" roared Keen from behind him.

Fearless slowed to a jolting trot and glared back over his shoulder. "Why, Keen? We have to find Thorn soon! It's important to get back to tracking Titan!"

"Because the cubs can't keep up, obviously." Keen paused to nudge Menace encouragingly on the flank.

"I'm sure she can manage." All the same, Fearless could see that the cub's paws were dragging on the ground.

"Yes, I can," said Menace wearily, picking up her paws again.

"No. She can't." Keen halted. "Fearless, they're just not as big or fast as we are."

Fearless wrinkled his muzzle. He found it hard to feel sorry for Menace, though Ruthless did look worn-out too, his ears drooping and his shoulders sagging. "I thought you'd be happy to have another mission, Keen," he growled. "We're not looking for Titan right now. Isn't that what you wanted?"

"What I don't want is two cubs dropping dead from exhaustion," snapped Keen, glaring at him. "If they can't keep up, they can't keep up. It's not like they're slacking deliberately."

"They could make more of an effort," retorted Fearless.

"No," growled Keen, "they can't. They're trying their best, believe it or not."

Fearless clenched his fangs. He didn't have an answer, and he knew it was because Keen was right, which irked him. He twisted his head to glare fully back at Keen. "Well, we need to hurry anyway. After this, there's still the matter of Titan, and—whoa."

A lioness had risen from the grass, not a hare's dash ahead, and stood there watching him. Fearless stumbled in shock. Then he froze, staring warily at the lioness. Keen too had halted, stock-still except for his twitching tail.

From the long grass before them, many lions rose to their paws, turning to study the newcomers. This new pride did not look friendly, thought Fearless. Menace and Ruthless had hesitated between Keen and Fearless, panting, trying to keep their eyes on all the strange lions at once.

Except, Fearless realized, they weren't strange at all. He recognized some of these lions.

"Titanpride," he growled.

"Or what's left of them," muttered Keen as he drew closer, shepherding both cubs nearer to Fearless and shielding them with his own body.

There was only one Titanpride lion Fearless wanted to see right now, and that was their leader. But there was no sign of the scarred, black-maned brute among these thin and weary lions.

"They didn't see us till we were almost on top of them," he whispered to Keen.

"We didn't see them either," Keen pointed out dryly.

"But we were walking," said Fearless. "Focusing on getting where we need to be. They just lay there. It's as if they can't be bothered defending their territory."

"Maybe," said Keen, licking his jaws thoughtfully. "But it's not as if they look scared."

The ragged pride was stalking around them now, their

shoulders hunched, heads low and menacing. Fearless bared his fangs in warning.

Then, with a mewl of delight, Menace broke away from Keen and bounded toward the lions.

"Titanpride? This idiot here says you're Titanpride!" The little cub jerked her head disdainfully at Fearless. "Are you? So where is my father? Call my father! Titan, I mean, obviously. I'm Titan and Artful's daughter." She tilted her head arrogantly high and surveyed the former Titanpride. "You've got to fetch my father, I tell you. This idiot wants to kill him. Ha!"

As one, the pride turned their heads to look at her.

"What are you waiting for?" demanded Menace. "Is Daddy out hunting? Well, kill Fearless yourselves, then. He's right here. Defend my father's honor!"

Silence and stillness followed her outburst; only a light breeze stirred the grass.

Fearless stared at the cub in shock. He'd never liked Menace, but this kind of betrayal? It cut as deep as a claw. At his flank he heard Keen give a threatening growl. Fearless moved closer to his friend and they stood shoulder to shoulder, ready to fight for their lives. Ruthless moved loyally to stand at Fearless's other flank and snarled at his father's former pride.

The biggest of the pride's males paced forward, then halted. Fearless could see that his mane was matted and straggly, his dull eyes deep-sunk. The lion stared down at Menace, his whiskers twitching with disdain.

"This is not Titanpride," he growled. "Not any longer. You know me, Gallantbrat. I am Forceful, and this is

Forcefulpride." He jerked his head at the lions behind him, who exchanged bored glances.

"You're Titanpride!" yelped Menace. "You are!"

Forceful shrugged. "Titan's gone, and good riddance to that maniac. He had us attacking grown elephants, the mad fool. Not that he ever joined in himself." He glared at Menace. "What do we care for Titan's honor after he sent so many of us to violent deaths?"

"Indeed, Forceful," snarled Defiant, padding to his side. "We don't want Titan back."

"True," put in Sly, curling her muzzle at Menace, "so throwing your father's name around doesn't mean rat dung to us, you ridiculous kitten."

Menace looked for a long moment as if they'd actually slapped their claws across her face.

Then she tensed every one of her little muscles and shrieked, "Traitors! Cowards! How dare you abandon my father!"

"That's enough of that nonsense, you snotty cub," growled Keen, gripping her tail in his teeth and dragging her back through the grass.

Fearless stared from one lion to another, confounded. So they'd disowned their crazed leader? It was good to hear— and an opportunity, too. . . .

He drew himself up, straightening his forelegs and tossing his head. "Then by the laws of our ancestors, I, Fearless of Fearlesspride, claim this pride of Forceful!"

Keen was staring at him, his jaw slack with surprise. Forceful made a face of amused disbelief.

Fearless cleared his throat, and deepened his roar. "I claim this pride! If Forceful won't fight me for it, who will?"

"I will," yelped Menace angrily, jumping forward through the grass.

Keen slapped his paw onto her tail and yanked her back again.

"Who?" demanded Fearless, scanning the other lions' faces. He was beginning to feel foolish, and he hated it.

"I'll do it," growled Forceful at last. "I, Forceful, fight to defend my pride. From this nonsense."

At Forceful's rump, though, there was a snort of contempt. "What do you mean, 'my' pride?" growled a younger lion.

"Yes, we keep meaning to mention that," drawled Sly. "This isn't Forcefulpride, whatever you tell other animals."

"Right," agreed an unfamiliar lioness. "Nobody ever agreed to that, Forceful."

"I'll fight him for the pride anyway," said Fearless grimly. He stalked forward to square up to Forceful.

"Careful, Fearless!" growled Keen behind him.

Fearless glanced back. Keen and Ruthless both looked far more worried than they had to be. With a grunt of dismissal, Fearless turned back to his opponent.

They might not regard Forceful as their natural leader, but all the former Titanpride lions seemed happy to gather in a circle and watch. Fearless eyed the rangy Forceful, taking his measure as they prowled around each other. The big lion had been strong and vigorous—once. But now his fur was dull and matted, his ribs visible, and there was a deep slash on his shoulder. The wound looked raw and black.

He was still fast, though. Fearless recoiled in shock as Forceful sprang at him. Dodging, Fearless rolled, and Forceful tumbled onto his flank.

Both lions scrambled back to their paws and glared at each other. Forceful was already panting harshly, and his legs looked shaky.

That swift preemptive attack, Fearless realized with relief, had been Forceful's one and only move. Fearless pounced, swiping a paw at Forceful's head. The bigger lion swerved, snarling in annoyance, and lunged for Fearless's shoulder with his jaws, but it wasn't hard to dodge that weary snap. Fearless ducked and slammed his head and shoulders into Forceful's neck. The big lion staggered.

Pressing his advantage, Fearless sprang onto Forceful's back, bearing him down. He sank his jaws into the back of the bigger lion's neck and shoved his head down into the grass.

Forceful went still. His flanks still heaved from the effort, and his paws twitched, but it was over already. Fearless knew it.

"Yield," he snarled through a mouthful of furred muscle.

The lion beneath him sagged, sighed deeply, and rolled limply onto his side. "Fine," he snarled. "Kill me. Fast, if you don't mind."

Fearless hesitated, his eyes narrowing. It was the custom.

"No," he muttered at last. Releasing Forceful, he stepped back, shaking his head as if he were tossing a mane. "No. Titan has wasted too many lives already. There is a new threat to

Bravelands, and all lions must stand together." He gazed out severely at the rest of the pride, who were exchanging doubtful glances. "Accept me formally as your leader, and Forceful lives. I'll make this pride strong and safe, and I give you my oath that I will be fair. That is my offer to you."

"I agree to this," said Forceful, staggering awkwardly to his feet, "and if you lot have any sense, you'll do the same."

Slowly and wearily, one of the lionesses nodded. It was Dignity; Fearless recognized her from his days in Titanpride. "All right," she said, and slumped back onto the grass.

Fearless turned to the others, a little apprehensive, but he kept his fangs clenched and his expression determined. Now that he was looking at the lions properly, he recognized most of them, despite their ragged and half-starved condition.

"Yes," agreed Defiant, nodding.

"It's fine by me." Sly shrugged.

Murmurs of weary acquiescence rippled around the pride.

"Be good to have a decent leader," growled Majestic, "if that's what you are."

"I promise," Fearless told them solemnly. He gave Forceful a nod of respect, then raised his head. "Welcome, lions of Fearlesspride!"

They looked sullen, almost bored, but it didn't matter. Triumph surged in his chest as Fearless surveyed the compliant pride.

He'd taken over Forcefulpride with barely a struggle; he was a leader again, with grown lions under his command. And to make the moment even sweeter, it was Titan's former pride.

No matter that he hadn't fought and killed Titan for it; the day of justice would come for that brute—eventually. What mattered was that he'd begun to fulfill his oath—and he'd done it before his mane even sprouted. Fearless had to repress the urge to roar his victory to the whole of Bravelands.

Oh, how he wished he could see Titan's face when that black-maned tyrant found out.

Menace plunged in among the grown lions, trying to roar her rage; all that she managed was a high-pitched and furious squeal.

"You're pathetic, all of you! How could you betray my father for the idiot here? You're cowards! All of you are cowards!" Spinning on her paws, she glowered at Fearless. "You'll pay for this. You'll be sorry, just wait!"

And before Keen could leap to pin her to the ground once more, Menace had darted between Defiant and Sly, shot into the long grass beyond them, and vanished.

Fearless sucked in an exasperated breath. Then he relaxed. Losing Menace made life easier, after all.

"Fearlesspride, we have work to do," he declared, slapping his paw on the ground. "First, we need to visit the Great Father, Thorn Highleaf. I need to stand side by side with my old friend as we face the threat of the golden wolves."

Forceful nodded. He seemed eager to cooperate with his conqueror, and to have been granted his life. The other lions swished their tails and scratched at their flanks, but they too bobbed their heads.

"It's an odd idea," remarked Honor, an old friend of

Fearless's mother. "It's not as if we even follow the Great Parent. But you're our leader now, so lead on. Which way?"

"To the forest of Tall Trees," declared Fearless. "Let's go!"

One by one, the lions turned and headed for the open plain. Delighted, Fearless watched them file away; he was about to overtake them at a trot and lead them on to glory, when he noticed that Keen hadn't moved. His young friend stood quite still, watching the pride leave, his expression unreadable.

Fearless padded back to Keen and licked his ear happily. "That went well. Aren't you glad I won?"

Keen turned to study him. "Of course I am. I'm proud of you, Fearless." His ears pricked up, and at last he began to walk after the pride. "And it'll be good to be part of a pride again. Normal life: hunting, sleeping, relaxing." He nodded at the broad sweep of grassland, dotted with shady thorn trees, then turned his head to gaze at a herd of impalas grazing in the shimmering distance. "This looks like good territory, despite the state of those lions."

"We'll soon get them hunting efficiently again," agreed Fearless, striding proudly at Keen's side. "And you know what the best part is, Keen? This completely isolates Titan. He doesn't have a pride now; they've abandoned him for me. And I'll have the strength at last to take him on! This development was unexpected, but I think I've made a genius move." He looked modestly at his paws as he walked. "Not that I'm boasting, mind you. Fighting Forceful wasn't even that hard."

He glanced up again, eager for Keen's approval, for some kind of reassurance that, yes, he had fought well, and after all,

Forceful was a much bigger lion. . . .

Keen only stared sidelong at him. His golden eyes were darker than ever, and Fearless couldn't read them at all.

"What is it?" Fearless prodded.

"So it's all about Titan," said Keen. "Again."

Fearless flicked his ears, confused. "Yes, in a sense. I mean, it always—"

"Titan. Titan's defeat and death. It's all you ever think about. I think I only just realized how true that is." Keen looked troubled and somehow very distant, and a shiver of unease ran along Fearless's spine.

"It really isn't," Fearless tried again. "After all, like you said, we'll have a proper pride again."

"For what purpose?" sighed Keen. "To help you beat Titan. When I say it's all you care about, Fearless, I really mean it. The only thing that matters is this vendetta of yours."

Speechless, Fearless stared at his friend. His pawsteps faltered.

"So I've had enough." Keen halted, turned, and faced him properly. "It's gone too far, and I can't do this anymore. I'm sorry, Fearless."

"Sorry . . . for what?" said Fearless hoarsely.

"I'm leaving. I'll join up with Mightypride; it shouldn't take too long to find them. I'll be all right."

"No!" yelped Fearless. He swung around in front of Keen, as if doing that would prevent his friend leaving at all. "You can't. I need you, Keen!"

"I don't think you do, Fearless." Keen hunched his

shoulders. "You need to kill Titan. That's what you need, deep down. And I can't be part of that obsession anymore; I can't keep encouraging you. Don't try to stop me leaving, Fearless." He wrinkled his muzzle wryly. "Let's part on good terms, my friend."

Fearless couldn't speak, not even to say good-bye. He could only watch as his best friend, the lion who had stood by him all this time, turned to pace away across the plain. He didn't know if he could bear it. Fearless watched Keen's diminishing silhouette as the young lion's outline shimmered into the distance and finally was lost in the trembling heat haze.

Fearless gulped. It had happened too fast. He hadn't been able to stop Keen from leaving. But what could he have done? For the first time, a tremor of doubt rippled through him. Was Keen right? What had his vendetta against Titan gained him?

He had lost his sister, Valor, and his first pride. Now his obsession had cost him his dearest friend, Keen Fearlesspride.

Keen Mightypride now . . .

He had to find and kill Titan, he knew. His honor demanded it. Only Titan's destruction could pay for the deaths of his adoptive father, Gallant, and his true father, Loyal.

But by the time Titan lay dead at his paws, Fearless wondered, and the debt was paid—what would he have left?

CHAPTER TWENTY

Craning his neck, rising on his hind paws, Thorn clung to the top-most branch of a mahogany. It was so high, he could feel the treetop swaying slightly in the breeze, and from here he and Spider could survey the expanse of the savannah, the line of its rivers and the dark smudges of distant forests. Agitated, the turaco flock swooped and fluttered around the heads of the two baboons.

"There!" cried a female bird. "There! Do you see?"

Thorn narrowed his eyes. At the farthest edge of the forest, a gray cloud seeped from its heart to billow out over the grass-land; a layer of it was thickening over the canopy. It was not the usual behavior of a rain cloud, thought Thorn, perplexed. But *something's not right.* His fur sprang erect, and a coldness ran down his spine.

"Look!" exclaimed Spider. "Flowers!"

Thorn looked at him askance. How could Spider claim to see flowers from this distance?

But staring back at the distant darkness of the forest, he saw that Spider was right. Flickering orange flowers bloomed through the cloud, licking out greedily before retreating. Within the deepest shadows of the trees, something glowed. How could flowers shine like the sun? Above his head, the turacos were rasping and cawing and grunting in distress.

"The fruit in those trees was good!"

"Fine trees. Good bushes. So many berries."

"All gone now, all gone!"

The racket was distracting. Thorn shook his head, then leaned forward. It was so hard to see, even from here, but there was something terrible and fascinating about that flickering glow. *What is it?* He leaned out farther, easing his grip on the branch. . . .

A hand grabbed his armpit, and he felt himself yanked back so hard, he fell back against the thin trunk. Spider craned over him, wagging a finger.

"Don't fall out, Thorn-friend!"

"I wasn't going to," objected Thorn.

"Yes." Spider nodded confidently. "You were."

Actually, thought Thorn, looking again at the thin branch he'd been holding, *maybe I was.*

"The cloud is called smoke," Spider declared, waving a paw toward the dark billowing fog. "It sheds little white feathers, and their name is ash."

Thorn stared at Spider. "This is bad. Do you think the

fire-plant caught Tendril and her troop?"

Spider shrugged and nodded. "Spider reckons so."

"It is the hot flower!" a turaco cawed to Thorn, its red underwing feathers flashing. "The hot flower that kills!"

Spider glanced up at the bird and mimicked its call. "Huh-roo, huh-roo! Ruh!" The bird shot him a confused look before soaring away.

"Since it attacked Tendril's troop, the fire plant's had all that time to grow bigger," said Thorn, appalled at the thought. "I didn't know the flowers could last so long!"

"Oh, they last forever if they get the chance," Spider told him knowledgeably. "They nurse their warmth and they kindle in the twigs and dry leaves and they grow. This looks like a disaster, if you want Spider's opinion."

"Spider knows a lot more about fire than Thorn does," Thorn told him grimly. "So I believe you. I've seen enough. Let's go, quickly!"

Heart thrashing, he scuttled backward down the mahogany trunk and bolted through the trees in the rough direction of the smoke. Spider's pawsteps were loud, crunching in the forest litter behind him.

"What's Thorn going to do?" called Spider. "I don't know what you can do."

"I don't know either," muttered Thorn. "I just need to get there."

At least his mind could go even faster than his racing feet. A creature was bolting from the forest onto the grassland. Scanning ahead, Thorn stretched out his consciousness toward it, and he was inside his head before he fully recognized what it was: a little dik-dik. He felt its panic and desperation, the heat of the fire on its rump, a sharp rasping pain as smoke filled its throat. Sparks fell all around, igniting dry grass blades that wizened and blackened. His small antelope heart hammered in his chest.

Jerking himself free of the dik-dik, Thorn clenched his jaw and put on a burst of speed, bounding through the trunks. Even in his head, the fire had been terrifying—and how many creatures were truly there, with the fire-flowers, in that forest?

As he sprinted across a clearing and shoved through a tangle of lantana, he could suddenly see the catastrophe far more clearly. The red fire-flowers bloomed out of control, licking up trees and along branches, devouring the leaves they touched, shriveling even the nearby ones to charred husks. Smoke poured between the tree trunks, looking as solid as a living animal. The fire roared like a lion, and it never ran out of breath; the closer Thorn drew, the more deafeningly it bellowed. But through its din, he could hear the death squeals of tiny trapped creatures.

Animals galloped and thundered out of the forest, stampeding over one another in their desperation to escape. A bushbuck almost trampled Thorn, but swerved at the last moment, its eyes wild and white.

Thorn scrabbled to a halt, breathing hard. Smoke stung his throat, and he spat out the bitter taste. But he was Great Father. Animals of Bravelands were trapped and dying. He had to go toward the flames.

Shutting his eyes, he dashed forward. But once he was within the smoke, he could hardly open them; it bit and burned, and his eyeballs seemed to dry up in his skull. The air around him was black, and hotter than any natural weather he had ever known. Suddenly there was something else in his face: a buffeting of huge black wings.

"Back!" screeched Windrider, her flock flapping behind her. "Go back, Great Father!"

"I can't," gritted Thorn, trying ineffectually to swipe her away. "Let me through!"

The vultures' broad wings clattered against leaves and charred branches. "You could die!" rasped Windrider.

"I have to take that risk." Ducking, Thorn darted past her.

Fire bloomed suddenly in front of his paws, and he dodged, only to see another patch burst into life, swallowing a grass tussock in an instant. A fallen log smoldered, then erupted in flame. Thorn staggered back, gasping for breath in the thick, scorching air. Fire swarmed up a nearby fig, twisting through its contorted limbs.

From behind, Spider grabbed his arm. "We shouldn't go in!"

"I have to!"

"Then Spider should put out the fire." Spider crouched, trying to pat one of the flickering flowers.

"No!" It was Thorn's turn to pull Spider away. "It can kill, Spider—you know that! And I need your help!"

More panicked creatures stampeded out of the burning forest, screaming with fright, and Thorn ducked and pulled Spider down with him.

"That's the right direction to run," observed Spider, watching them flee toward the open grassland.

"No." Thorn summoned all his courage and determination and bounded forward through the smoking tree trunks. With a loud sigh of exasperation, Spider followed at his heels.

In a confined clearing, a family of zebras stampeded in a wild circle, bucking and rearing, neighing and squealing and pawing the ground. Thorn raced toward them and skidded to a halt before the biggest mare.

"That way!" he pointed. "Don't stop running till you're beyond the trees!"

The mare was too terrified even to speak. Whinnying to her herd, she led them at a frantic gallop toward the way Thorn had shown her. Rats, ground squirrels, mice: they all scuttled and scurried after the zebras, not stopping even when some of their companions were crushed beneath pounding hooves.

A monkey burst from the bushes ahead of Thorn, her tail and fur smoldering and crackling with greedy flecks of fire; her eyes were crazed with pain and fear. Thorn had to crash into the terrified creature to bring her to a halt.

"Spider!" he yelled, trying to hold the monkey while avoiding the flames. "What can we do?"

"Knock her over!" shouted Spider.

It seemed wrong, but Thorn did not have time to argue. He sprang onto the monkey's back, forcing her to the ground while she fought and squealed. Spider loped to his side, his paws crammed with damp earth; he began to smear it on the monkey's burning fur. Grabbing up more clods, he did it again.

It seemed to quell the flames. Thorn copied Spider, snatching up lumps of earth and grass, crushing them against the monkey's hide till only a few smoking trails were left.

Thorn rolled off her. "Go!" he screamed. "Follow the zebra tracks!"

She sprang up, and with a screech she bolted.

"Thorn?" Spider glanced anxiously toward the heart of the fire. "What's that?"

Even over the roar of the fire, Thorn could hear it: a crashing thunder of huge feet. He had barely time to take a breath before an elephant smashed through the burning trees.

Thorn recognized him. Rock! This was Sky's betrothed mate, the elephant who had joined the Great Herd to battle Stinger and Titan. But there was no time for surprise, no time to ask Rock what had brought him here. The massive, dark-hided bull cradled a tiny dik-dik between his tusks and trunk. *The one whose mind I entered*, realized Thorn, *I'm sure of it!* This fire must have almost caught up with it before Rock arrived.

The dik-dik panted, its tongue lolling, but when Rock set it gently on the ground, it sprang to its hooves and fled. Rock nodded to Thorn.

"Great Father. Forgive me, but I can't stop. More need my help." He turned, and Thorn saw that his flanks and hind-quarters were mottled with raw red burns.

"Rock! Wait!" Thorn bounded forward. He glanced swiftly around at the trees. There was a pattern to this terrible flower's growth, and he thought he was beginning to work it out.

"What?" said Rock impatiently, glancing back into the forest. "I mean, I'm sorry. But I have to go!"

"The flames," said Thorn quickly, nodding as he saw the fire swarm along another tree and leap to the next. "It travels—look. It needs to follow a trail. It has to touch things to grow on them!"

"And?" demanded Rock.

"We must deny it a path," cried Thorn, smacking his paws together. "I think we can stop this thing in its tracks. With your help!"

Rock blinked, shook his ears, then nodded. "Yes. All right. There's sense in what you say. But where is its next path? Who can tell?"

"See the trees? It follows the trees." Thorn pointed at the flames crawling along branches, swallowing leaves. "Knock enough of them down—a row of them, or—no, better, a circle! Then it will have nowhere to grow."

"A break in the fire-path?" Rock's ears flapped forward with eager desperation. "It's worth a try, Great Father!"

"But even you can't do it alone," said Thorn. "Sky and her herd—I know they're on migration. But do you know where they are, Rock? Are they close?"

Rock had already placed his huge head against a tree and was shoving hard, his great feet raking channels in the earth as he sought purchase. "I know exactly where they are," he grunted. "The Plain of Hearts. It lies below Baboon Mountain, in the south."

"I saw them in my mind, near a mountain like a baboon!"

exclaimed Thorn. "I'll send for them!"

"But that will take too long!" Rock glanced back toward the fire, his eyes wild.

"Not the way I'm going to do it," growled Thorn. Twisting, he sprinted back to the edge of the forest, leaping burning branches and smoking tufts of grass.

"Windrider!" he yelled.

She stooped instantly, soaring down to his side and hopping to a halt. She tilted her head and eyed him—with some disapproval, Thorn knew. The vultures hadn't wanted him to go near the burning forest at all.

"I have no time for a scolding, Windrider," he told her. "I need your help—Bravelands needs it. Summon the elephants!"

CHAPTER TWENTY-ONE

"I didn't want to know," Sky told the gathered herds of elephants. "I was afraid to find out what had happened to River Marcher. But now I'm glad I did. It was a terrible accident—an awful tragedy, but an accident. No elephant intended to kill her, not even in the Rage." Her head drooped with sadness. "That's the truth."

A high, hot sun beat down on the herds as they stood listening to Sky's tale, but no elephant complained or turned to hurry for the shade of the cliff walls. Apart from twitching their tails to swat flies or stretching their ears wide for coolness, they all remained still and somber, their dark eyes thoughtful.

A tall and rangy matriarch moved forward from the listening herds. "I am Mahogany Marcher," she told the herds, "as you know. River was one of us." She turned back to Sky. "I knew her from the time she was a calf. I speak for my whole family when I say that we thank you. We know River's fate now, and we know her resting place. It will be hard, but we will retrieve all her bones from where the cheetahs found them. We will take River to the Plain of Our Ancestors, where she belongs."

Sky dipped her head. "I know she would be glad," she said softly. "Her spirit waits for you."

There was a stirring to Sky's left. Elephants shifted out of Boulder's path as he stepped forward, his eyes lowered.

"And I too speak for my herd," he rumbled. "We are sorry, Sky, for the way we treated Rock. We were wrong. I especially should have known."

Yes. You should. Sky fought to suppress her anger; Boulder looked so remorseful. Now was not the time to remonstrate with him.

"You were in the grip of the Rage, brother," murmured Sky, her throat tight. "I saw what happened. Neither you nor Rock was thinking clearly, that was obvious. I daresay it would have been hard to remember details, even at the best of times."

"All the same, I rushed to judge Rock, and so did my brothers." Boulder butted Sky gently with his trunk. "And we are sorry. We have caused you—and Rock—needless heartache." He lifted his head and angled his ears toward River's family. "To you also, Mahogany, we owe an apology. I declare before all the herds that I am so sorry for the pain I caused the Marcher herd, however unwittingly. My sister Sky is wrong about one thing: I am partly to blame. I will live with that, and I will never forget River."

Mahogany nodded. "We accept your apology, Boulder. But it was, in truth, a terrible accident. If anything killed her, it was the ravine itself."

Slowly, subdued and thoughtful, the herds dispersed. Boulder, though, lingered at Sky's side. She could sense his discomfort, and he seemed to find it hard to speak; he opened his mouth, but he only gave an agonized groan. It took him several attempts to form words.

"Sky, I . . . I mean it," he rumbled at last. "I should never have tried to keep you and Rock apart. I didn't know enough, and I assumed too much."

Pity for him warred with resentment over her broken relationship with Rock; she couldn't help it. "You truly didn't know how River's death happened." Sky took a breath. "What you did know was that you were in the grip of the Rage, that you couldn't remember anything properly! So why did you tell me with such certainty that Rock killed River?"

"I was trying to protect you," he mumbled.

"I can protect myself. Haven't I proved that, over and over again? I don't need you to defend me!" Sky drew a shaking breath, trying to control the anger in her voice. "And I don't need you to make decisions for me."

"I give you my word, it won't happen again." He bowed his head to hers. "Are you truly angry with me?"

Sky took a pace back. "Because of you, I've lost Rock. I drove him away because of what you said. I loved him, and now he's gone. That's why I'm angry, brother."

"I wish I could change what happened. I wish I could take back all that I said." He scuffed the ground with a foot.

She hesitated, trying to find words. But she couldn't forgive Boulder, not yet. So what else was there to say to him?

Glancing up, she caught a glimpse of a black dot, high in the blue arc of the sky. She squinted against the light. The black dot became several; then, as they dropped lower, they became broad, flying shapes. A flock . . . In moments she could make out their wings. The vultures stooped, angling their flight feathers to land.

Leaving Boulder behind, Sky trotted anxiously toward them. The largest of them was an elegant bird, with vast wings, a noble, aged face, and black bright eyes that locked at once on Sky.

"Windrider!"

The great vulture's talons touched the ground, and she folded her wings and hopped to meet Sky. In her beak she held a thin, blackened bone. She dropped it at Sky's feet.

Sky started. Leaning close, she peered at the bone and reached out her trunk to sniff. It smelled bitter, acrid. She glanced up, and her eyes met Windrider's. The vulture nodded once.

With a deep breath, Sky curled her trunk around the bone's charred surface.

She was a warthog, a frightened and desperate one. Panic buzzed through her blood like a mosquito swarm, as she ran squealing from some terror behind her. Her body felt heavy, her legs too stumpy; she could not run fast enough. What could she do? *Only run! Run!*

But where to? The monstrous black smoke billowed behind her, and ahead were only hungry, scorching yellow tongues. They licked around her hooves, and she stumbled, screeching with terror. A solid burst of heat erupted at her flank, searing her flesh, and her bristling fur was being eaten now, and there was nowhere to go, nowhere to run, no escape—

Sky, tearing herself from the vision, almost stumbled to her knees with the horror. Panting, she tossed the bone aside. She could still taste ash and smoke, she could still feel the unbearable, burning pain in her parched throat.

"What's happening?" Her voice was high-pitched and breathy with fear. How she wished she could still understand Skytongue.

Windrider only stared, her black eyes intense.

"Great Father," Sky gasped. "Does he know? Of course he does! He needs my help?"

Windrider dipped her head.

"No!" cried Sky. "I've been gone too long. I should never have left him!"

Windrider made no response. Turning away, Sky cantered urgently back toward the herds. Raising her trunk, she gave a blaring trumpet of summons.

Heads and trunks lifted, and ears flapped forward. One by one, the elephants turned toward her, startled.

"A fire," she declared, her voice shaking. "Fire has come to Bravelands!"

Mahogany strode forward, as did Flint and another big male.

"Fire?" asked Mahogany. "Sky Strider, you are still young. You have never seen fire."

"Don't dismiss her," rumbled Flint. "Sky is wise for her years."

"I've heard about fire," insisted Sky. "Great Mother described it to me and warned me about its dangers. Fire is a deadly thing, isn't it? And one that can't be fought."

"Indeed," said Flint, nodding. "All that living things can do is run from it."

"Well, fire has taken hold in Bravelands again," said Sky, craning desperately forward. They had to believe her! "The Great Father needs our help."

The older elephants exchanged skeptical glances, and Mahogany looked doubtful. "What Flint says is true. There is no fighting fire."

"It's too dangerous even to try," put in another matriarch, shaking her ears.

"It's not as if the Great Parent is an elephant anymore," rumbled a young bull. "We don't have the same obligation to a baboon. It's not our job to protect Bravelands—it's Thorn Highleaf's."

"That's not true!" exclaimed Sky. "The elephants have always been the protectors of Bravelands. It doesn't matter if the Great Parent isn't an elephant—the Great Spirit lives in Thorn, just as it did in Great Mother! Our loyalty and duty are to the Spirit, and Thorn has it within him."

"Sky is right." To her surprise, Boulder thundered up to her side and turned to face the herds. "My sister here—she carried the Great Spirit for moons, for seasons! If any creature knows what is owed to the Great Spirit, it's Sky."

This time, as the elephants looked at one another, there was a touch of shame in their expressions. A few stared at the ground; others nodded solemnly.

"Very well," agreed Mahogany. "When you put it like that, Boulder, it makes sense."

"We need to follow Sky," Flint told them all sternly. "When it comes to the Great Spirit, this is an elephant who knows what she's talking about."

"I have known Sky since her mother birthed her," declared Comet, striding forward. "Great Spirit or no Great Spirit, she herself has wisdom far beyond her years. I trust her word."

Sky gazed at her matriarch, hoping the depth of her gratitude showed in her eyes. "Thank you, Comet," she whispered.

"It is agreed, then: we will go with her." A huge, dark-hided female nodded. "All of my herd."

"And mine," said another matriarch.

"We will stand with you!"

"We go with Sky!"

More calls came from every direction, every herd offering their strength to help Sky in her battle against this new and deadly threat.

"The Walker bull herd follows Sky Strider," bellowed an

old male, the last to speak. "What do you need us to do?"

Sky felt her muscles sag with relief. "Thank you," she rumbled. "Thank you, all."

Then she raised her trunk and made her declaration in a ringing trumpet that echoed from the cliff walls.

"Follow me now, all of you. As fast as we can travel. We will go to the Great Father's aid!"

CHAPTER TWENTY-TWO

The fire was a breathtaking sight. Sky stood with the herds behind her, staring in awed horror at the flames as they ravaged the forest, turning ancient and venerable trees to black skeletons, burning the bushes in swift infernos, sending columns of thick black smoke upward to blot out even the sun. Flecks of ash and shriveled bits of wood drifted down onto Sky's ears and shoulders; even at a distance, she could feel the force of the heat against her hide. Her eyes watered, and her throat stung, and yet she still stood on the edge of the grass plain. What it must be like within the forest itself, Sky could hardly bear to imagine.

The herds behind her were shifting, milling, blaring cries of distress.

"We can do nothing!" bellowed an old bull. "This is a hopeless mission."

"It's an insane one," agreed a female, pulling her yearling calf closer.

Sky heard more anxious mutterings.

"We should leave."

"Yes, now."

"Not even elephants can help the Great Father. Not in this inferno."

Sky swallowed hard. She couldn't blame the other elephants. She had never seen fire before, and now that she was witnessing it for herself, she had no wish to go closer. Deep in her gut, instinct churned, and she understood its almost irresistible command: *Run. Just run.*

She shook her ears hard and tossed her trunk. "No. We have to go on. Follow me!"

A small brown shape was rushing toward her across the ash-strewn grassland. "Sky! Thank the Great Spirit, you're here!"

"Thorn!" She reached for him with her trunk, but after hugging it quickly he brushed it gently aside.

"I'm fine," he told her, "so far. But we need you elephants, badly. I have a plan that I think might work."

"You do?" Sky blinked and swallowed. Thorn's optimism was a wonder, she knew, but surely even he couldn't hope to conquer this enemy? Sky felt her heart stutter and lurch.

"I want to clear the fire's path," Thorn told her.

"Clear its . . . ?" began Sky, bewildered.

"Yes. It's a flower that eats things. Spider, explain the plan to the elephants!"

Spider bounded up to stand next to Thorn, nervously clenching and unclenching his paws. "We reckon . . ." he said. "Spider and Thorn, well . . . we reckon if the fire can't eat, it can't move. So if we take things away, see, it'll have nothing to eat. It'll die." He cocked his head. "But it has to have absolutely nothing to eat, nothing at all."

"Won't it just stop anyway, when it reaches the grassland?" asked Comet anxiously.

Spider shook his head and poked ash out of his ear. "Nope. It'll eat the grass, the flowers, the whole savannah. It eats everything. We must break its way. A fire-break!"

"The Great Father is right about how fire travels." Flint nodded. "I've seen it myself. But I would never have thought to clear its path."

"It's certainly an interesting plan," rumbled Boulder, "if he and Spider are right about the way the flames travel. Let's get to work!"

"Good." With a plan to accomplish, Sky felt suddenly more sure of herself. "Mahogany and Flint—each of you take some strong elephants and some weaker ones. It seems to me that if this is going to work, the fire's food has to be removed equally, all around the forest where it was born."

Spider nodded. "Otherwise it'll just change direction and go the other way. The way where there is something for it to eat. Spider knows. He's seen it happen."

"Boulder and I will stay here." Sky felt hope and excitement rise in her chest. "We'll try to starve the fire on this border of the forest."

Leaving the other elephants to organize themselves, Sky trotted toward the edge of the wood. She raised her trunk, seeking scents, but thick fumes clogged her trunk immediately, and she felt ash scald its sensitive interior. Shuddering, she felt her feet burning; the ground itself was hot.

We must beat this thing!

Choosing a tree, she butted her head against its trunk and began to shove. Her feet slipped in the churned earth, but she found purchase and strained. Hot feathers of ash drifted onto her ears; flapping them away, she tried to beat down the rising fear. This would be just like creating the Great Father Clearing, she told herself firmly.

Except for the deadly flames advancing toward us . . .

The roots of the thorn tree lurched suddenly out of the ground, with an eruption of mud and dead leaves. Sky rolled the fallen tree out of the way, kicking and pushing it away from its neighbors, and began on the next. A little way to her side, Boulder was already starting to push at his third tree.

"This old kigelia," he trumpeted to her after a while. "It'll take two of us. Come here!"

Despite her aching chest and legs, Sky knew she simply could not be exhausted. It wasn't an option. Gritting her teeth, she lurched to Boulder's side and stood shoulder to shoulder with him, shoving hard on the tree.

As Sky worked next to her brother, she barely had time to notice Thorn. But she was vaguely aware that he and Spider were dashing in and out of the forest, guiding animals to safety, urging them to hurry. Always they came out with some small creature: a mouse cupped in a paw, a ground squirrel cowering on furred shoulders. Thorn's energy never seemed to flag.

And neither will mine, she thought.

Her head pounded, her trunk was in agony, her shoulders ached. Everything ached. Sky's tormented throat was harsh and dry, and the soft inner skin of her trunk felt scalded. But the sight of Thorn, unflinchingly returning again and again to the forest, filled her with hope and courage. Even the terrified animals Thorn rescued seemed inspired by his determination; their eyes glowed with gratitude, and some, when they had recovered their breath and their strength, ran back with him to help others.

As she glanced at her brother, their eyes locked, and Sky nodded. She could see he felt the same. And while she had no way of making out the elephants on the other side of the forest, Sky knew without a doubt that they were still there, working desperately, making the same effort she did for Bravelands.

Turning to the next tree and the next, she and Boulder struggled on, shoving, tearing, ripping.

Thorn appeared from the bushes ahead of Sky, sagging into a crouch for a moment as he regained his breath. He glanced up at her.

"It's going well so far, Sky," he gasped, "I think."

Panting, Sky took a moment's respite to survey the woodland around her. The ground was scraped clear of brush in a big circle around Sky and her brother. The earth was churned mud, the grass beaten into pulp, and trees young and old had been smashed down. Tomorrow, Sky knew, this would be a matter of sadness, especially for the creatures who had made their home here.

But right now, the destruction of the forest's borders was beginning to look like a triumph.

"Thorn, how did you know where to find us?" asked Sky. She paused as she tore at a clump of thin saplings. "The elephants, I mean. In your vision you saw the baboon-shaped mountain, but you didn't even know where it was."

"Your friend told me," he said.

"My friend?"

Thorn watched her intently. "Rock."

"Rock?" Her heart stuttered and lurched. "Rock was here?"

Thorn nodded, reaching out to pat her trunk. "I found him rescuing animals, Sky. He kept going back. I told him not to go so deep into the trees, but he was determined. Last time I saw him . . ." Thorn hesitated. "He went back in to find a monkey family that was trapped."

"And . . ." Sky cleared her throat. It felt hotter and rougher than ever, and she could barely get the words out. "You . . . you haven't seen him since then?"

Slowly, Thorn shook his head. "I'm sorry, Sky. That was some time ago. I'm sorry."

"No!" Sky's voice returned to her and she gave a great, harsh cry of despair. "No!"

Boulder hooked his trunk over her shoulders, stroking her frantically. "Oh, Sky—"

She shook herself, dislodging her brother's trunk, and

stumbled away from him. "There isn't time," she said hoarsely. "There isn't time for grief. We have to keep working. . . ."

The smoke was growing worse, but Sky no longer cared. Her eyes streamed as she tore and shoved violently at the trees. She was dimly aware of the huge bodies of other elephants, away to her left flank, becoming visible as the trees and the undergrowth were cleared. But she could focus only on her own mission. Intently, she hauled down trunks and branches, trying to think of nothing but the job: putting an end to the fire that, it seemed, had taken her beloved Rock.

But at last, a sound did penetrate the chaos and her own misery: the deep trumpeting of a male elephant in distress.

Sky jerked her head up, ears flapping forward. It was him. *Rock!*

CHAPTER TWENTY-THREE

Sky drew a deep breath of clear air and charged toward the trees. Behind her, Boulder gave a trumpet of alarm.

"Sky, you can't!"

"I must!" she cried over her shoulder. "Boulder! Stay here, please! I have to look for him!" Without waiting for his answer, she plunged into the forest. At once she felt the scalding heat of the fire on her hide, the choking smoke in her throat.

A judder of terror went along her spine as she thundered on. This was crazy. She could die.

No. She would not think that way. If there was a chance, she had to look. She couldn't lose him again; not when there was still life in her body. Gasping, she raised her trunk, blaring Rock's name over and over again. Smoldering saplings blocked her way, and clusters of leaves burst into flame; she

swung her tusks and trunk and smashed them aside. Tendrils
of smoke coiled around her legs.

"Rock! Where are you?"

Above her there was a crashing rumble, and Sky glanced
up just in time to dodge the blazing branch that collapsed
toward her. Panting, turning, she blinked in the thick fumes
and coughed violently.

"Rock!"

More flames, more smoke. Sky knew how close she must
be to the heart of the inferno: the blast of the heat on her skin
was almost intolerable. She could almost feel her hide begin to
shrivel and char, and her mouth and trunk felt thick with soot.

From above came a deep cracking sound, then a shower of
hot ash. Sky looked up in time to see a huge branch, aglow
with fire, falling right toward her. She lurched away, but not
quickly enough, and the weight of it smashed over her back.
Her knees buckled and she stumbled through a rain of cin-
ders, crashing into a blazing lantana bush and collapsing onto
her side.

She lay huddled in the center of a ruined glade. All was
shifting cloud and licking flame. She tried to stand, but it felt
like her legs were sapped of strength. Just as in her vision of
the comet, she was weak as a newborn calf, staring up at the
trails of fire jumping between the branches and turning the
leaves of the trees to black.

As the heat grew, so did Sky's despair. There was nothing
she could do now. No way to escape. All she could hope was

the smoke overcame her before the terrifying fire. She thought of her herd, of Horizon and Breeze, Comet and the others. She thought of Flint, and Boulder, and the males. Would they look for her in the cooling ashes? If they found her, there'd be nothing left but charred bones, left to turn to dust, far from the elephant graveyard on the Plain of Our Ancestors. The worst thing of all was that she hadn't even found Rock. Hadn't managed to speak to him one last time. Would their spirits ever meet? Would she ever be able to make amends?

The ground began to shake, with a regular pounding that felt like the heartbeat of Bravelands itself, coming closer until it vibrated through her. Sky blinked her eyes against the stinging heat, and the breath she drew was more smoke than air. *Is this the end? Great Spirit—take me. . . .*

Then the pounding stopped suddenly as a shadow fell over her. Something touched her side, and a croaking voice rumbled close to her ear. "Sky? Is that you? Sky!"

She managed to turn her head, but her mind was slow to understand until she laid eyes on the speaker. Rock's massive head bent over her—his trunk gently touching the base of hers.

No. It can't be. . . .

It had to be some final, desperate vision—her mind playing tricks as she faded from life. Sky felt her head reel. It was a strange vision indeed.

On Rock's shoulders crouched a family of monkeys, hanging on to his singed and ripped ears for dear life. And in his trunk, the bull cradled a tiny baboon. It had huge pale eyes, wide with terror. Perhaps it had been bitten by the fire; there was a splayed tuft of black fur, like a baobab leaf, on the crown of its head.

"Sky, you have to stand," said Rock. He nudged her.

"Too weak," she mumbled.

"No, you're not," said Rock. "You're the strongest elephant I've ever met."

She felt his trunk snake under her foreleg and prize her up a little. She managed to get one foot on the ground. A trunk creaked and snapped somewhere to the left, and a great wave of heat swept over them, following by a cloud of black and blinding smoke.

"On your feet!" said Rock with more force. More desperation and fear too. As he heaved with his trunk, she pressed herself upright on shaky legs, only to fall against him. He stood his ground, supporting her.

Sky hardly recognized the clearing in which she stood. Fire blocked the way on every side. The scorched earth was littered with black tangles of branch and log and trunk. And as she walked, she feared every step might be her last. She knew if she fell now, no amount of encouragement would get her upright again.

"Follow my lead!" said Rock.

Sky kept her trunk in constant contact with his shoulders as he guided her through the dark and smoky shambles. Sky coughed violently again, feeling panic rise to constrict her throat. Her head swam. For all she knew, they could be heading deeper into the heart of the flames.

Another creature stepped out of the burning tangle ahead of them. Sky gasped. She had not known she could feel any greater terror, but this horrible apparition froze her where she stood.

It was a wolf; that was all she knew. But its golden fur was gone, burned away to leave only charred black skin. It stared at Sky.

How is it even alive—?

The wolf, unhurried, opened its jaws very wide. Its fangs gleamed startling white against the blackness of its burned throat. Those awful jaws went on opening, impossibly wide, and Sky glimpsed something within them: a flash of golden fur.

But it wasn't the wolf's pelt, of course it wasn't. Even fire did not turn creatures inside out, she told herself as terror squeezed her heart. No. It was the face of a lion, its dark eyes brilliant and mesmerizing.

As swiftly as it had appeared, the lion vanished. And then, so did the wolf.

"Sky! Hurry!" said Rock. "It's isn't far now."

Sky stared at the empty space, flabbergasted. It was a vision!

Where the wolf had stood, the air looked thinner, cleaner. Sky could make out the murky, twisted shapes of half-familiar trees and bushes.

Rock urged her on with his trunk, and Sky summoned all her last reserves, stumbling toward the lighter air.

Dimly, she was aware of great shapes rushing to meet her:

Comet, Star, Breeze. She couldn't greet them; she couldn't even hold herself upright any longer.

"Rock?" Sky's mouth tasted bitter and smoky, and it hurt her throat to call out, but she had to know if what she had seen had been real.

A trunk stroked her head, and she heard Comet's soothing voice. "He's fine, Sky. You did it. You found him."

"No," she mumbled. "He found me."

Her vision was blurred, clouded with ash. She did not know how long she had lain in a daze of pain and exhaustion, but it could not have been long; the fire still raged and crackled behind her, its heat fierce against her rump.

With what seemed more effort than for anything else she had done, Sky raised her head. Nearby, Horizon stood trembling between Breeze's legs. The baby's hide was pallid with ash, and her eyelashes were singed, but she seemed otherwise unharmed. Rock waited at a distance, surrounded by other elephants. Yes, he was really there. His hide was very pale, but much of it was marred with red, black-rimmed patches of charred skin. One of his ears was badly torn. The baby baboon now sat across his back, splayed in sleep.

Thank the Great Spirit—he's alive!

Slowly, painfully, Sky staggered to her feet. She stood swaying, with Comet and Breeze flanking her for support.

Those long tusks. Those green eyes, bright with terror and determination. That pale hide—but it was not pale, of course.

It was a dark gray hide, coated with ash. Sky stumbled forward toward her betrothed.

Rock's green eyes opened wide. He hesitated, swaying, then reached out, twining his trunk around hers. An almost unbearable surge of joy rocked her where she stood. She pressed her head to Rock's, desperate to feel the solidity and warmth of his living body.

"It's really you!"

"Sky," he murmured. His voice was so feeble, she barely heard it, but he had spoken her name with deep love.

"Rock, I'm sorry. I know now that River's death was an accident. I saw what happened. I'm so sorry. So very, very sorry . . ."

"Hush," he croaked. "It doesn't matter."

"It does," she moaned. "Will you forgive me, Rock? Will you be my life-mate as you were before? Can we start again? Please."

He rubbed his head desperately against hers.

"It's all I want, Sky. All I ever needed or wanted."

The happiness drove out all her pain and exhaustion. Resting her head against him, Sky thought: *I'll never leave you again. Never drive you away.*

Boulder trotted toward them, and they broke apart a fraction.

"We're done!" he rumbled. "We did it, Sky, all of us. A ring is cleared around the fire." He glanced uneasily at the forest and the pall of black smoke that swathed it. "Now we can only wait. And hope the Great Father's plan was a good one."

Sky stood with her brother and Rock and watched, her

legs still shaking, her heart in her throat. The other elephants gathered too. The cleared track that surrounded the forest was a wasteland of smashed twigs, excavated red earth, and great ruts and craters where elephant feet had strained to hold on as they felled the forest. The broken trees themselves had been rolled aside; they lay outside the ring of destruction, their leaves shriveled and wrinkled. In any other circumstances it would have been a heartbreaking sight, but right now, hope stirred inside Sky's breast. She shifted closer to Boulder, her heart stuttering.

On the other side of the devastation, the flames raged like living things—furious, frustrated creatures, devouring all that was left to them. Sky held her breath. If the fire crossed that new line of wasteland, it had all been for nothing.

But it didn't. A few sparks kindled into life in the litter that was left, but they were extinguished quickly, burning to nothing. A jet of fire roared out from a burning fig tree, as if stretching for a hold on the next; but it found nothing, and it subsided, sputtering.

The forest within the elephants' fire-break blazed and burned, but however hard they raged, the flames could not cross. Sky closed her eyes and sagged with exhausted relief.

"It worked," whispered Boulder.

"So many animals must have died," said Comet sadly.

"We did what we could," added Boulder.

On Rock's back, the small baboon lifted its head, before falling back into slumber.

Talk of the poor animals trapped in the fire crystallized in

Sky's mind her vision of the burned ghost wolf. It had seemed to show her the way out—a spirit guide leading her from the forest, but now that she dwelled on it once more, a tiny shudder of foreboding went through her gut. A lion, bursting forth from a wolf. It was more than strange. . . .

And with a lurch of horror, Sky knew exactly what it meant. "No . . ." she muttered.

"What is it?" said Rock. "What's the matter, Sky?"

She turned to her beloved, struggling to find the words to express the terror in her heart.

CHAPTER TWENTY-FOUR

Something cool splashed onto Thorn's fur, and he glanced up. Another drop of water fell, and then another, hitting his snout and trickling down his jaw. In moments the spatters of rain had become a steady downpour, and he opened his jaws in delight, letting fresh rain fall onto his tongue and run down his parched throat. Then a horrible thought struck him.

"Rain! It'll feed the fire-plant!" he gasped. "It will start to grow again. . . ."

"No!" shouted Nut, pounding the ground with his paws in delight. "Look—there—it's killing the fire-plant!" He pointed at the devastated forest.

Thorn stared in wonder. Where the rain lashed down, the fire-flowers sputtered, spat, and dwindled to wet-looking smoke.

The stench of charred wood was still overwhelming, but

the fire-flowers were dying swiftly. Thorn could hear their last angry hisses as rain drenched the wasteland of burned trees. A pall of smoke still hung heavy over the land, but it was starting to dissipate, torn to wisps by the freshening breeze. The smoke, thought Thorn with relief, looked far less threatening when set against the great black storm clouds that raced across the sky.

Exhausted animals were gathering around him. A big female elephant swayed, and her mate shouldered against her to support her. Sodden creatures huddled in small groups, their fur gray and bedraggled; Thorn saw baboons, monkeys, a couple of zebras. Many of them had raw scars and fresh scorch marks on their hides, but they all wore expressions of triumph and happiness. Many must have died, Thorn realized—he had seen their charred corpses among the trees—but many, too, had been saved, and many had returned to the terrifying inferno to help rescue others. Today had been a terrible day for Bravelands—but also an inspiring one.

"Great Father saved us!" neighed a zebra, pawing the scorched ground.

"Yes! Thank you, Thorn!" chorused a group of baboons.

"Praise to the Great Father," whispered a weary-looking vervet. She was hunched, her paws dangling, as if she was too tired to stand upright. "If it hadn't been for Thorn, many more would have died."

"And for the elephants," added a rhino, his pale leathery hide almost white with ash. He nodded respectfully toward Boulder and Comet and the herds. "Without their strength, this blaze could not have been contained."

"Yes!" declared Thorn, rising onto his hind paws. He ached all over, but he didn't care; the plan had worked. "The elephants have our endless thanks—but the fact is, you all contributed. All the creatures of Bravelands worked together in the face of this disaster, and to every one of you, I am more grateful than I can say."

Nut moved a little closer to Thorn, as Spider bounded through the elated crowd toward them. "It was your plan, Thorn," murmured Nut. "I know you want to share the glory, but that was amazing. Well done."

"Spider agrees," announced Spider, sitting back on his haunches and picking ash out of his ear. "Thorn is one smart Great Father."

Nut nudged Thorn and grinned. "So believe in yourself a little more," he said.

"Nut's right," said a voice.

Thorn glanced around to see Sky looking over at him. She was smiling, her eyes soft. Next to her stood a bull elephant, keeping protectively close to her side; the bull's eyes were dark green, his hide a strange mottled mixture of ashen pale and black dark where the rain streamed down it. *It's Rock*, realized Thorn with delight.

Sky's trunk stroked Thorn's shoulder gently. "You made good decisions today," she said softly. "You saved so many and protected Bravelands. You will be one of our finest Great Parents, I'm certain. The Great Spirit is truly with you, Thorn. Don't ever doubt it."

In her voice and in her dark eyes, Thorn thought he detected something else . . . relief maybe? Sky had never been anything but supportive, a strong and sturdy tree that he could lean on, even though, inside, she must have found it hard to imagine a baboon as Great Parent.

"I'll try not to." He laughed hoarsely. All the same, despite the victory, there was a nagging tug of anxiety in his gut. Thorn turned, staring around. "But where's Berry? And Mud? They should be back by now too."

"I'm sure they're fine." Nut patted his shoulder.

Thorn wished he could feel so certain. Of course Mud and Berry were all right, of course they were. . . . There was chaos here, and many more of the animals had not yet assembled. His friend and his mate were fine. They would appear at any moment, exhausted but smiling. . . .

Except that something didn't feel right, and if Thorn had learned anything over the last season, it was to trust his instinct. Drawing a nervous breath, he pushed through the hubbub of excited animals and loped back toward the smoldering ruins of the forest.

Thorn paused, leaning on a blackened trunk; it still felt very warm. He closed his eyes, reaching out toward her mind.

Berry . . . where are you . . . ?

He squeezed his eyes tighter shut, concentrating as hard as he could. The forest was big, but he knew he could find her; he knew her mind, that gentle, kind, sometimes severe presence. Dizzy, he felt his awareness flicker through the ruined trees. His eyes still closed, he frowned. She was nowhere in this part of the forest. Taking a steadying breath, Thorn expanded his senses beyond it, out toward the unspoiled trees of the forest, to the river at its edge and the grass plains that surrounded it; reaching, searching . . .

He gasped with relief and blinked. Here she was. Berry, his love. Thorn submerged his mind in hers as if it were the most natural thing in the world, as if his brain was made by the Great Spirit to fit with hers, like strong roots in deep, rich earth.

He stood in the Great Father Clearing. Why had Berry come here of all places? Was she looking for him? But she knew where Thorn was right now, so why—

And then he saw the wolves who crept out of the trees.

Berry, he thought with the part of him that was still Thorn. *Get out of there!*

"Where is your Great Father?" A rangy wolf took a pace forward. "Great Father of Bravelands, yes. Thorn of the Baboons, with his powerful heart! Where do you keep him, hmmm?"

"Idiots!" Berry spat her contempt. "You think Thorn Highleaf is the Great Father? He had you fooled. We had you all fooled!"

"What?" growled the wolf.

What? echoed Thorn inside her head. What was she saying? Berry swallowed hard.

The wolf laid back his huge ears, as his pack exchanged perplexed glances. "What are you talking about, monkey?"

"Thorn? Be serious!" Berry straightened, eyeing the wolves

with disdain. "Thorn was not truly even a Highleaf baboon, let alone a Great Parent. You thought he—ahahaha!"

Her laughter was strained and false, but it seemed to convince the snarling wolves. Angry slaver dripped from their jaws.

"You know nothing of the ingenuity of baboons," Berry went on. "Thorn was a decoy. Nothing but a stooge, an illusion to draw away attention from the true Great Parent. Not a very smart stooge, it's true, but he played his part well, I give him that."

Thorn wanted to put his paws over his ears. But they weren't his paws; this wasn't his body. He had to hear her. *Please stop, Berry. Please stop. Why are you saying these things?*

"So who," growled the wolf silkily, "is the real Great Parent?"

Through Berry's nostrils, Thorn could smell the creature's rancid breath.

"Why," said Berry, "I am. I stand before you! Berry, the Crownleaf of Dawntrees Troop. The daughter of Stinger, the cleverest baboon who ever lived. Who else would the Great Spirit choose?"

Now he understood, too late. All Thorn wanted to do was clench Berry's jaws shut. But he had no power over the body he occupied, and no power over its mind. All he could do was watch.

"You are Great Parent?" Those huge wolf ears pricked forward. "Then our Alpha will eat your heart and be strong! And we too, for we will be he!"

No. No no no. Berry. No! She was afraid; Thorn could feel it. So afraid. *She must run now, she must!*

The heart within Berry's body pounded so hard with terror, Thorn felt faint.

"No pathetic wolf can eat my heart," sneered Berry. She laughed again. "The Great Spirit lives in me, and it will protect me."

"We will see," growled the wolf. "All of we. We will see. We will taste."

The ranks of the wolf pack parted. Through them stalked the Alpha: it had to be. He was no more than shadow, but he was huge and menacing, and his eyes were clearly visible: they burned with power and violent hunger.

Thorn could bear it no longer. He had to do something. Breaking out of Berry's mind with a violent jolt, he twisted and leaped through the forest toward the Great Father Clearing, running faster than he had ever run. The rain was a torrent now, a dark gray shroud over the whole of Bravelands; it soaked him instantly, drenching his fur, pouring into his eyes. The burned skeletons of trees did nothing to shelter him; even when he reached the unburned forest, the rain fell so hard and heavy that he might as well have been on the open grassland.

Thorn's heart pounded, and he felt as if he was running through a river of thick mud; he could not make his limbs move swiftly enough. His paws slithered and slipped on sodden grass and leaf litter. This was like a dream, a terrible nightmare.

Except that it was no dream. He had seen it all. *Berry, I'm coming.*

The trees of his own part of the forest were before him now; Thorn recognized this log, that branch, this fig tree. He plunged into familiar woodland, running, springing, leaping, his heart in his throat. *I have to make it in time. I have to.*

One last log to bound over; then he staggered and slid into the glade, gazing around frantically, gasping for breath.

The silence was dreadful. There were no wolves here. There was only his friend Mud, crouched over a shapeless thing in the center of the clearing.

Thorn's breathing was harsh and loud. Mud turned. The little baboon's eyes were wider than ever, his face racked with grief.

Thorn's mind felt oddly cold and detached; his own limbs somehow felt distant as he stumbled toward Mud.

He did not want to look. But he had to. Thorn tore his eyes away from his friend and forced himself to stare at the thing that lay on the ground: limp, torn flesh and tattered fur. That could not be his mate, his love. It could not.

He was Great Father. . . . He would not allow it. Surely, the Great Spirit itself would stop this from being true.

Berry.

No, it couldn't be. This baboon was lifeless. She was already cold. Her eyes, the eyes that had been so warm and golden and full of love, held no spark at all. Wide-open, they stared almost peacefully at the edge of the glade.

"No. No. No." Thorn's legs would no longer hold him. He collapsed to a crouch, hunched in the torrential rain.

Mud didn't speak; he didn't seem able to. He had piled flowers on the body, Thorn noticed—but only on Berry's chest. All along the center of her rib cage Mud had placed heaped clusters of blossoms, red and yellow and green and gold. Only on her chest. And with a sudden wrench of unbearable grief, Thorn knew why.

They had taken her heart. The wolves had taken Berry's heart, her spirit, everything she was.

"I tried to stop her." Mud's voice, when he at last managed to speak, was a racking wail of sorrow. "I tried, Thorn. She wouldn't listen. She said it was all that would save you. She said if they took a false Parent's heart, the wolves wouldn't come for you."

Thorn wanted to comfort his friend, but it wasn't possible. His voice had died in his throat. There was only a fiery, thudding pain, worse than the flames of the destroyed forest behind them. Yet the pain seemed to be that of another baboon; somehow it was as if his body did not belong to him.

Crawling to Berry, Thorn reached out and took her in his arms. He dislodged the flowers, exposing her ravaged chest, but it didn't matter. It had been kind of Mud to try to shield him, but Thorn needed to know. He needed to know what she had gone through, after he had torn himself from her brave and terrified mind.

Holding her close, Thorn stroked her beautiful golden fur.

How could he let her go? She had died defending him, and he knew he should stay here, cradling her body, until death came for him too.

She loved me so much. And now he would never have a chance to tell her how much he had loved her back. If only he could reverse time, he could be back with her in their secret ravine, meeting in the darkness, happy just to be with each other. He could be showing off for her in the Three Feats, striving to be good enough in the troop's eyes to be her mate. He could be back in the Tall Trees glade that had been their home, shyly offering her a mango and watching her golden eyes light up.

But they would never light up again. The eyes he loved were dead and staring, and her spirit was gone. A new surge of pain racked him. The wolves had taken her spirit. Berry would never run among the stars, climbing the shining trees full of golden fruit that waited for baboons when they died. When Thorn himself died, she would not be there waiting for him, starlight glittering on her golden pelt, moonlight glowing in her warm and loving eyes.

What use was it to be Great Father if he couldn't turn back time? Thorn buried his face in her fur, desperate to cling to her beloved scent. But even that was contaminated by the stench of wolf.

. . . And something else. Somewhere in his grief-stricken mind, Thorn realized it and registered the scent.

It was a scent he knew, feared, and hated.

Earth, and blood, and darkness.

CHAPTER TWENTY-FIVE

Fearless's hopes were higher than they had been for a long time as he padded across the golden expanse of grassland toward the watering hole. The lions behind him followed without question, and on this cloudless morning, all of them kept up with his pace. None dropped back, limping and whining; none roared complaints of exhaustion or hunger. Since he had taken them under his command, the former members of Titanpride had rested, hunted, and eaten well. Fearless felt a deep sense of accomplishment and contentment. It almost eased the nagging pain in his heart. But not quite.

At his left flank trotted Ruthless, quiet and loyal as always. On his right, though, was an empty space where Keen should have been. Once again, a twist of aching regret tugged at Fearless's gut.

He hoped Keen had made it safely to Mightypride, that

they had accepted him and welcomed him. But Fearless missed his friend's stalwart, thoughtful company. He could no longer even scent a trace of Keen on the air—

Fearless halted. He raised his head, flaring his nostrils. His eyes narrowed.

The odor was like nothing he'd ever smelled before. A dark and acrid tang drifted from the forest ahead. *That's Thorn's forest.*

Around and above the tree canopy lay a pall of thick black cloud. Fearless felt his hide prickle with a fear that seemed to come from very deep inside.

He swung his head to glance at his pride behind him. They stopped too and gazed at him expectantly.

"I don't know what's going on ahead there," he growled, "but we should take a look."

The lions nodded, without even exchanging glances. Not one of them questioned Fearless's decision. He should have found that satisfying, but oddly, his optimism felt shakier than before. If he couldn't explain or confront that frightening cloud, what kind of a pride leader would he be?

But he'd made his choice now. Straightening his shoulders, tightening his jaws, Fearless headed for the forest.

Instinctively, his steps slowed as he drew closer to the trees, and his jaw slackened. They were barely recognizable as trees anymore. The lions behind him were silent, and when he glanced back, he saw that their eyes too were wide with shock.

Fearless could no longer tell mahogany from fig, or kigelia from sapwood. Every tree was a charred skeleton, its leaves gone. Even the earth beneath them was blackened, stripped of shrub and grass. Flecks of gray drifted in the breeze that whistled eerily between the trunks; one soft flake landed on Fearless's nose, and he shook himself violently to get rid of it. The horror that rose inside him was bone-deep.

"What happened here?" he growled, bewildered.

His paws trembling a little, he advanced to the edge of the forest. His pride followed, hesitantly.

What creature could do this to an entire forest? And could anything have survived its attack?

Fearless tensed. Yes. Something had.

Shadows were slinking through the trees toward him, thin and eerie. His eyes watering from the sharp stench of the devastated forest, Fearless blinked and peered harder.

His heart chilled. The shadows were pale golden, with narrow snouts and bushy tails. Vicious yellow eyes gleamed at him.

The wolf pack.

At their head stalked a big wolf with a scar across one eye. It gave Fearless an unnervingly lopsided stare, then opened its blood-soaked jaws in a malevolent grin.

And then the wolf stepped aside.

Another animal strode out of the forest shadows, his huge paws crunching on the desiccated ground. And though the wolves turned to gaze up at him with eager adoration, this creature was no wolf. Fearless gaped in disbelief.

The black mane was streaked with ash and blood, the scarred jaws drenched in gore. The eyes that met Fearless's were every bit as crazed as he remembered. Perhaps they were touched with even more insanity.

Fearless's sworn enemy. The killer of Gallant and Loyal. The lion he hated with all his heart.

Titan.

EPILOGUE

The intense blue arc of the sky had vanished behind roiling storm clouds. At the edge of the Great Father Clearing, Windrider perched with her flock on the branches of a dripping mahogany, her head hunched in her shoulders. She felt no urge to take flight. There was no joy in stretching broad wings, in soaring over the expanse of the savannah: not when gray rain lashed the grass flat and turned the earth to red mud; not when that black cloud bank hung heavy, blotting out the horizon.

Silent, the birds watched Great Father. He had not moved for a very long time. Since daybreak, he had crouched over the body of his mate, and he did not seem to feel the rain that drenched his fur and ran in rivulets to the ground.

Distantly, lightning flashed, and thunder rumbled through the dense trees. Windrider shook water from her feathers, feeling them brush the leaves, then folded her wings once again. She tilted her head. One of the younger vultures shuffled along the branch, closer to her.

"This storm, Windrider . . ." he rasped, with a nervous glance at the sky. "Is it natural? I've never seen one this powerful."

She opened her beak to scold him, but remembered that young Darkfeather was barely fledged, at least when compared to her.

Windrider paused, then nodded. "I have. It happens when the Great Spirit is angry."

"The Spirit has been angry before," he said hesitantly. "In my time."

She turned to eye Darkfeather. "Yes. But Bravelands has never faced an enemy like Titan. No lion follows the Great Parent, but all follow the Code. All, except for Titan. That lion abandoned it long ago—but even so, this is new and deadly. He sinks deeper into evil. In leading the golden wolf pack, he breaks the boundary between creatures who should never hunt together."

"This has happened before," suggested Darkfeather. "The lion, Fearless, and the baboons. And the young elephant, Sky—"

"All worked together for the good of Bravelands," Windrider interrupted him. "This is not the same. Titan works with the wolves against all creatures. He threatens everything we know, everything we love."

Darkfeather looked as if he was about to reply, but then something caught his eye. He tensed, craning down to peer at

Thorn Highleaf. "Look," he whispered.

Windrider turned back to the Great Father. The young baboon had risen to his paws. For long, aching moments, he stared down at the corpse of the baboon he had loved.

Then he turned and bounded away into the forest.

"Where's he going?" asked Blackwing from a branch above Windrider.

"Who knows?" croaked old Swiftflight.

"I do." Windrider's heart clenched with dread. "And I must go after him."

Without another word, she beat her wings strongly and lurched from the branch, diving through the clearing into strong and steady flight.

She was not built for forest flying. Angling her wings abruptly, she swerved to avoid a kigelia and its heavy fruits, then ducked under the branches of a mango tree, half closing her eyes against the slap of foliage. Several times she had to tilt herself sideways to veer between trunks.

An unaccustomed desperation gripped her as she wobbled in flight, steadied herself, and soared on. Her flock, she thought, would not recognize their coolheaded and serene leader—but she must catch up with the Great Father. *I must stop him—*

And there was Thorn, a blurred brown shape running swiftly through the drizzly murk ahead of her. With a burst of speed, Windrider shot forward, dodged a last jutting branch, and swerved ahead of the baboon.

Spreading her wings, she skidded and hopped to a halt,

facing him down. Thorn slid in wet leaves, startled, panting. His eyes narrowed, and he glared at her.

"Get out of my way, bird," he growled. He sprang forward, shoving her aside.

Windrider stumbled for only a moment, wings flailing. Steadying herself, she flapped into the air once more and swooped past him, landing to block his way again. She flared her wings as wide as she could, sweeping the scrubby foliage aside.

Thorn thumped both his forepaws on the sodden ground, sending up a shower of rain. "Leave me alone!" he screamed.

The Great Spirit, thought Windrider, should have warned Thorn not to try the same trick twice. As he lunged forward, Windrider flapped up, extended her scaly feet, and plunged down at him. The full force of her curled talons slammed into his shoulder, and he sprawled hard in the mud.

There was shock in his expression, but to Windrider it seemed a distant sort of astonishment. Mostly, what those golden-brown eyes held was grief.

Thorn struggled up, slithering in the mire. Water ran in rivulets down his face, dripped from his ears and tail.

"Titan and his wolves. They murdered Berry," he croaked. "Let me go. I'm going to make him pay for what he's done."

"No, you're not." Windrider placed a firm claw on his shoulder, pressing him down. "Titan will pay. There will be justice for Berry Crownleaf, just not today, Thorn Greatfather."

"But—" His breath came in harsh rasps. "Titan killed her. With his wolves. He—"

"You cannot defeat Titan in a fight," Windrider told him brusquely. "Don't be foolish, Great Father."

"I don't care if I live or die," snarled Thorn, "so long as he dies with me!"

"Do not be foolish," Windrider snapped. More gently, she added: "Where would the justice be for Berry then, Great Father? Titan would have killed you both. And he will take your spirit, and with it, the power of the Great Father."

"I don't care." But Thorn's voice was almost a sob, and under her strong grip, he slumped down in the torrential rain.

"You must care! Do you know how close you came, with your wild plan to sacrifice yourself? The Great Spirit would not have taken flight with your death. . . . The wolves would have possessed it!"

He shivered, silent, beneath her talons. For an age, he said nothing. She realized it was the first time Thorn had faced the truth of the calamity he had almost unleashed.

"You have wits," murmured Windrider at last. "Your mind is your strength, so use it. You are angry, and you are filled with sorrow, but your own vengeance needs you to be calm. Reject the madness, Thorn Greatfather. Make a plan."

He panted, shutting his eyes tight. His shoulders slumped, and he hunched in a miserable crouch.

"You're right," he said at last. "I know."

Tentatively, Windrider shifted her talons from his shoulder, releasing him. He did not spring up or try to shove past. All the passion and energy seemed to have drained from his body into the sodden earth of Bravelands.

There was a rustle and crack of twigs and leaves in the trees above them, and Windrider tilted up her head to glimpse her flock. Black shapes flapped awkwardly through the forest toward her, and one by one the vultures landed in a circle around Thorn, shifting on their claws, shaking their wings. They eyed him with a kind of detached pity.

Windrider nodded to Blackwing. Stretching out her wings, she raised her head and began to chant. Blackwing, his eyes fixed on hers, joined the song. In moments all the vultures had raised their harsh and eerie voices in chorus.

It was a strange impulse, thought Windrider as she sang. This song had come naturally to her throat; she had not even considered it, much less chosen it. Perhaps the Great Spirit had sent it to her; she had not known that she remembered these ancient Skytongue words. It must sound even more unearthly to Great Father, who stared at the vultures in shock and wonder.

But it seemed that deep within her, Windrider knew the chant well. It had stayed with her for an age, after all, and she knew what its words meant.

Strong and fierce and wild, it was the song of battle.

KEEP READING FOR A SNEAK PEEK AT A
NEW WARRIORS ADVENTURE!

WARRIORS

As a bitter leaf-bare season descends on the lake territories, the five warrior cat Clans face moons of cold and darkness— and far worse, the voices of their ancestors in StarClan have grown dim and silent. Only one medicine cat apprentice still hears them, in a strange vision that warns of a looming shadow within their borders. One that may threaten the warrior code itself.

CHAPTER 1

Shadowpaw craned his neck over his back, straining to groom the
hard-to-reach spot at the base of his tail. He had just managed
to give his fur a few vigorous licks when he heard paw steps
approaching. He looked up to see his father, Tigerstar, and his
mother, Dovewing, their pelts brushing as they gazed down at
him with pride and joy shining in their eyes.

"What is it?" he asked, sitting up and giving his pelt a shake.

"We just came to see you off," Tigerstar responded, while
Dovewing gave her son's ears a quick, affectionate lick.

Shadowpaw's fur prickled with embarrassment. *Like I haven't
been to the Moonpool before,* he thought. *They're still treating me as if
I'm a kit in the nursery!*

He was sure that his parents hadn't made such a fuss when
his littermates, Pouncestep and Lightleap, had been warrior
apprentices. *I guess it's because I'm going to be a medicine cat. . . .* Or
maybe because of the seizures he'd had since he was a kit.
He knew his parents still worried about him, even though it
had been a while since his last upsetting vision. *They're probably
hoping that with some training from the other medicine cats, I'll learn to
control my visions once and for all . . . and I can be normal.*

1

Shadowpaw wanted that, too.

"The snow must be really deep up on the moors," Dovewing mewed. "Make sure you watch where you're putting your paws."

Shadowpaw wriggled his shoulders, praying that none of his Clanmates were listening. "I will," he promised, glancing toward the medicine cats' den in the hope of seeing his mentor, Puddleshine, emerge. But there was no sign of him yet.

To his relief, Tigerstar gave Dovewing a nudge and they both moved off toward the Clan leader's den. Shadowpaw rubbed one paw hastily across his face and bounded across the camp to see what was keeping Puddleshine.

Intent on finding his mentor, Shadowpaw barely noticed the patrol trekking toward the fresh-kill pile, prey dangling from their jaws. He skidded to a halt just in time to avoid colliding with Cloverfoot, the Clan deputy.

"Shadowpaw!" she exclaimed around the shrew she was carrying. "You nearly knocked me off my paws."

"Sorry, Cloverfoot," Shadowpaw meowed, dipping his head respectfully.

Cloverfoot let out a snort, half annoyed, half amused. "Apprentices!"

Shadowpaw tried to hide his irritation. He was an apprentice, yes, but an old one—medicine cat apprentices' training lasted longer than warriors'. His littermates were full warriors already. But he knew his parents would want him to respect the deputy.

Cloverfoot padded on, followed by Strikestone, Yarrowleaf,

and Blazefire. Though they were all carrying prey, they had only one or two pieces each, and what little they had managed to catch was undersized and scrawny.

"I can't remember a leaf-bare as cold as this," Yarrowleaf complained as she dropped a blackbird on the fresh-kill pile.

Strikestone nodded, shivering as he fluffed out his brown tabby pelt. "No wonder there's no prey. They're all hiding down their holes, and I can't blame them."

As Shadowpaw moved on, out of earshot, he couldn't help noticing how pitifully small the fresh-kill pile was, and he tried to ignore his own growling belly. He could hardly remember his first leaf-bare, when he'd been a tiny kit, so he didn't know if the older cats were right and the weather was unusually cold.

I only know I don't like it, he grumbled to himself as he picked his way through the icy slush that covered the ground of the camp. *My paws are so cold I think they'll drop off. I can't wait for newleaf!*

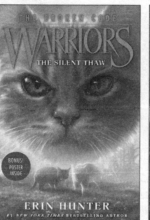
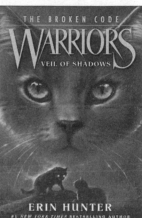

WARRIORS

How many have you read?

Dawn of the Clans
- ○ #1: The Sun Trail
- ○ #2: Thunder Rising
- ○ #3: The First Battle
- ○ #4: The Blazing Star
- ○ #5: A Forest Divided
- ○ #6: Path of Stars

Power of Three
- ○ #1: The Sight
- ○ #2: Dark River
- ○ #3: Outcast
- ○ #4: Eclipse
- ○ #5: Long Shadows
- ○ #6: Sunrise

The Prophecies Begin
- ○ #1: Into the Wild
- ○ #2: Fire and Ice
- ○ #3: Forest of Secrets
- ○ #4: Rising Storm
- ○ #5: A Dangerous Path
- ○ #6: The Darkest Hour

Omen of the Stars
- ○ #1: The Fourth Apprentice
- ○ #2: Fading Echoes
- ○ #3: Night Whispers
- ○ #4: Sign of the Moon
- ○ #5: The Forgotten Warrior
- ○ #6: The Last Hope

The New Prophecy
- ○ #1: Midnight
- ○ #2: Moonrise
- ○ #3: Dawn
- ○ #4: Starlight
- ○ #5: Twilight
- ○ #6: Sunset

A Vision of Shadows
- ○ #1: The Apprentice's Quest
- ○ #2: Thunder and Shadow
- ○ #3: Shattered Sky
- ○ #4: Darkest Night
- ○ #5: River of Fire
- ○ #6: The Raging Storm

Select titles also available as audiobooks!

HARPER
An Imprint of HarperCollins*Publishers*

www.warriorcats.com • www.shelfstuff.com

SUPER EDITIONS

- ○ Firestar's Quest
- ○ Bluestar's Prophecy
- ○ SkyClan's Destiny
- ○ Crookedstar's Promise
- ○ Yellowfang's Secret
- ○ Tallstar's Revenge
- ○ Bramblestar's Storm
- ○ Moth Flight's Vision
- ○ Hawkwing's Journey
- ○ Tigerheart's Shadow
- ○ Crowfeather's Trial
- ○ Squirrelflight's Hope

GUIDES

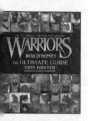

- ○ Secrets of the Clans
- ○ Cats of the Clans
- ○ Code of the Clans
- ○ Battles of the Clans
- ○ Enter the Clans
- ○ The Ultimate Guide

FULL-COLOR MANGA

- ○ Graystripe's Adventure
- ○ Ravenpaw's Path
- ○ SkyClan and the Stranger

EBOOKS AND NOVELLAS

The Untold Stories
- ○ Hollyleaf's Story
- ○ Mistystar's Omen
- ○ Cloudstar's Journey

Tales from the Clans
- ○ Tigerclaw's Fury
- ○ Leafpool's Wish
- ○ Dovewing's Silence

Shadows of the Clans
- ○ Mapleshade's Vengeance
- ○ Goosefeather's Curse
- ○ Ravenpaw's Farewell

Legends of the Clans
- ○ Spottedleaf's Heart
- ○ Pinestar's Choice
- ○ Thunderstar's Echo

Path of a Warrior
- ○ Redtail's Debt
- ○ Tawnypelt's Clan
- ○ Shadowstar's Life

A Warrior's Spirit
- ○ Pebbleshine's Kits
- ○ Tree's Roots
- ○ Mothwing's Secret

HARPER
An Imprint of HarperCollinsPublishers

www.warriorcats.com • www.shelfstuff.com

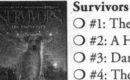

Watering Hole

Titanpride Territory

Hyena Den

Ravine

Great Father Clearing

Lightning Tree

BRAVELANDS